"Ms. Poitevin ripped my heart out, left me for dead and then stitched everything back together"
—*Romancing the Dark Side*

"The Grigori Legacy series has become the benchmark that other Urban Fantasies are compared to for me."
—*Book Mood Reviews*

"Poitevin's series is a passionate and emotionally powerful written story combined with a gritty urban fantasy detective mystery."
—*I Smell Sheep*

"A dark urban fantasy novel like you haven't read before. It is electric, thrilling and extremely intelligent. Linda Poitevin's world building is rich and layered and her writing is excellent. A fantastic new series which will appeal to urban fantasy, paranormal romance and thriller fans!"
—*Ex Libris*

"Urban Fantasy deeply infused with a richly developed mythology, excellent world building, characters you'll love, and villains you'll love to hate."
—*The Qwillery*

"An epic battle story of good and evil with so many scrumptious twists and turns . . . Using scintillating character development and fast-paced action, Linda Poitevin has crafted an amazing series in the Grigori Legacy."
—*Fresh Fiction*

"It's got sexual tension, angels, Lucifer, and amnesia. What more can a girl want? Oh! A kick ass storyline that keeps on moving even when your eyes try to close and go to sleep. Definite late night read!"
—*Heroes and Heartbreakers*

SINS OF THE LOST

THE GRIGORI LEGACY

LINDA POITEVIN

MICHEM PUBLISHING

MICHEM PUBLISHING
Published by Michem Publishing
Canada

This is a work of fiction. Names, characters, places, and incidents either
are the sole product of the author's imagination or are used fictitiously, and
any resemblance to actual persons, living or dead, business establishments,
events, or locales is entirely coincidental.
SINS OF THE LOST

September 2015

Cover design by Designs by Lynsey
Interior design by Book Ninjas

ISBN: 978-0-9919958-5-1

MICHEM PUBLISHING

For Pat...
because you know I couldn't do this without you

PROLOGUE

"You want me to *what*?"

The Archangel Mika'el stared at his Creator. For more than a week he had awaited her summons. He'd been prepared to endure her wrath, her bitterness, her disappointment . . . but this?

Nothing could have prepared him for this.

The One gazed back at him with equanimity. "I want you to convince Seth to take back his powers."

Her words made no more sense the second time around.

"You can't be serious," he said, because it wouldn't do to tell his Creator, *"You're insane."*

Steel formed in the silver depths of her eyes. He held himself rigid against the desire to look away. He'd earned his place as Heaven's greatest warrior through strength and counsel, not by folding at the first sign of the One's displeasure. Straightening his shoulders, he met her glare with his own.

"Two weeks ago, your son's instability damn near

cost us the mortal realm," he said. "We have no reason to think he has changed, so why would you give him his powers back?"

The One sighed. "I'm not giving them back."

"You just said—"

"I said I want you to convince him to take them back."

Mika'el's irritation stilled. As her words sank in, he let his mind sift through to their underlying meaning. To what she wasn't saying. Understanding glimmered.

"The earthquake," he said. "In Vancouver."

The One stared out the window, her gaze unfocused. "When Seth chose the mortal woman over his destiny, the energy he discarded put the entire physical world in flux. I've been dealing with the consequences ever since. Earthquakes, storms, tsunamis. They've been manageable so far, but if we don't contain what he released soon, it will destroy the planet. Perhaps the entire universe."

Mika'el's blood turned cold. He'd seen the consequences of Seth giving up his power in the first place: buildings reduced to rubble, an already earthquake-prone city made more unstable. If the One was right, they'd removed one threat posed by her son only to have it replaced by this, an entirely new problem. And if her proposed solution was to have Seth take back his powers, it could only be because—

He whirled to face her. "The energy. You can't control it."

"I can't so much as touch it." Bitterness laced the Creator's voice. "Every time I reach for it, I make it more unstable. Its very nature makes it reject my presence."

As much as he'd expected the confirmation, it still

stunned him. Still made his universe drop from under his feet. "You're certain?"

You're certain that you—the All-powerful, the Creator, Mother of everything—cannot control this? Cannot contain an energy that is—should be—so much less than your own?

Raw honesty gazed back at him, piercing deeper than any steel might have done. "The energy is not mine to hold, Mika'el. It was created by my union with Lucifer. It belongs only to the product of that union. I wish it could be otherwise, but—yes, I'm certain."

"If he does this, if he takes back his powers, how strong will he be?"

If something goes wrong, if he chooses not to return to Heaven, can you stop him?

"I don't know."

Her answer, he knew, encompassed both questions, spoken and unspoken.

He pivoted on his heel and stalked the width of the room in one direction, then the other. "There must be another way."

"We tried your way."

The words held no recrimination, only a statement of fact, but they stopped him in his tracks. She was right. He'd created this mess. He'd let himself be ruled again by the arrogance that had separated him from her side all those years before, and in that arrogance, had loosed an unknown, unquantifiable force upon the world when they could least afford it.

When war between Heaven and Hell already threatened humanity with Armageddon.

He cleared his throat. "One—"

The tiny, silver-robed figure by the window held up a hand. "What's done is done. There is no point in belaboring the issue. I just need you to convince Seth. I'll hold things together as best I can, but I don't know how much time I can give you."

"He will never listen to me."

"No. But he might listen to the woman."

The Naphil. Of course. After choosing her over his own destiny, Seth would almost certainly listen to her. Still Mika'el hesitated. He wanted to ask what would happen afterward, if Seth did take back his power. Wanted to know . . . and already did. The measures he'd taken—the risks—none of it had changed her mind.

"You know we're not ready to lose you," he said gruffly.

Infinite sadness gazed back at him from silver eyes. "Loss isn't something you're ever ready for, my Archangel. It's something you survive."

ONE

Alexandra Jarvis jolted awake, heart racing, lungs sucking for air. Bathed in sweat, she lay rigid, waiting for reality to replace the nightmare. Again.

As she had every night since Lucifer had raped her.

Then, through the horror she'd begun to think she might never come to terms with, came the touch of a man's gentle hand. She flinched, fighting back a shudder, and made herself relax.

"Again?" Seth's deep voice asked quietly.

She nodded. It didn't matter that he couldn't see her in the dark; after two weeks, he was as familiar with the nightmare as she was.

He tugged her close. She let him slide an arm beneath her and curled into him, head resting on his chest. She focused on the steady *tha-dump* of his heartbeat, the rise and fall of his breath. Slowly her fingers uncurled. She matched her own breathing to his. Inhale, exhale, inhale.

His voice rumbled beneath her ear. "It's not getting

any better, Alex."

She tensed anew, but his arm held firm. "I'm doing my best," she muttered.

"I know. But I've been doing some reading"— his hold tightened against a second attempt to free herself—"and I think maybe you need help with this. I think it might be post-traumatic stress—"

She succeeded in pulling away, scowling down at him in the dark. "I know what it is, Seth, and you're right. I probably should talk to someone, but who the hell do you suggest? Being raped by Lucifer himself isn't something I can discuss with just anyone, for chrissakes. We mortals tend to medicate people who spout off about things like that. Especially people with my history."

And you refuse to talk to me about any of it.

Seth stroked her hair. The faint tension in his hand told her he knew full well the words she'd swallowed back, but once again he avoided the subject. "I know. And I know you're trying. But you can't go on like this. We can't go on like this."

Like this. Words too small to contain all that lay behind them: the disappointment; the recriminations never stated but always underlying; the hurt she knew she inflicted whenever he reached for her and Lucifer loomed between them yet again. Lucifer in Seth's form. Lucifer turning her into nothing more than another pawn in the cosmic mockery of a game he played with the One.

Reassurances gathered in her throat but refused to move farther. She couldn't make herself say what she didn't believe to be true, couldn't promise that everything would be all right. Not anymore. Not knowing what she did of Heaven and Hell and the

Nephilim and—

On the bedside table, her cell phone shrilled. She extricated herself from Seth's hold and rolled over to grab it.

"Jarvis."

"I need you at a scene."

Surprise made her fumble the phone. "Staff?"

"Does anyone else call you at three a.m. to attend a murder scene?" Staff Inspector Roberts growled.

Well, yes. Usually dispatch. She kept the observation to herself and reminded him instead, "I'm not cleared for active duty."

Beside her, Seth switched on the lamp. She squinted against the glare.

"You are now. I'll text you the address. You have twenty minutes to get your ass down here. Pick up coffee on your way."

"Wait—"

The phone went dead. Alex stared at it, trying to gather her muddled thoughts and sort through her myriad unanswered questions. How many victims? Why call her? Was everyone else tied up on other cases? She thought back to the mass murder wrought by Caim and shuddered. *Please don't let it be another like that . . .*

Setting the phone down, she turned to find Seth propped up on one arm, his black eyes watchful.

"My supervisor wants me at a scene."

"Did he say what it is?" Seth's voice took on the hint of a growl, the way it did whenever they spoke of her job.

"Beyond a homicide? No." Slipping out of bed, Alex stripped off her pajama bottoms and reached for the panties and slacks she'd hung on the back of the door in anticipation of her meeting with Roberts later that day. A meeting that was supposed to determine whether or not she could return to investigative duties.

She assumed it was canceled now.

"But you think it has to do with *them*," Seth persisted.

Them. Angels, Fallen Ones, Heaven, Hell . . .

His parents.

A whole other world paralleling her own, controlling it, threatening its very existence. Her fingers clamped onto the duvet. No. Michael had told her she was done with all that. He'd assured her the worst she would face would come from her own world, from humanity's knee-jerk reaction to its own fear. Which, given what she'd come to expect of her fellow mortals, would be bad enough.

Still . . .

She shook off the creeping tentacles of doubt and continued dressing. "I'm sure it's just an ordinary homicide," she said. "Not that any homicide is ordinary, but—" She broke off. Sighed. "You know what I mean."

"But what if it's not? What if it *is* them? I want to come with you."

"We've been over this." She slipped into her blouse and then dropped onto the edge of the bed, reaching to stroke the hair, dark as his eyes, back from Seth's forehead. "This is my job. It's what I'm trained to do. Even if it is them, there's nothing—"

She stopped, but not before Seth's eyes hardened into obsidian.

"Nothing I can do?" he finished.

She bit back her denial. They both knew that's what she'd been about to say. Just as they both knew it was the truth.

Silence stretched between them, thick with arguments already had and words scrupulously avoided. They'd been over this same territory at least once a day since their return from Vancouver a week ago, their ongoing disagreement adding to the tensions between them.

Seth was right. They couldn't continue like this. *She* couldn't continue like this.

She curled her fingers around his. "I know this is hard," she said. "I'll try to find someone I can talk to, all right? Just . . . give me time. I'll get past this."

Seth turned his hand palm up and linked his fingers with hers. For a long moment she let his love, his strength, seep into her. Then she rose, dropped a kiss on his lips, and left.

TWO

Aramael drew back from the rooftop edge as the door of the apartment building across the street opened. A woman stepped into the night, blond hair glinting briefly in the glow of the light above the door. A tiny thread of awareness tugged deep inside him. Alexandra.

He didn't need to see her features to be certain. He just . . . knew. The way he knew when she slept or woke. Or when she moved from one room to another in the apartment she shared with Seth Benjamin.

The thread inside him drew tight.

All things he wasn't supposed to know anymore because he wasn't supposed to care. He'd assured Mika'el that he didn't, that any connection between him and Alex had been severed.

But here he was. Day after day, night after night, using his patrols of the earthly realm as an excuse to stay near, to check on her. To torture himself with the tiny, too intimate glimpses into her life without him.

The life she'd chosen with another.

At first he'd told himself he only wanted to be sure she was all right. That she suffered no ill effects from her run-in with the second most powerful being in the universe. On his third night standing in this same spot on the sidewalk, however, he'd given up the pretense. For him, the soulmate connection remained. He knew now that it always would.

Mika'el would be furious if he found out.

So would Alex.

Flexing the massive black wings at his back, he wondered briefly if he would ever become accustomed to their weight, so much greater than that of the Power's wings he'd once worn. Then he launched himself into the air above the city.

SETH WATCHED Alex's car roll out of the apartment parking lot and onto the night-emptied street eight stories below. Letting the curtain settle back across the window, he turned to face the apartment. Just him, the furniture, and who knew how many hours before her return. He flicked a glance in the direction of a soft *tick, tick, tick.*

Him, the furniture, and that damnable wall clock, ever so helpfully keeping count of those hours.

He lowered himself onto the sofa, elbows resting on knees, and traced a thumb across his bottom lip. This wasn't how it was supposed to be. None of it. Not after what they'd been through together, not after he'd brought her back from the brink of death—twice— and sure as Hell not after they'd chosen each other the way they had.

He'd given up all he had been, all he'd been destined

to do. For her. For mortality.

For this.

He surveyed the room, lit by a single floor lamp standing alone in one corner. A rental property, it exuded not a hint of the woman he loved. Alex claimed she hadn't had time to deal with rebuilding after Aramael and Caim's battle had burned her former home to the ground, but Seth knew better. He saw in the hardness of her eyes there was more to it. She might not have said so—might not have admitted it to herself—but the real reason she hadn't rebuilt was because she didn't see the point.

And he couldn't argue with her.

Not with what he knew was coming.

It was bad enough that Lucifer and the One insisted on going to war, a war that would inevitably spill over into the mortal realm. But if Lucifer had been telling the truth about the eighty thousand Nephilim his followers had bred. . .

Closing his eyes, he pinched the bridge of his nose. The human race didn't stand a chance. It was just a matter of time until every mortal soul on the planet was wiped out, including Alex—and now that he'd given up his immortality, him.

Which was why none of this was how it was supposed to be. Alex trying to stem an unstoppable tide, him staring at a featureless beige wall, both apart for hours at a stretch instead of spending their time together, away from all of this. Away from her job, the constant threats, the relentless insanity gripping the universe. None of which he could do a bloody thing about.

Dissatisfaction gave a sinuous roll in his belly. Perhaps he'd been too quick to—

He opened his eyes, cutting his thoughts short. No. His former powers had no bearing here. He'd given them up because he didn't want them, damn it. Because he'd wanted no more part in the endless battle between his parents. He'd chosen Alex over all of that. Had chosen . . . he stared at the featureless room again.

He'd chosen this. Of his own free will.

It was time he made the best of it.

THREE

"Two sugars, no cream." Alex handed one of the disposable coffee cups to the tall, overcoated man standing beneath a streetlamp.

Doug Roberts, staff inspector for Homicide Section, took the cup from her with a grunt of thanks. His assessing gaze swept over her from head to toe, then traveled back up to meet hers. "You look sane enough."

"Excuse me?"

"The Voice of Doom has been trying to convince me otherwise for the past week."

She raised a brow. "Bell?"

"The highly qualified Doctor Bell," Roberts corrected. "In whose esteemed opinion, you're ready for the loony bin."

"What the hell is with that guy? Why is he so determined to trash my career?"

"It's more about his own career. And his ego. He's pissed that I'm allowing you back to work based on the judgment of an unknown psychiatrist on the other side of the country."

"A psych—you mean Elizabeth Riley? Wait a minute. She contacted you, and you still made me suffer through a week of meetings with Bell?"

"I contacted her," Roberts corrected, "and yes. CYA, Detective."

Cover your ass.

Alex thought back over the excruciating hours of verbal sparring she'd endured as the department shrink tried and failed to elicit details about things she would never—could never—tell him. To her mind, Roberts's ass could go straight to hell for making her go through that.

That, however, was an opinion best kept to herself. She surveyed the parking lot. With the question of her sanity out of the way, it was time to get down to business—and to her first murder scene since their serial killer more than a month before. A killer that had turned her entire reality upside down when she'd learned he was a Fallen Angel. She hunched her shoulders and gripped her coffee a little tighter.

A handful of personnel dismantled the powerful floodlights used to light the scene. Roberts had called her in late on this one. Odd. She shot him a sideways glance.

"So what do we have?"

"A goddamn mess."

Noting the thin line of his mouth, she raised a brow. "Can we be a little more specific?"

Roberts pointed toward an ambulance across the lot. "In the body bag. Female, Caucasian, twenty to twenty-five years of age."

"And?"

"She was pregnant. The baby is . . . gone."

Gone. An innocuous enough word, if it hadn't been for Roberts's slight hesitation before speaking it. Gone. Gone how? Gone as in she'd given birth and the baby was missing? Gone as in the baby had died with its mother?

Or gone as in this was the reason Roberts had called her?

As in Seth was right and this had to do with *them*.

Tossing her still full cup into a nearby Dumpster, she took a deep breath. "Right. Let's have a look."

Roberts's hand on her arm stopped her before she'd taken more than a step. "It's bad, Alex."

"I'm—" The word *fine* died on her lips. Had those haggard lines always been around his eyes? That gray tinge under his skin? She stared at him, then nodded once in acknowledgment of the warning.

Roberts released his grip.

Alex walked toward the ambulance, passing the mobile command post, a forensic technician packing up equipment, two others winding up extension cords and shutting down generators. She tried to steel herself for what she knew was coming, but what had once been an automatic defense felt rusty from disuse. Whatever awaited her, it was going to be rough.

With Roberts at her side, she reached the ambulance and waited for the coroner to unzip the body bag strapped to a gurney.

Heavy-duty black plastic parted to expose a young woman's face, its unnatural pallor speaking to massive blood loss. Silently, grimly, the coroner pulled open the rest of the bag. Alex's gaze traveled down the body. Settled on the raw, gaping hole where the abdomen should have been. Where a baby would have been.

If it hadn't been ripped out of its mother.

Not cut.
Ripped.
Brutally, viciously torn.
Alex's stomach heaved.

FOUR

"You cannot avoid me forever, Mika'el."

The careful neutrality of Verchiel's voice made the words all the more accusatory. Mika'el paused in the task of honing the sword laid across his lap. He stared down at the gleaming metal, its edge now beyond lethal. It hadn't needed sharpening, but the rhythmic act of sliding stone over metal had been calming. Mindless. Requiring no conscious thought as long as he continued.

Given a choice, he would have continued for eternity.

He laid the broadsword beside him on the garden bench. Then he leaned back and stretched his arms wide along the backrest. "I'm not avoiding you, Highest."

"Fine. Then you can't avoid *yourself* forever."

He grimaced at the diminutive, crimson-robed female in the arched entry of the rose garden where he'd taken refuge. "You're very astute."

Verchiel, Highest Seraph and executive administrator of Heaven, shrugged. "I've had my share of practice at reading angels," she said. A reference, no doubt, to her past position as handler of the volatile Powers—particularly Aramael. "My point—"

Mika'el waved her silent. "Your point is that you want to know what the One told me yesterday."

"She holds you responsible, doesn't she? But she knew—"

"She knew I would task Aramael with Seth's assassination," Mika'el cut in. "All that happened after—the Nephilim army, permitting Lucifer to manipulate me, my plan to strike the first blow and plunge Heaven into war again—all of that I kept from her."

"*We* kept it from her because if we'd told her—"

"Then she would have stopped Lucifer the only way she could, and we would have lost her."

"Surely she cannot blame you for trying to protect her."

He played idly with the whetstone in his hand, moving it between his fingers. "She can if she prefers not to be protected."

Silence met his words, broken by the faintest whisper of a breeze passing through the stone-walled garden, the lazy drone of a bumblebee, the call of a distant bird, Verchiel's swallow.

"She *wants* to end herself?" the Highest asked at last. "You must be mistaken."

"Not end," he said. "Alter. She wants to go back to what she was before she divided herself into so many pieces—or at least closer to that state. She's worn out, Verchiel. Weary of the struggle between her and Lucifer, of trying to maintain balance in the universe, of being the All to so many souls. She's given so much of herself that there's nothing left. She tried to tell me before, but I didn't want to listen. And now my actions might have made it impossible."

Leaving his sword on the bench, he stood and paced the gravel path. "If we—if I hadn't interfered," his voice was harsh in his own ears, "she could have done what she wanted to do all along. She could have eliminated Lucifer as a threat and left us to deal only with the Fallen. We would still have faced a difficult battle, but we would have prevailed. We would have saved humanity."

Verchiel's head moved in convulsive denial. "Without the One? How will we live without her?"

Mika'el stopped to watch a honeybee buried in the pale pink folds of a rose, its buzzing at a frenzied pitch. The internal chaos he'd held at bay by endlessly sharpening his sword, by refusing to think, had begun swirling inside him again. How *would* they live without the One? He had no idea, but she had made it clear they had no choice. Their time with her had run out. It was up to him to lead the way.

But not to lie.

"We don't," he answered Verchiel. He met her shock with the grim implacability that had carried him through six millennia of alienation from his Creator. "We learn to survive. One day at a time."

Another silence fell, this one filled not with shock but with their shared, fathomless anguish. Not even the birds intruded. After what felt like an aeon but could only have been a few moments, Verchiel softly cleared her throat.

"You said your actions might have made it impossible. Because of the Nephilim?"

His eyes closed. Involuntarily, briefly. He made himself open them. He wouldn't hide from the Highest. Wouldn't keep secrets. Not anymore.

"Them—and Seth."

"Seth? But he gave up his immortality, his power . . . what threat can he possibly—?" Verchiel broke off as a shudder, barely perceptible, rippled through the ground beneath their feet. She stared down, then lifted startled, questioning eyes to Mika'el's.

"That kind of threat," he said, rising to his feet and replacing his sword in its scabbard at his waist. "Now, if you'll excuse me, I have a mess to clean up before Lucifer realizes what's happened and finds a way to use it to his own advantage—if he hasn't already."

FIVE

A swirl of dust and litter lifted from the street and traveled toward the parking lot, bringing with it the exhaust fumes from the early morning traffic. From behind Alex came the solid *thunk* of the ambulance doors closing, then the steady footfall of Roberts's approach. He stopped at the edge of her vision and cleared his throat.

"Well? Is it what I think it is?"

That depends, a part of her—one that still believed in keeping secrets—wanted to hedge. A greater part of her knew there was no point. Not with Roberts. With someone else, perhaps, but not Roberts. He'd seen too much, guessed at too much, and he needed to know. He deserved to know.

"If you're asking whether I think this is related to our serial killer, the answer is yes."

"Our killer died two months ago."

Almost taking her out in the process, despite her Heavenly soulmate's best efforts. The scars across her throat prickled with memories. "Yes."

"So there's another one?"

More than one. More than you can imagine.

"It looks that way."

Massaging the back of her neck with fingers made icy by the November wind, she struggled to find the words she needed to tell her supervisor that the bizarre pregnancies happening worldwide had nothing to do with the virus being postulated by the medical community—or the bioterrorism theories rampant in the media.

She tried to remember what she'd told Hugh Henderson when it had become impossible to put off the Vancouver detective any longer. How she'd explained that Heaven and Hell were real, and Armageddon itself was about to unfold. But Roberts forestalled her, his tone brisk.

"All right. As soon as the preliminary autopsy confirms what we're thinking, I'll pass the file on to Bastion. Are you going home again or straight to the office?"

Her fingers curled into the hair at the nape of her neck. She stared at her supervisor. "Excuse me?"

"I asked if you're—"

"I heard, but that's it? That's all you want to know?"

"It's all I need."

Her mouth flapped three times before she found her voice again. "A woman's baby is ripped—not cut— *ripped* from her, and you don't have any questions other than am I going home or straight to the office? What the hell, Staff? You must realize we're not dealing with a human killer here. You need to know—"

"Stop."

She did, if only out of sheer surprise.

"I don't *need* to know anything, Detective. In fact, the less I know, the better. Because regardless of who—or what—did this, as it stands right now I have no choice but to investigate the homicide as I would any other. And if I'm going to place you back on active duty, I need deniability. *Has Detective Jarvis ever mentioned hallucinations to you?* No. *Has she reported hearing voices?* No. *Does she appear mentally sound?* Yes."

The buttons of Roberts's wool peacoat strained under the sudden thrust of his hands into his pockets. "As good a cop as you are, your career is hanging by a thread right now. The rest of the world wants a rational explanation for what's going on. Our bosses want a rational explanation. So if you go around spouting off about killers who aren't human, I either have to back you up or shut you down. If I back you up, I get shut down and we're both finished. Whatever the hell is going on, neither of us will be of any use without a badge behind us. Are you getting this?"

If I back you up. Not when. *If.*

Because it didn't come down to whether or not the rest of the world wanted to believe her, but whether or not he did.

The truths she'd wanted to speak gathered in the back of her throat, piling one on top of another until they threatened to cut off her breath. She hadn't realized until now, until this very moment, how much she needed to share her burden. To tell someone here in Toronto, because Henderson was just too damned far away in Vancouver, about all the things no mortal should have ever known.

The broken pact that had triggered war between Heaven and Hell; a Nephilim army, eighty thousand strong, growing in the bellies of human women; Heaven's attempt to assassinate the One's own son when his love for a mortal woman, for Alex, had threatened the existence of humankind.

Archangels. Lost soulmates. Rape at the hands of Lucifer.

She nudged at a pebble near the toe of her shoe. "Can I ask you something?"

Roberts waited.

"If you didn't want to know, why call me?"

"I called you for confirmation, Detective. Because I do know. Maybe not everything, but enough." Her supervisor opened his car door. "There's a meeting this morning. Ten a.m. I expect you there."

MIKA'EL STARED DOWN from the rooftop at the woman in the parking lot below—and at the Archangel watching her from the shadows of a building.

Aramael.

Damn it to Hell and back again.

At first, when he hadn't found the Naphil at either her apartment or office, he'd been at a loss as to where else to look. With any other human, it would have been a simple matter of contacting his or her Guardian, but those of Nephilim descent had no Guardians, making them essentially untraceable—especially in a city of several million. Then, about to give up and post a watch at the two most obvious locations, he'd sensed Aramael's presence.

The coincidence had been too great to ignore.

And now he'd confirmed his suspicions. Aramael, newly promoted from exiled Power to Archangel, had lied to him about having severed the connection between him and Alex. Mika'el tipped back his head and stared at the still-dark sky. He should have expected this. He of all angels should have known that one's soulmate, Naphil or otherwise, could not be so easily dismissed.

His years away had made him careless. It was time—past time—to get his act together. The One needed her son back, and Mika'el needed to know he had a united force of Archangels at the ready.

With a last glance streetward, he stepped back from the roof's edge and out of the human realm.

He'd start with Aramael.

SIX

Raymond Joly looked up at her from the couch as Alex walked into the coffee room.

"Look what the cat dragged in," he said, his enormous mustache giving an upward twitch indicative of a grin. "It's about time you got off your ass and back to work."

"He said as he lazed on the couch," she retorted, walking between him and the newscast he'd been watching, headed for the counter. She indicated the television with a lift of her chin. "More good news?"

Joly thumbed the remote control, and the screen went blank. Linking fingers behind his head, he leaned back. "Earthquakes in the Middle East, a massive hurricane that hit more Caribbean countries than I knew existed, flooding in Australia, and a volcanic eruption off the coast of Japan. Oh, and pregnant women lining up by the thousands to demand DNA tests for this virus they still can't identify. Shall I continue?"

There was more?

"I'm good, thanks," she told Joly.

"I know this stuff happens all the time, but I swear it's getting worse," he muttered. "It's like somebody hit the self-destruct button on the bloody planet. So I heard Roberts called you in on our thing this morning. What did you think?"

"I thought it looked like someone got killed."

"You know what I mean."

She did, but she wasn't going to answer. Not after that speech from Roberts. She took down a mug from the cupboard and reached for the coffeepot. Joly heaved himself off the couch with a grunt. Joining her at the counter, he held out his own cup, and she poured for them both. Her colleague leaned back against the counter, one ankle crossed over the other, and stared down into his coffee while she stirred cream and sugar into hers. The silence moved beyond a lapse in conversation to being obviously deliberate.

She dropped the spoon into the sink with a clatter. "If you're waiting for me to—"

"It's not about the case."

"What, then?" she asked, settling against the counter beside him.

"Nothing, really." Joly shrugged. He slurped at the coffee from under his handlebar mustache. "It's just . . . Vancouver. What the hell happened out there, Jarvis?"

"You've read the report."

"I have," he agreed. "I've also got a cousin who's married to one of their emergency response members."

Hell. Sometimes the thin blue line was a little too thick for comfort.

"He won't talk about what he saw that night—"

Good.

"—but that Sunday he got up and went to church."

Alex flashed him a look and found him studying the floor at his feet.

"Garth is—was—the staunchest atheist I've ever met in my life," he said. "Our discussions on the issue of faith rarely end well, at least according to my wife, and now he's going to church and taking his kids to Sunday school. My cousin is freaked. So I repeat: what the hell happened out there?"

She wondered how he would react if she told him. Just blurted out the truth, the whole truth and nothing but the—

"Your career is hanging by a thread," Roberts's voice echoed in her memory.

She scowled at her coffee. Hell, who was she kidding? Even without Robert's warning, she'd become so adept at keeping secrets at this point that she wasn't sure she knew how to let them go.

Bastion poked his head into the room. "Meeting's in two minutes," he said, then gave Alex a nod. "Good to have you back, Jarvis."

Alex detached herself from the counter.

"You haven't answered me," Joly said.

She turned when she reached the door. "You know what happened, Joly? Shit happened. A lot of it."

Joly's mustache twitched. "What kind of answer is that?"

"The only one you're getting."

ALEX TOOK A PLACE against the wall in the conference room, returning various greetings. She'd wondered how it might be, coming back after all that had gone down, but apart from Joly's questions . . .

She watched the subject of her thoughts take a seat beside his partner at the table. Abrams leaned in to ask Joly something, Joly responded, and both men looked across the room at her. She lifted a brow, and they turned away. Right. So Joly wasn't the only one with questions.

Roberts came into the room and dropped a stack of files on the conference room table. The resounding thud silenced conversation.

"All right, people, listen up. Those of you who have been following the news will know that this pregnancy virus has the nut-jobs crawling out of the woodwork. Attacks on women have more than doubled across the country. The demand for DNA testing—and abortions—has gone beyond the capacity to provide those services. Ob-gyns are canceling appointments and refusing to handle anything but straight-up deliveries. Every emergency ward, medical lab, and private clinic in the city has hired security guards, and we are fielding dozens of calls a day to those locations. This means we are stretched seriously thin."

Roberts pushed back his suit jacket to rest hands on hips. "As of today, all leave is canceled until further notice. You'll have your regular time off but nothing more. If you're looking for overtime, see me after the meeting. You can have as much as you want. If you're not looking for overtime, you're about to get more than you bargained for. From this moment forward, you will do the bulk of your paperwork in your cars. You will have your radios on at all times, and if you hear a call for backup in your vicinity, you will respond forthwith. I do not want to see you in this office unless you're picking something up or dropping it off. Are we clear?"

Heads around the room nodded.

"Good. Now these"—Roberts slapped his hand on the files—"are the sixty-seven files we currently have open. I want them updated before you go home tonight. All of them. If there is nothing new to add and the case has nothing to do with the current state of affairs in our city, put a note on it to that effect and pass it to Detective Jarvis—"

Alex abandoned her study of the wall behind her supervisor. "Me? But—"

"—who will be on desk duty until we find her a partner," Roberts finished. "Class dismissed. Jarvis, stay."

The others cleared the room, Joly taking the stack of files with him for distribution except for one their supervisor had set aside. The door closed. Roberts settled into a chair. With a nod, he indicated another, but Alex paced the edge of the room instead, coming to a halt in the far corner.

"Seriously, Staff? Desk duty?"

"My hands are tied where policy is concerned, Detective, especially when my decision to allow you to return at all is under scrutiny."

"I thought you'd taken care of that."

"So did I. Bell went to the chief, the little—" Roberts broke off and scrubbed a hand over his short-cropped hair. He sighed. "It's not ideal, and it's certainly not my preference, but it's how it has to be for now. And frankly, it might not be a bad thing to have your eyes on all the files right now."

He slid the file he'd held back from the pile toward her. "That came in from Alberta's RCMP this morning."

Alex stared at it, then stepped out of the corner and walked back to join him. She flipped open the folder and scanned the single page inside. "Militia? In Canada? Seriously?"

"End of the world nutcases," he corrected. "They're claiming the pregnancies and the recent rash of natural disasters are a sign of God's wrath. They've barricaded themselves into a compound outside Morinville, north of Edmonton. The news crews are going insane."

She could just imagine.

"We've had three similar reports out of the States," Roberts added. "Tech crime units across the continent are monitoring dozens of other groups that look to be moving in the same direction. I want you reviewing every file that comes through this office for the same reason."

Threading her fingers through her hair, Alex stared at the file. She understood the need for consistency, but to be cooped up in the office with all hell breaking loose in the world? She couldn't do it.

Roberts stood. "I'll light a fire under staffing and have you back on the street by the end of the week. You have my word."

One week.

Alex handed the file to her supervisor and watched him leave the conference room. She did a mental calculation. Today was Saturday, so that would make the end of the week the following Friday, six days away.

Just in time for the birth of Lucifer's army.

SEVEN

A ramael stared out at the barrens, mile after mile of dry, lifeless soil stretching as far as he could see in every direction. Scowling, he shot a look over his shoulder at Mika'el. "You're serious. You really want me to stand here and do nothing."

"No, I want you to keep watch. There's a difference."

Aramael snorted. "Forgive me if I fail to see one."

He surveyed the desolate landscape, featureless but for the stony outcrop on which he and Mika'el stood, the occasional bit of dead scrub brush . . . and the distant band of Hellfire that marked the edge of Heaven itself.

Raised against the Fallen when the One had created Hell, its flames had burned steadily, powerfully, and without cessation for millennia. Until Aramael, one of Heaven's own, had murdered his brother and broken the One's pact with Lucifer. Until the downward spiral into Armageddon itself had been triggered.

The wall of flames flickered, danced, steadied again.

Aramael's mouth twisted. "How long am I here for?"

"As long as it takes," Heaven's greatest warrior returned, his voice and expression implacable.

"Can I have a best guess?"

"A day. A year. A century."

"A century?" Of sitting out here in the middle of nowhere, far from Alex, waiting for something that might or might not happen? The possibility chafed.

"Perhaps a millennium." Mika'el flicked him an unreadable look. "We don't know how fast the Hellfire will break down enough to be breached, or how many of the Fallen will cross when it happens. We can't afford to leave it unprotected."

"With all the patrols you have going, I'd hardly call it unprotected," Aramael muttered, scanning the unwelcoming landscape again.

"I still prefer to have an Archangel keeping watch."

And as the newest member of the choir, the task fell to him. Great. Aramael shifted under the weight of his armor. "Shouldn't we be more concerned with the mortal realm? With no barrier to protect it, it seems more likely the Fallen will strike there first."

"The others can look after Earth."

"But—"

"And they're more likely to look after all of it, rather than just one Naphil."

Aramael shot a startled look at the other warrior. Hell. "How did you—?"

"You really expected otherwise?" Hard green eyes pinned him. "You assured me the connection between you was severed."

"It was. It is." His heart cringed at the lie. "I can manage it."

"By watching her?"

I just want to make certain she's happy. To see that Seth treats her well, that he cares for her. To reassure myself that I did the right thing in not fighting for her, in letting her go, even though I know I could never have had her.

"Habit," he said wearily. "It's just a habit. I'll break it."

"And being here will help you do so," Mika'el retorted, his voice brooking no argument. "Now, any questions before I leave?"

"Many. What are we waiting for? Why not just go after the Fallen and make sure the fight is on our terms rather than theirs?"

A muscle in the other Archangel's jaw contracted. "The agreement might have fallen, but Heaven's own rules remain unchanged. The One will not strike the first blow, Aramael. Good may *de*fend, but not *off*end."

Aramael thought about how Mika'el had come to him during his exile in the mortal realm and tasked him with the assassination of the One's son, the Appointed. How he would have carried out the order if it hadn't been for the interference of Alexandra Jarvis. How close he and Mika'el had skated to the very edge of *good*.

"Have you ever noticed how the rules for good are more constricting than those for evil?" he growled.

"Have you ever considered those restrictions are what keep us good?" The other Archangel countered. He drew himself up, topping Aramael's six-foot height by a good four inches. Massive, coal-black wings unfurled and stretched wide. "Remember who you are, Aramael. *What* you are. Angels are the final line of defense between Hell and Earth, and Archangels the last hope of—" He broke off, his face going bleak.

"Of what?"

"Nothing," Mika'el said. "It doesn't matter. Not anymore. Just remember we have no more room for mistakes."

With a great rush of wind, he launched upward, leaving Aramael alone on the boulder-strewn hill. Alone for days, weeks, months—maybe centuries— with nothing but his thoughts to keep him company. Thoughts of how he came to be in this place to begin with, memories of Alexandra Jarvis and how he had chosen her over his very purpose . . . and how she had chosen Seth over him.

Thoughts, memories, and that lingering tug of a connection he continued to deny to Mika'el.

EIGHT

"Shouldn't you be done for the day?"

Alex looked up from the news report she'd been reading on the computer monitor and met Seth's dark gaze. The breath hitched in her throat. Arms crossed over his chest and broad shoulders nearly filling the doorway, the man was sheer physical perfection from the top of his black-haired head to the soles of his exquisitely proportioned feet. Despite the exhaustion of her first day back in Homicide, a fragile warmth unfurled in her.

Seth might no longer be of Heaven, but his presence still packed a powerful punch. Time and again since she'd made her choice, moments like this had dispelled any lingering concern that her feelings for him might simply be tied to his divinity or, worse, a misguided sympathy. What she felt for the son of the One and Lucifer was far more than that . . . and far from simple.

The specter of his father complicated it further.

Seth's expression darkened. He knew she'd thought of Lucifer again. He always knew, sometimes before she did. A familiar, automatic apology rose into her throat. She held it back. After this morning's discussion—following which she still hadn't made a move to talk to anyone—her oft-repeated words would just rub salt into an already festering wound.

"I just need another ten minutes or so," she said. "I'm waiting for Henderson to call me back from Vancouver."

Seth's shoulders tensed, so imperceptibly that only a skilled interrogator would have noticed. Not for the first time, Alex wished she could turn off that part of herself, that she could take a person's words and actions at face value and not always be looking for what they hid from her. Such as Seth's ongoing displeasure.

"Is it about this morning's case? I thought you said Roberts gave the file to someone else."

This morning's case. File. Words that didn't begin to encompass the details of the day she'd shared with him over dinner. The immensity of a pregnant woman's murder, the child missing from her belly, Alex's hollow certainty about who—or what—might have taken it. Seth's disinterest in the same.

She snuffed out a flicker of irritation. He was still new to this mortal thing. He hadn't had a chance to develop a connection to humanity yet, apart from her. He just needed time.

She kept her voice even. "He did give the file to someone else. But if the killer is a Fallen One—"

"Then it won't matter. There's nothing you or Henderson can do."

"I can't stand by and do nothing, either."

The phone on the desk rang. Seth stared at it, then turned on his heel and left.

ALEX LIFTED THE RECEIVER on the third ring, when she was certain her voice could be trusted. "Hey, Hugh, thanks for calling me back."

"It was about bloody time you called *me* back," came the unceremonious rejoinder. "When I call you at eight a.m., Jarvis, and again at ten, noon, two, and four, you don't bloody wait until after nine at night to call me back."

Refraining—only just—from hanging up on the Vancouver detective who had become her friend, Alex let silence be her answer for a long moment. Then, her voice silky sweet, she inquired, "Done?"

A deep exhale sounded on the other end of the line. She pictured Henderson slumped at his desk, rubbing one hand over his cropped, graying hair.

"I was worried about you," he said, his voice quieter. "We both were."

"Both? Hell, don't tell me you called Riley." She didn't care how many good words the Vancouver psychiatrist put in for her with the brass, she still didn't like her—or her habit of poking at the unseen scars Alex preferred to think of as healed.

"She's my friend," Hugh answered her, "so yes, I stay in touch with her, and yes, she's worried, too."

"I'm fine, Hugh. I was fine when you called yesterday, I was fine when you called the day before, I was fine when I left Vancouver—"

Henderson snorted.

"—and I'm fine now," she finished. "Really."

"Right. You damn near die sticking a knife into

your own gut, get buried under a goddamn building, and now you're living with Lucifer's son. Of course you're fine. How could I possibly think otherwise?"

Alex pushed back the images his words conjured. Extracting her nails from her palms wasn't so easy. "Did Riley put you up to this?"

"I told you, she's worried about you," Hugh replied.

"I'm—"

"If you say *fine* again—"

"Surviving," Alex said. "I'm surviving. But I have to tell you, conversations like this don't make it any easier."

"Well, I guess that answers my next question of whether or not you're talking to anyone."

She snorted. "Right. And who do you suggest I talk to? I already have the department shrink watching my every move. If I so much as breathe a hint of what's going on—"

"You have Seth there. Talk to him."

Seth, who wanted nothing more than to put his past life behind him and have nothing to do with his parents' machinations. Who, through no fault of his own, had become another insurmountable barrier in her life—and one of her greatest sources of guilt.

"I don't want to talk to anyone," she said, her voice harsh. "I just want to do my goddamn job."

"Saving humanity from imploding is a little more than doing your job."

"Is this all you called for? To harass me?"

"You can be awfully stubborn, can't you?"

"You have no idea."

"Fine," he growled. "But just for the record, you're the one who wanted to talk to me, remember?"

Alex tried to think past the headache forming at

SINS OF THE LOST

the base of her skull. She considered reminding him he'd actually been the one trying to call her all day, but an argument over semantics would take way too much effort. Massaging her neck, she re-focused her thoughts. "Two things. First, Roberts called me in this morning. We had a woman turn up in a parking lot with her belly ripped open and the baby missing."

Silence. She listened to the faint ringing of a phone at Henderson's end. Another long exhale.

"We found one in a Dumpster two nights ago," he said. "Same thing."

Alex's own stomach tightened, cramped. She touched the scar that remained from her brush with a Naphil pregnancy, drew back her fingers as if scorched. "Are you sure?"

"That she was ripped open? Fairly." Henderson's attempt at gallows humor fell as flat as his voice. "I spent the better part of last night on the phone with Interpol," he continued. "There have been four others reported in the last twenty-four hours. One in India, one in the States, and two in China."

Her gaze returned to the computer monitor and the article she'd been reading.

"If that keeps up, it'll seriously screw with the bioterrorism theories," she said. "There's no group in the world organized enough to steal babies from across the planet. At least, not a human one."

"Interpol is setting up a task force anyway. They have no choice."

For a moment, she envied the cops who would be a part of that task force, analyzing, investigating, doing all the things they'd been taught to do in their mortal world. She wondered what it would be like to go back to that state of blissful ignorance. To forget all that had happened, all that was still to come. Would she do it if she could? Even if it meant losing Seth?

"You said there were two things," Henderson reminded her.

She switched off the monitor, then changed the subject. "Morinville."

"Yeah, I saw that."

"You don't think the scrolls—?"

"A leak? No. Anyone with access to them would have been able to give the press more specifics. This is just pure knee-jerk fanaticism. You have to remember how much practice the Vatican has at keeping secrets."

"Even the Church has rumors."

"True, but the press would straight-up say where they'd got that kind of information."She grunted a concession, then added, "That doesn't mean something won't get out eventually, and when it does, we're screwed six ways to Sunday."

"Let's worry about that when—if—it happens. Now, how is Seth doing?"

"Settling in. It's hard for him."

"Still not talking about it? Because we could really use some insider information. He does realize the Nephilim could wipe us out, right?"

"He's also been betrayed by both his parents, used for millennia as a pawn in their twisted little game, and given up everything he ever was in order to put all that behind him," she snapped. "How happy would you be to rehash your parents' attempts to kill you?"

"Easy, Jarvis. I was only asking."

She bit the inside of her cheek, creating a physical pain to distract herself from the one in her heart. It didn't help. "I know. I'll keep working on him."

In between working on her own issues.

Henderson cleared his throat, but his voice remained gruff. "It's late there. Get some sleep, and I'll talk to you tomorrow."

Murmuring a good night, Alex replaced the receiver in its cradle. The headache had spread, filling her skull, throbbing in time to her heartbeat. She closed her eyes against the pain. Against the fine thread of constant tension that caused it.

Her brain replayed Henderson's words. *"He does know the Nephilim could wipe us out, right?"*

Yes, he knew. She just didn't know how to make him care. Especially when she couldn't—

Warm hands settled onto her shoulders, massaging at the knots that never went away anymore. She sat quietly, letting Seth's strength seep into her and chase away the shadows that wanted to gather at her core.

Long minutes later, when his hands left her shoulders to link with her own, she opened her eyes, let him draw her up out of the chair, and followed him to their bedroom. There would be no pressure tonight, no demand for anything she wasn't ready to give. She knew that, because she knew he cared for her.

And if he cared for her, he could learn to care for others.

He just needed time.

NINE

Lucifer looked up at the sound of a tap on his office door. His aide, Samael, stood in the opening, an aura of apology surrounding him. Lucifer scowled.

"Still nothing?" He tossed down his pen. "Bloody Heaven, how hard can it be to trace them?"

Samael leaned a shoulder against the door frame, his reluctance to venture inside clearly written across his expression, right beside the scars that served as Lucifer's permanent reminder about who truly ruled Hell.

"I warned you this could take a while," he said. "They're Nephilim. Without Guardians we can eavesdrop on, we have no way to trace them other than through the woman."

Lucifer's nostrils flared, and the hand he rested on the desk curled into a fist. Across the room, Sam shifted. Lucifer didn't bother telling him it was the thought of the woman that irritated him and not Sam's news. He liked the former Archangel this way: a little nervous, a little cautious, a lot respectful.

No, Sam wasn't the issue. The woman, on the other hand . . . now, she infuriated him. The defiance, the sheer insolence . . . His fingers curled tighter. Killing his child, maiming herself so she could not bear another . . .

He glowered at his aide. "Have we made *any* progress?"

"We've located where the woman works, and we're watching her around the clock. It's just a matter of time until she reaches out to her sister."

"*Watching* her? Why in bloody Heaven would we sit back and *watch*? Take her, damn it. *Make* her tell you where to find the sister."

"That might not be wise. The Archangels have been watching her, too. At first it was only Aramael, and I thought it was personal, but now Mika'el is hovering over her. We don't know what his interest is, but if we take her and he wants her . . ."

His aide's voice trailed off.

"Bloody Heaven!" Lucifer thrust back his chair and rose, stalking to the window. Weariness wound through him. What was the Archangel up to now? The warrior had been such a thorn in his side. The only being in all of Heaven, other than the One, powerful enough to take him on and not be decimated in the process. First rallying the Archangels to force him across that damnable Hellfire barrier, then derailing his attempt to mold his son, and now returning to interfere yet again.

Bracing a hand on either side of the window, he stared out at the gray, brittle landscape. The gardens that defied his efforts to recreate Heaven had declined yet further. Nothing remained but the withered corpses of what he'd intended. Bitterness filled him, settling like dry dust on his tongue.

For the first time in his existence, disquiet slithered down his spine. A possibility he'd denied for more than six thousand years took form low in his belly, gelled into certainty.

I'm going to lose it, he thought. *I'm going to lose it all.*

Maybe not now, maybe not even soon, but eventually.

It was inevitable.

For an instant, the realization paralyzed him. Held him as a fly might be held by a spider, passive and unmoving, tangled beyond hope in strands of unbreakable silk. He shook off the suffocating cling of the metaphor. Loss might be inevitable, but it wouldn't happen yet. Not if he could help it.

Not until he had ensured humanity's absolute, total destruction. He spun back to face Samael.

"What about the Nephilim? Are we at least ready for them?"

"We're working on it. The city we chose has been abandoned for a long time. It's not an easy task readying it without drawing attention to ourselves."

"You've had human interference?"

"Not in Pripyat itself, no. We caused the radiation levels to spike, so they've shut the area down tight. The only way in is through checkpoints, and we control those. Making arrangements for supplies without alerting the Guardians has been interesting, but so far we've managed. The pregnant humans, however, are another matter. We've had to assign a watcher to each of them to prevent them from ridding themselves of the babies."

"Can we not just move them to the site right now?"

"And end up fighting the war with Heaven in the midst of your unborn army? That might not be the wisest course of action. We're better off waiting until after the births. We'll only need a few Fallen to tend the children then, and the rest of us can draw the host away from them. Keep them occupied. Besides, we're not sure what the radiation levels in the city might do to the mothers. If they became ill, they might not be able to carry the babies to term."

"But the infants themselves won't be harmed." A statement, not a question, and one that dared contradiction.

Samael shook his head. "Not as far as we can tell. We've harvested a few over the last week as test subjects. So far they seem to be thriving."

"And how long before the rest are born?"

"Only a week."

Lucifer gritted his teeth at the placating tone of his aide's voice and resisted the urge to throw something at him. Such as his desk. "Fine. Then that's how long you have to find the Naphil's sister."

Fleeting exasperation crossed Samael's face, and then he nodded. "I'll see that the trackers step up their effort."

"No. Not the trackers. You."

"Me? But I—"

"The others don't know how important this is. You do. The Nephilim need a leader. They need this child I will father. If their place is as ready as you claim, then you're free to pursue this for me. Find the Naphil's sister, Samael. And don't come back until you do."

TEN

Verchiel found the One seated beneath an arbor in the rose garden, eyes closed, so still that she might have been one with the wood. Loath to disturb her, Verchiel paused, studying the lines in the beloved face. Lines she was certain hadn't been there before. Her heart squeezed in on itself. *She looks so . . . fragile.*

Her hesitation deepened. Perhaps she should leave, come back later.

"Come," her Creator said. "Sit with me."

"If I'm disturbing you . . ."

A moment's silence, then the One's eyes opened, and some of the lines smoothed away from her forehead. She patted the bench beside her. "Not at all. I was just containing my son's folly. Again."

Verchiel crossed the sweep of lawn and settled on the seat. "How is that coming?"

"It isn't. Every time I think I have it under control, it finds another escape. I'm not sure how much more the planet can take without self-destructing."

"And you? How much more can you take?"

"A good question." The One pulled a spray of roses toward her, inhaling deeply. "I suppose as much as I must. But we're not here to talk about me."

Guilt ensnared Verchiel's voice and held it captive. It was true. She had come in search of the Creator for other reasons. More selfish ones.

The Creator's hand covered her own in her lap and squeezed. "Tell me."

"It's just—" She blinked away the sheen of moisture blurring the garden. "You have always . . . been. The very idea you can cease to do so terrifies me."

The One's hand pressed hers. "Not cease, Verchiel. Alter. I'll still be here, just not like this."

"But this—this is how we know you, One, and I don't know how to go on without that." Verchiel turned her hand over in the One's until their fingers linked. "Your counsel, your guidance, your very presence . . ."

"All of that will still be yours. You'll just have to pay closer attention. I'll still be a part of you, as all mothers remain a part of their children. My voice will be in yours if you choose to hear it. My counsel and guidance in your heart if you choose to heed them."

A tear spilled over onto Verchiel's cheek. With a rueful sigh, the One reached out her free hand to wipe it away.

"Close your eyes," she commanded.

Verchiel did.

"Now breathe."

She inhaled.

"Do you smell the roses? The grass and trees and a thousand other scents that mingle with them?"

A nod.

"Those are *my* scents, Verchiel. The scents of my

skin, my breath, my very essence. Every breath you take, every inhale, every exhale—that is me. The sun warming your skin and the breeze playing with your hair—those are me, too. Holding you, loving you, cradling you close. And the beat of your heart inside your chest? My very life force, made manifest in you."

The One lifted her hand, pressing it against a soft, lined cheek. "This, the physical part of me to which you cling, this is but a tiny fraction of what I am, my angel. I am so, so much more than what you can touch or see or feel. I am everything. All you have to do is want to understand that."

Verchiel sat. Listened. Strained to feel what the One described to her. She shook her head.

"I'm so sorry," she whispered, "for not being strong enough."

"Hush, child. After all you have been, all you have done, you have nothing for which to apologize. You are as strong as you need to be. The rest will come in time."

Verchiel pressed a hand against the ache in her chest. This struggle was her own. The One did not need the extra burden of her doubt; she needed her help. Even if helping meant losing her.

"Tell me what you need me to do."

"Watch over the Archangel Mika'el for me. He takes on too much—more than he needs to—and he's terrible at asking for help."

"He doubts Seth."

The Creator of All looked out over the garden. Her gaze became distant again, her face shadowed with a sorrow that made Verchiel's own pale in comparison. .

"As do I, Verchiel," she murmured. "As do I."

ELEVEN

Alex steered down the ramps and around the pillars of the underground parking complex. Fatigue sat heavy behind her eyes, the result of another mostly sleepless night spent staring at the ceiling. Returning to work had seemed like a good idea, but now she wondered how long she could keep it up. Playing at being a cop, pretending everything was normal and not teetering on the edge of total destruction.

Just another day at the office.

Yawning, she rounded the final corner to her parking level. The sedan straightened out again—

And bore down on a man directly in its path.

Adrenaline shot through her and she jammed her foot onto the brake, but it was too late. She had no room to get around him, nowhere to go, no time. She braced for the impact. The car jerked to a halt, and she stared in horror out the windshield at—

Nothing.

No one slumped across the hood. No one hurled to the pavement by the collision of steel against flesh. No one at—

A tap sounded at the window beside her.

"Christ!" She whipped around in her seat, then froze. An emerald gaze met hers, holding it with a familiar, shoulder-knotting intensity. She stared at the arrogant features, the watchful stance, the broad expanse of black wings.

Michael.

A hundred possible reasons for his presence flitted through her mind, none of them good. For a second, she considered putting the vehicle back into gear and driving away. She might have done so if she thought she could get away with it.

But she didn't think one ignored an Archangel.

Reaching for the electric window button, she saw that the glass between them had already dissolved. The desire to run away grew exponentially. She clamped her teeth together.

"Naphil." Michael's tone was reserved. Guarded.

Irritation sparked. They were back to that, were they?

"Archangel," she responded.

Annoyance flared in the green depths. Good. Maybe he'd get the message . . . eventually.

"We need to speak."

"About what?" Glancing in the rearview mirror, she saw another vehicle pull up behind her. "Wait. I need to move. There's a café across the street from the main door. I'll park and meet you there."

Michael hesitated, most likely weighing the chance she might not show up. The car behind Alex tooted its horn. His gaze flicking toward the sound, Michael nodded, withdrew behind a concrete pillar, and vanished. Alex stared at the emptiness left behind, convinced she would never, ever get used to the disappearing act.

A second impatient toot jolted her back to the present. She waved a hand out the windowless opening—hell, she'd forgotten to ask Michael to undo that particular trick—and took her foot off the brake.

SHE FOUND MICHAEL seated by the window in the back of the crowded café. Sliding into the chair opposite, she shook her head at the waitress's offer of a menu and asked for a coffee. Michael declined to order anything. With a huff of displeasure, the harried-looking woman stomped off to serve other, presumably higher-paying clients. Michael cleared his throat.

"You look well."

Alex raised a brow. Small talk? From an angel? She reached past him for the sugar dispenser, taking in the stiff lines of his shoulders, his fists resting on the chipped tabletop.

"And you're not here to exchange pleasantries," she replied. "So you might as well get to the point."

"I need your help."

"I thought you said my part in your affairs was done."

"It was supposed to be. Something has changed."

She frowned. "This morning's murder?"

It was Michael's turn to raise an eyebrow.

She cast a look at the crush of breakfast patrons crammed into the restaurant. At the table nearest them, a lone man turned the page in his newspaper, giving it a snap to straighten it out. She lowered her voice.

"One of the pregnant women turned up dead. The baby was ripped out of her. Detective Henderson says there have been others. Five altogether that we know of. If I had to guess, I'd say the Fallen Ones are to blame."

Beyond a brief flash of annoyance, however, the Archangel looked unperturbed. "I told you, the Nephilim are your concern, not ours. That's not why I'm—"

She slammed down the sugar dispenser. "Maybe you didn't hear me right. We're already dealing with the Nephilim problem, Michael. Women across the globe are terrified of becoming pregnant, demand for DNA testing has soared beyond all capacity to provide it, and religious fringe groups are all over the Internet spouting off about the end of the world being nigh. But this? This is the Fallen Ones killing human women. That sounds like direct interference to me. The kind of interference you're supposed to have rules about."

Michael regarded her. She scowled back, silently daring him to say what they were both thinking: that the women would die anyway. He sighed.

"Fine. I'll increase our surveillance. Now can we please move on?"

"To what?"

Hesitation flickered across her companion's face, just enough to make ice crystals form in her veins. Hell, maybe she *should* have driven away when she had the chance.

I could still leave. Before he tells me why he's here, I could walk out. Just like that. Stand up, pay for my coffee, and—

"We need Seth to take back his powers."

The air hissed from her. "Excuse me?"

"His choice has had repercussions—"

"Stop." Holding up both hands against his words, she leaned back in her seat, as far away from him as the chair would allow. "Why hasn't Seth told me this?"

Michael's expression turned wooden. "He doesn't know."

"You haven't spoken to him?"

"I thought it best to speak to you first."

"Then this conversation is over."

"You don't understand. The world—"

"No, *you* don't understand." She glared at him. "You wanted to kill him. His own mother wanted to kill him. You would have cut him down where he stood in that alley if Aramael hadn't helped me get to him, even after you promised to give me time to help him. You lied. To him, to me—" She broke off, remembering their very public location.

"I did what was necessary," Michael growled. "You don't know all that's going on—"

"And I don't want to. The only reason you're coming to me is because you know Seth won't give you the time of day on this. He made his choice, and you made yours."

"Damn it, Naphil—"

Alex slammed a fistful of change on the table beside her untouched coffee. She stood. "You told me once that I was done with your affairs, and now I'm telling you. I'm done. And so is Seth."

Iron fingers clamped over her wrist.

"If Seth doesn't take back his powers—"

"What, you'll put out an assassination order on

him?" she hissed. "Oh, wait, I forgot. You already did that. For God's sake, Michael"—how ironic that she should invoke the Almighty's name at a time like this—"you've done enough to him. You know that, or you'd be talking to him, not me. Just let him go. Please."

Michael's jaw flexed. "We can't."

"Then grow a set and talk to him yourself. Because I'll be goddamned if I'll do your dirty work for you." Tugging free, Alex pushed past the man with the newspaper and stalked out of the café.

TWELVE

Mika'el watched Alex stalk across the street and into the police station, her every line rigid. Leaning an elbow on the table, he raked his fingers through his hair. Well. That had gone just swimmingly. He grimaced.

Who was he kidding? It had gone exactly as he'd expected. Except for her parting shot, perhaps. His grimace became a scowl. *Grow a set?* Bloody Hell, she had a nerve.

Still, he couldn't fault her reaction. Every accusation she'd made had been accurate. He'd given her no reason to trust him—or to listen to anything he had to tell her. Even though he knew damned well what Seth's reaction would be, he should have at least talked to him first. Maybe if he had—Mika'el went still.

Across the street, the man who'd followed the Naphil from the restaurant, newspaper tucked beneath his arm, stopped to speak with another lounging against the side of the police station. Another that would appear human to mortal eyes, but Mika'el saw what they could not. An aura of power that marked him as an Archangel—but not one of Heaven. Not anymore.

Samael.

Halfway out of his chair, Mika'el froze as the other looked up, locking gazes with him. Golden eyes gleamed with bitterness, hatred, challenge.

Thrusting back the chair with a force that sent it crashing to the floor, he put his hand to his side. It closed over nothing. He hadn't brought his sword, hadn't thought he would need it. And if he'd had it, he still couldn't have gotten to his foe without pulling out of the mortal realm, something he and Samael both knew he wouldn't do in full view of dozens of people.

As if he'd read his thoughts, Samael bared his teeth in a mock grin, sketched a salute in his direction, and strolled around the corner. All sense of his presence disappeared. The man with the newspaper looked around at Mika'el, his

Bloody Hell. Mika'el picked up the chair and slammed it back into place at the table. A murmur of alarm washed through the restaurant. The waitress reached for a telephone behind the counter. Reining in his fury, he strode through the crowded restaurant and pushed out onto the sidewalk. He scanned the street for the newspaper man, but he, too, had disappeared.

Bloody, bloody Hell.

What was the sole Fallen Archangel doing watching the Naphil?

MITTRON, former executive administrator of Heaven, sagged back into the grimy building entrance, staring at the posters of barely clad women plastered against the glass. He struggled to think through the fog that had become his brain. To sort out the unexpected turn of events.

He'd spent weeks making his way here, using every spark of ingenuity he possessed—in his coherent moments—to find the woman. To discover where she lived, where she worked. To see if maybe, impossibly, the connection he'd tried so hard to sever between her and her soulmate might have survived. Because if it had, if she could call Aramael to her in a time of need, if enough of the immortal survived in the former Power to do for Mittron what he had done for Caim . . .

He inhaled shakily, pressing palms against the rough brick behind him. So many ifs. And such a crude plan, born of desperation and a far cry from the beautiful, intricate schemes he had once woven. He hadn't held out any real hope that it would work. He'd just needed to focus on something—anything— to keep the insanity at bay.

When he'd found Aramael—now an Archangel with the ability to take his life a thousand times over— already camped out on the Naphil's doorstep, it hadn't just been fortuitous, it had elevated crude to possible. Desperation to a soul-consuming need for oblivion.

But now Mika'el and Samael hovered around her, too? What purpose could either of them possibly have for a Naphil? Especially one so far removed from her bloodline as to have been rendered useless? A faint whisper touched the edge of his consciousness, and his fingers spasmed into fists. No. Not now. Not yet. He needed to think, to focus.

He gritted his teeth against the wound reopening

in his soul. He would have to leave soon, before the whispers became wails. Before they turned to the mind-destroying screams of every soul lost to the Fallen, his to bear for eternity, underscored by the anguish of the One he had betrayed.

Grinding already lacerated knuckles into the brick, he slammed his head back against the wall, trying to mask mental agony with physical pain. Needing to think clearly for a few minutes more.

Mika'el and Samael didn't matter. This was about the woman. He needed to catch her alone. Force her to call for Aramael the way Caim had done. If Aramael's connection remained strong enough, he would be able to do for Mittron what he had done for his own brother and put him out of his misery, end the suffering inflicted by their Creator.

But he had to move soon. He didn't know how much longer his mind would survive. So many of the human drugs had already lost their efficacy, and he was running out of new ones to try. If he couldn't mask the voices anymore, his Judgment would become the torture the One had intended. An eternal, soul-shattering persecution he would never escape.

Another moan, this one his own. He clamped his teeth down on his tongue. The metallic, salty tang of blood filled his mouth. Through a haze of tears, he focused on the building into which the Naphil woman had disappeared. Screw Mika'el and Samael and Aramael. If she returned, if she came outside again now, before the pain took over and immobilized him completely, he'd take the chance.

A shriek broke through the incessant buzz of voices. He slammed his head against the brick again but felt nothing. No impact, no pain, no distraction.

He'd run out of time. He had to find relief while he still could. Winding fingers into his hair, he pressed bloody, scarred knuckles against his skull. Forced air into his lungs. *Stay focused. It helps. Think about the woman . . . about Aramael . . . Mika—*

Anguish shredded his already tattered core.

Sometimes focus helped.

Sometimes it didn't.

Sobbing, he staggered down the street.

THIRTEEN

The outrage that had powered Alex's exit from the café deserted her by the time she stepped out of the elevator on the fourth floor, leaving her deflated, shaking, and wanting nothing more than to go home to Seth.

Or to puke her guts out.

Leaning against the corridor wall, she rested hands on knees and stared at the thinly carpeted floor.

And if I do go home? What do I tell him? That the Heaven that turned its back on him—tried to kill him—needs his help? That they want him to take back what nearly destroyed him in the first place?

Her head sagged. Hell, she couldn't even tell him why. She hadn't stuck around long enough to find out what lay behind the Archangel's announcement because whether or not Michael had been willing to tell her more had been a moot point. She hadn't been in any shape to hear it.

She shuddered. She couldn't get involved again. Not

in the battle between Heaven and Hell. She'd nearly died the last two times—*had* died, for all intents and purposes. She didn't think she could survive a third time, even if Seth *could* bring her back again.

Which he couldn't.

Unless he took back those damned powers.

The cell phone at her waist vibrated. Taking it from its holster, she stared at the caller ID. Home. Seth. Hell. Her thumb lingered on the answer button, moved sideways, pushed ignore. She replaced the phone, then, inhaling deeply, stepped into the chaos that was Homicide.

"THAT'S IT?" Lucifer asked. He didn't look up from his desk.

Samael risked a scowl at the top of the Light-bearer's head. "I'm not sure I understand."

Lucifer continued scrawling in yet another of the damnable journals in which he recorded his every move, his every thought. "That's all the news you have. Speculation about the Appointed, garnered from a human, no less. Nothing about the Naphil's sister or niece." His tone remained conversational. Even. Too much so.

Samael shifted, assuring himself that he did so for comfort and not as a way to move closer to the door. "No, but—"

"Perhaps I didn't make myself clear enough with regard to my expectations."

"I understand the woman and her sister are a priority, Lucifer"—bloody Heaven, how he hated that placating tone in his voice—"but this is important, too. If Mika'el is right and Seth is able to take back his powers—"

"What my son does or doesn't do has no bearing on me."

"I disagree. Any battle with Heaven is already weighted against us—heavily. If they convince him to take back his powers and align himself with them, it could very well have *great* bearing."

At last Lucifer laid aside his pen and the journal in which he'd been writing. He sat back, eyes closed, resting one elbow on the chair's arm. He pinched the bridge of his nose.

"Exactly how many times must we go over this, Archangel?" he asked wearily. "I don't care about Heaven. I have what I want—or I will, if you can focus long enough. Once the Nephilim army is in place and my child born to lead it, the One will be able to do nothing to stop humanity's annihilation. With or without Seth on her side."

"Maybe not, but she'd have an excellent chance of destroying Hell."

"That could be a problem," Lucifer conceded. "If I cared any more about Hell than I do Heaven."

Samael's breath left him in a hiss. So. They were back to that, were they? He scowled. "Damn it, Lucifer, if we're to survive, this has to be about more than just the mortals."

"Again you assume I care."

Samael stared at the One's former helpmeet, at his slumped shoulders and closed eyes. He thought he had seen the Light-bearer's every mood, every frame of mind, but this—this was new. And it bore far too great a resemblance to defeat for his liking.

"With all due respect," he said, "those of us concerned about our continued existence do care.

Wiping out the mortals is one thing, but what about the ones who followed you, who remain loyal to you? We deserve—"

Lucifer's eyes snapped open, purple fire burning in their depths. "You deserve *what*? My undying gratitude? My return loyalty? For fuck's sake, Archangel, when will you get it through your head that I don't care? I *can't* care. Not about you, not about the others, not about myself. My entire existence is about *her*. For *her*. Because of *her*. Heaven and Hell and the whole damned universe could implode, and it wouldn't matter to me because I just. Don't. Care."

A thick, bitter sense of betrayal rose in Samael's chest and sat heavy on his tongue. "So that's it? We're just supposed to admit defeat? Throw away our lives for you without trying? That's what you want from us?"

Across the room, Hell's ruler held up one hand, rubbed his thumb across his fingertips and formed a fist. His gaze locking with Samael's, he tightened his fingers until the knuckles stood white against his already pale skin, then spread his fingers wide. Agony shocked through Samael, driving him back against the door, holding him there.

Through streaming eyes, he watched Lucifer rise and stroll across the room. The Light-bearer stopped before him, placing a hand on the shoulder he had once ruined.

"No, Samael, I do not want an admission of defeat. Do you know why? Because my definition of defeat differs from yours. You do know what I would consider that to be, don't you?" His fingers squeezed, and the pain of a thousand knives sliced down Samael's arm and across his chest. Lucifer leaned in, close enough for the warmth of his breath to stir against Samael's ear. "Well?"

"Mortals," Samael ground out from between clenched teeth. "Allowing mortals to live would be defeat."

"Exactly. And your deaths, Sam? The deaths of each and every Fallen One who chose to follow me? How do you think I would define those?"

"I don't—"

Another tightening of Lucifer's grip.

Samael's knees gave way, but he couldn't fall. Couldn't escape the hold on his shoulder pinning him upright. His sweat-slicked hands scrabbled at the doorknob.

"Think hard," the Light-bearer encouraged.

"Sacrifice!" he choked. "Death is sacrifice!"

"*Necessary* sacrifice," his tormentor clarified. "Excellent. You *do* understand."

With a final, vicious squeeze, Lucifer released him. Samael slid to the floor, fighting back the black that threatened, the nausea that would surely bring further punishment. He listened to Lucifer's retreating footsteps. The creak of leather told him the Light-bearer had settled into the chair behind the desk; the scratch of quill tip against paper said he continued writing.

Bit by bit, the pain receded. When it became bearable, Samael groped for the doorknob, pulled himself upright, and opened the door enough to slip into the corridor. Lucifer's voice stopped him halfway through.

"One last thing, Archangel."

Samael looked over his shoulder. Cringed. Waited.

"Just so we're clear, death as sacrifice for success is

infinitely preferable to that which would accompany defeat. You'll want to remember that."

Samael stood in the corridor for a long, long time, staring at the closed door, waiting for the vestiges of pain to ease. Slowly the terror that had claimed him under Lucifer's grip gave way to cold fury.

Necessary sacrifice? Was the Light-bearer serious? He really expected all of them, all of the Fallen who had followed him out of Heaven and believed in him, to throw themselves on the swords of their kin as *sacrifice*?

Samael exhaled a long hiss into the silence.

Of course he did.

He always had.

He'd told him so, when the Pact had been shattered and the remains of peace between Heaven and Hell had hung in tatters: *"War was never my priority. I've never pretended otherwise."*

Samael hadn't wanted to believe him then. He'd clung to the certainty that, when the time came, Hell's ruler would come to his senses and lead them in the war to reclaim their rightful home.

Now, however . . . Samael put a hand to his shoulder. Now he believed him.

And there wasn't a bloody thing he could do about it.

Because while the others might welcome battle as much as he did, might even turn their backs on Lucifer's idea of success for the chance to return to Heaven, they would never be able to pull it off without a leader. Jockeying for control would begin immediately, and Samael didn't kid himself for a moment that he was powerful enough to replace Lucifer as ruler. If he had the backing of a half dozen

Archangels the way Michael did, perhaps. But alone? Not a chance. Once the infighting began, Hell would be awash in the blood of its own occupants.

Footsteps approached on the other side of Lucifer's office door, jolting Samael back to the present. If the Light-bearer found him standing out here dithering over his future, there would be questions. And, when he couldn't or wouldn't answer, more pain. Or worse.

He needed to stop worrying about a future if he intended to live long enough to have one. More importantly, he needed to find a Naphil.

FOURTEEN

"It didn't go well."

A statement, not a question.

Head tipped back against his chair, Mika'el didn't bother opening his eyes. "No," he said. "No, Verchiel, it did not go well. Did we really expect otherwise?"

He listened to the Highest Seraph settle into one of the chairs on the opposite side of the desk.

"What did she say?"

"She told me to grow a set and talk to Seth myself."

Silence. Then what sounded like a muffled snort. Cracking open an eyelid, he found Verchiel struggling to hide a smile. He scowled. "The world is ripping itself apart, and the one mortal who might have helped me hold it together has refused. I fail to see the humor."

Steady blue eyes regarded him. "It's not humor that makes me smile, Mika'el, but admiration. You're the most powerful warrior in all of Heaven. You led the battle against Lucifer himself. Do you know of any other being, mortal or otherwise, that might have the nerve to tell you what she did? This Naphil has great courage."

He closed his eyes again, this time pinching the bridge of his nose. "I don't need her courage, I need her cooperation."

"Then earn it. Speak to Seth. Perhaps he will surprise us."

"Neither of us believes that. The Appointed has twice tried to avoid his responsibility. We have no reason to believe he will do otherwise now."

He avoided adding what he privately thought, but peering through his fingers at Verchiel, he saw the same concern—no, the same certainty—written across her face, too. Seth, son of their Creator, was weak. Very possibly too weak to do what they needed of him. Which would leave them all—Heaven and Earth alike—in an unspeakably fragile position.

Verchiel's chin lifted. "Even if you're right, even if he refuses you, at least you'll have tried. Perhaps the woman will be more inclined to step in then."

"I have no time for *perhaps*, Seraph. I need certainties."

"Fine. You *certainly* won't solve anything sitting behind your desk."

Sheer surprise at the tart rejoinder made him drop his hand. "Excuse me?"

"You heard me, Mika'el. The One has given you a task. No matter how distasteful you find it, you cannot avoid the inevitable forever."

He glowered at her. "There's another complication."

"Is that possible when things are already so complicated?" Verchiel asked wryly.

"Samael is watching her."

All hint of amusement dropped from the Highest

Seraph's expression. "What possible interest could he have in her?"

"If I knew, I wouldn't be sitting here racking my brain for answers instead of going after the Appointed."

Verchiel raised a brow at his thinly veiled snarl. Then she frowned. "Wait—you haven't left her unguarded?"

"Samael would have taken her by now if he wanted to do so."

"Unless he noticed you hovering around her."

"He did see me, but only today. He could have taken her anytime before—" Remembering how Aramael had watched over the woman before him, he stopped. He rotated a quarter turn one way and then the other in his swivel chair.

"There has to be a reason Hell is interested in her," Verchiel pressed. "We can't afford to take chances, not with the state things are in right now."

She had a point.

"I'll put a watch on her." Seeing her shoulders straighten, he held up a hand. "No. I know what you're thinking, and it's out of the question."

"This isn't just any Fallen One we're talking about. It's Samael. If he makes any kind of move, none less than an Archangel can stop him."

"There are five other Archangels." Well, four that he could use, because putting Raphael anywhere near his traitor of a brother would be just plain stupid.

"None of whom have any experience inhabiting the human realm. Aramael was a Power before he was an Archangel, Mika'el. He has walked among the humans before, and is less likely to draw attention to himself."

"He still feels a connection to her."

Her lips pursed. "Another reason it should be him. The others will follow orders as best they can, but in their eyes, the woman remains tainted by her bloodline. None will fight harder to keep Samael away from her than he will. None will give up his own life for hers."

"Is that what we want? An Archangel giving up his life for a Naphil?"

"Of course not. But if Hell is interested in her, then you can't risk her, either. Not until you know *why* they're interested."

Twisting the chair back and forth again, Mika'el studied her. "You never used to be this"—he hesitated to use the word *cold*—"pragmatic."

"I never used to be responsible for Heaven trying to save the world, either. I don't like what I suggest, but neither do I see a choice."

Verchiel rose with a rustle of robes. Crossing to the door, she reached for the handle, then looked over her shoulder. "And, Mika'el, just so you're clear, you *will* need the Naphil's courage. If we're to convince Seth to return to his rightful place here, with us, you'll need all the courage she possesses and more."

FIFTEEN

The scuff of boot against rock snagged Aramael's attention. He looked down the mountainside to see Raphael emerge from a crevice. The Archangel's dark skin was almost indistinguishable from the black armor he wore, making him little more than a massive shadow amid the many other shadows.

Albeit one with a sizable grudge.

Raphael paused and stared up. Aramael couldn't see his eyes, but he felt his gaze—and the animosity behind it. He returned to his vigil, resting his right hand on the hilt of his sword. Raphael's glowering looks over the last few days had made it clear their previous encounter hadn't been forgotten. Frankly, Aramael was surprised it had taken him this long to get around to a confrontation.

The other Archangel crested the hill, the reflection of the distant flames of Hellfire dancing across his burnished face.

"News?" Aramael asked, careful to keep his voice

even. Mika'el would be pissed in the extreme if two of Heaven's protectors went at each other; Aramael had created quite enough conflict in the world without starting something else here now.

"You know that's not why I'm here." Raphael stopped a half dozen feet away.

Aramael's fingers contracted on his sword's pommel. He stared out across the barren wastelands and the band of Hellfire beyond, the last, thinning barrier between two armies sworn to fight to the death. If Lucifer ever got around to taking the first swing.

"I don't suppose an apology will do any good, but in the interests of maintaining peace, I'm sorry I called you a bastard. As I remember, the circumstances were somewhat extenuating."

If that's what one wanted to call being ripped out of the human realm by force and handed over to the Seraph responsible for engineering his downfall.

Raphael shifted his stance, settling his feet more firmly into the sparse, arid soil. "I've been called worse, Power. That's not why I'm here, either."

Aramael raised a brow at the other Archangel's use of his former designation. So that's what this was about. "Issues with my promotion?" he inquired.

"Issues with your track record."

"You think Mika'el made a mistake."

"I think he has a lot on his mind and might not have thought this through as well as he should have. I think you're more liability than asset."

A flare along the fiery border drew their attention. Aramael stared in its direction, waiting. Brilliant yellow turned red, and the ripple of tension across his shoulders faded. If the flare had turned blue, it would have meant an attempted breach. But red was good.

He looked back at the other Archangel, who still stared across the wasteland. "Was there something else, or was that the only insult you wanted to deliver?"

"It wasn't an insult. It was a statement of fact. You're a liability, and I'll be watching you. We have enough to worry about in this bloody war without having one of our own screw things up for us. One misstep, one hint that you've lost control . . ." Raphael made a snick sound as he drew a finger across his throat. "Am I clear?"

Seeming satisfied his message had been delivered, he started down the hill. Aramael held back a *fuck you* and waited until the other had taken several steps. Then he cleared his throat. Raphael slowed, stopped, and looked over his shoulder.

"The decision was Mika'el's," Aramael reminded him. He was all for keeping the peace, but he'd be damned if he wouldn't respond to whatever Raphael wanted to start. "The One sanctioned it. Like it or not, I'm one of you now, and—"

The other Archangel's blade pressed against his throat before he could finish. Aramael froze, staring into the vicious golden eyes inches from his own.

"You are *not* one of us," Raphael hissed. "We have passed through Hellfire itself, and we bear the scars on our souls to prove it. You might wear the armor and carry the sword of our kind, but you will never be one of us. *Ever.* Do you understand?"

Even if he'd wanted to nod assent, the finely honed metal nestled below Aramael's jaw discouraged him from doing so. Wordlessly, he held Raphael's glare until the Archangel sheathed his sword. Stalking down the hillside once more, Raphael flicked a last glower over his shoulder.

"Remember what I said, *Power*. I'm watching."

SIXTEEN

"All quiet?" Mika'el asked as he topped the rubble knoll where Aramael stood.

Aramael shrugged. He adjusted the armor chafing under his arms. "One flare-up that settled down," he said. "And one visit from Raphael. The latter was by far more exciting."

Mika'el settled a foot on a boulder and leaned forward, bracing his forearms across his armor-clad thigh. His lips quirked. "He's a little gruff, but to coin a human phrase, his bark is worse than his bite."

Aramael shot the Archangel a sidelong look, remembering the edge of steel against his throat. "I somehow doubt that." He returned his attention to the distant strip of Hellfire. "Can I ask you something?"

"Of course."

"When you chose me to take Samael's place among you, did you consult the others?"

"The decision was mine to make." Mika'el's words held no arrogance, only a statement of fact. "There was no need for consultation."

"Did you know they would"—Aramael sought the right word—"object quite so strongly?"

"I figured you were a big enough boy to handle it. You aren't the only one in Heaven to lose a brother to Lucifer's allure, Aramael. Raphael would have had a difficult time with anyone replacing Samael. You just raised more issues for him than another might have. As for the others, they're understandably protective of one of their own. Give them time. They'll come around."

Raphael—and Samael? Aramael turned his attention back to the band of Hellfire. He hadn't expected that. A grudging sympathy edged out the memory of Raphael's sword. His presence would have hauled a lot of unwanted memories back to the surface for the other Archangel—along with an accompanying sense of betrayal with which he himself was all too familiar.

"I don't suppose you could have thought to mention this to me at the time," he said.

"My job is to protect Heaven and the One, not your feelings."

"Seems to me you'd do a better job of it if you weren't pitting your own warriors against one another."

Mika'el went silent for a moment. "No Archangel would turn against another," he said finally, "but your point is taken. I'll speak to Raphael."

More silence. Aramael's gaze narrowed on the other Archangel, who still stared into the distance. "You didn't come here just to check up on me."

"No." With a heavy sigh, Mika'el straightened up. "No, I'm not here to check up on you. We've run into a complication. Samael is watching the woman."

"The—" Aramael's heart jolted. "You mean Alex?"

A scowl crossed the other's features. "The Naphil, yes. We've no idea why he's interested in her, but I think we can safely assume it's not a good thing. We need someone to watch her."

It took several seconds for Mika'el's intent to sink in. Several more to force a swallow in a throat that had gone as dry as their surroundings. Of all the Archangel might have divulged, this would have been what Aramael least expected. Watching Alex on his own, in secret, had been one thing. He'd been careful not to let himself get too close. But what Mika'el suggested—watching her with Heaven's permission? Its blessing? That was something entirely different.

He stared toward the Hellfire. He was an Archangel now. He couldn't afford to give in to the baser instincts. Not anymore. Not again.

"You know I still have feelings for her," he said at last, feeling duty-bound to tell the other warrior.

"I suspected as much, yes."

Aramael's fingers curled around his sword hilt. "Then you've chosen me because . . . ?"

"Two reasons. First, because without a Guardian to help you, you'll need to track her on a physical level. Your experience as a Power means you'll fit into the human realm better than the others. And second, because you do still have feelings for her. We need more than just a watcher, Aramael. If it becomes necessary, we need her protected. The others would stand in Samael's way, but . . ." Mika'el's voice trailed off.

"But they wouldn't die for her as I would," Aramael finished. He scuffed the toe of one boot against the hardened soil, remembering Raphael's accusations. "And you trust me to do this."

"I have no choice."

Well. That had been nothing if not blunt.

"May I at least know why I'm being asked to play sacrificial lamb?"

Again.

"We need her help. With Seth."

Slack-jawed, Aramael stared at him. "You have got to be kidding me. You want me to protect the woman to whom I am soulmated so she can help you with the one she chose over me? Even if I wanted to—"

"The One is leaving us."

Aramael stared at him. He snapped his mouth closed. "I don't understand. Leaving us how?"

"Permanently."

"She can't leave. She's the Creator, the All. Heaven cannot survive without her."

"And the world can no longer survive with Lucifer. It's the only way she can stop him." The tightness in Mika'el's voice told how much the words cost. "She needs to bind with him, to become what she was before she created him from herself. Seth stands in the way. Giving up his power created an imbalance that's ripping the mortal world apart. Controlling it is making her weak. We need him to take back what he gave up."

Take back . . . Despite the gravity of the situation, Aramael's heart leapt beneath his ribs. "You mean become immortal again?"

Mika'el glowered at him. "Don't even think of going there. Regardless of what happens with Seth, the Naphil remains out of your reach, is that clear? This isn't about you—or her, for that matter. It's about honoring the One's wishes."

"I should think it would be about *saving* the One

rather than honoring her wish to die."

The other Archangel's eyes darkened with an anguish that lanced through to Aramael's own core, making him wish he could retract his words. His cruelty. None in all of Heaven had been more loyal to the One; none would do more for her than the Archangel Mika'el. To suggest otherwise verged on blasphemy.

"I spoke out of turn—" he began.

Mika'el cut him off. "I have been over this a hundred thousand times," he said quietly, "and every time, I reach the same conclusion as our Creator has. There is no other way to do this. No way to both stop Lucifer and save her."

"But how in Hell can we survive without someone to—?" Aramael stopped. A cold knot formed deep in his gut. "Not Seth."

Mika'el said nothing. He didn't have to.

Aramael tested the idea. The Appointed, who had already abdicated his role twice, returning to Heaven, taking over from his mother, ruling over all of Creation. No matter how hard he tried, he couldn't imagine it. The knot drew tighter.

Bloody Hell, if Seth was the best they could come up with . . .

He looked back to Mika'el.

"Protect the woman," the other Archangel said. "However you must."

SEVENTEEN

Alex placed the dishes in the sink and then stood, hands braced against the counter. She stared at her reflection in the darkened window, blocking out the voices of Seth and her sister and niece in the dining room behind her—if the miniscule apartment cubbyhole could be called such. She should be pleased with Seth's sudden display of interest in something other than her. Should be thrilled with the first attempt he'd made to fit in with her life instead of insisting she remake it to suit him. He'd gone to a lot of trouble, surprising her by inviting Jen and Nina, making dinner . . .

And all she wanted was for her only family to leave.

Because all she'd been able to think about was the same thing that had eaten at her all day. Michael's visit. His words.

"We need him to take it back."

Take back the power that had been the price of his choice to be with her. That had caused the implosion of the alley in which they'd stood when he had given it up. That had connected him to the divine and made him the pawn in some bitter, cosmic game of chess played by his parents.

How could Michael think for an instant that she would help convince Seth to do such a thing? And why would he ask?

Damn, she wished she'd let him at least state his reasons.

"Are you clearing the table or hiding?" her sister's voice intruded. Alex opened her eyes to Jen's reflection beside her own in the window, the smile on her sister's lips at odds with the furrow between her brows.

"Long day," Alex said. "Sorry."

"Long many days."

While Jen's words were neutral enough, her voice held an underlying accusation. A guilty part of Alex wondered again when her family might leave.

She forced a smile. "I know I should have called, but things are a little chaotic at the moment."

"Which I might know if you'd bothered returning any of my two dozen voice messages." Jen scraped the remains of dinner from a plate into the garbage. She rinsed the dish and placed it in the dishwasher.

A quick glance into the dining room told Alex that Seth and Nina had retreated to the living room, out of earshot. She folded her arms and settled back against the counter, waiting for the lecture. Jen wouldn't rest until she'd had her say.

"I'm worried about you, Alex." Another plate went into the dishwasher, this one with a little more force behind it. "Ever since everything before—the killer, Nina, the fire—you just haven't been the same. I'd hoped you'd make progress with Dr. Bell's help, but—"

"Bell can't change what's real."

"It's not about changing what's real, it's about coping with it. And you didn't give him a chance."

"What chance? If I told him half of what's going on in my life right now, he'd have me in a straitjacket," Alex retorted. "Shrinks don't care about real, they care about normal—and in case you haven't noticed, nothing about my life qualifies as that anymore. Neither does yours, but you don't want to admit it."

Jen stared at her, fine lines around her mouth marking her tension. "Well. Do feel free to get your feelings off your chest, Alexandra. Don't hold back on my account."

Alex put a hand to her temple, where a wrecking crew threatened to take up residence. The tension of the day—the last many days—thrummed through her like an overextended rubber band.

"This is why I don't return your calls," she said. "Because whatever you might tell yourself, you'd rather not know what's going on in my life. You can't handle it."

Jen's chin lifted. Stubborn denial darkened her doeskin-brown eyes. "That's rather harsh, don't you think?"

Alex stared at her. The internal rubber band snapped.

"Harsh?" she echoed. "*Harsh*? Goddamn it, Jennifer, you can't keep pretending things are just fine. A Fallen Angel tried to kill me because I—*we*—descend from the Nephilim. The angel sent to stop him is the soulmate I can never have. The man I'm sleeping with is the son of the One and goddamn *Lucifer* for chrissakes, and he gave up his divinity to be with me."

She paused to swallow against the tightness building

in her chest—and the admission of her rape by Lucifer, a detail she hadn't yet shared with her sister and one Jennifer didn't need to know.

"Heaven and Hell are at war because of me, Jennifer. Our world is coming apart at its seams because of *me*." A whisper deep inside her suggested she might be oversimplifying things just a little. She ignored it. The Archangel Michael had been right. She'd been the cause of Aramael killing his brother and breaking the Pact. Everything happening now—the war, Seth's presence on Earth, all of it—stemmed from that. Stemmed from her.

She forged on, her voice thick and ragged, "*This* is what I live with. *This* is my reality. And you're right, I'm not *coping* with it. I'm trying to goddamn *survive* it."

Jen stared into the dishwasher for a long moment before reaching to tear a sheet of paper towel from the roll suspended beneath the cupboard. She folded it, dabbed at her eyes, blew her nose, added it to the garbage can. Then, in typical Jennifer fashion and at complete odds with what she preached about opening up and sharing, she said, "Thank you for dinner. It was nice getting to know Seth a bit better. It will make Nina's birthday dinner more comfortable for everyone, I think. That is, if you're still planning on coming to her birthday."

The tightness in Alex's chest rose to grip her throat. She crossed her arms against the desire to reach out to her sister, because she didn't trust herself not to choke Jen instead of hugging her. Despite what she'd said, a part of her did want to talk. Desperately. She would like nothing more than to unburden herself to someone who wouldn't brush off what she said, wouldn't try to rationalize, wouldn't judge, wouldn't have her committed. Someone she could talk to about Seth and Lucifer and how the two had become so entwined in her psyche. About the war she was certain was brewing in a realm she had never seen but knew to be real.

About the panic that gripped her when she thought of how humanity's potential savior had chosen her over his responsibility to the very universe itself.

Panic that had increased tenfold in the wake of Michael's visit.

Hell, she'd give just about anything to talk to someone. But not Jen. As strong as her sister had seemed over the years, as much of an anchor she had been after their parents' deaths, the events of the past couple of months had shown Alex that it was Jen who had taught her to bury her feelings in the first place. Jen who had always shut down the emotional discussions before they started. Jen who had truly failed to cope.

And who would almost certainly fail to appreciate the irony if Alex were to point it out.

Heart aching, Alex mustered a smile. She nodded. "Of course. Thursday night, six thirty sharp. We wouldn't miss it for the world."

EIGHTEEN

S amael watched the females get into the vehicle:
the Naphil's sister and niece that Lucifer wanted
so desperately to find. This was it. His chance to
redeem himself with the Light-bearer. Here. Now.
All he had to do was follow them to their home, and
Lucifer would have what he wanted. An heir to lead
the Nephilim army that would wipe out the One's
mortal children. And then . . .

And then what? War with Heaven but without a
leader?

He looked up at the roof of the apartment building
and the impassive Aramael, too far away to have
sensed his presence. What was it about the Naphil
that commanded such watchfulness?

A car engine sputtered to life, pulling him back to
the departing girl and woman. Damn. Stay or follow?
A cold breeze swept bits of debris past him. The sweat
on his brow turned icy. His gut insisted Heaven had a
reason for keeping vigil over the Naphil. If he helped

Lucifer kick his plan into action now, he might never have the chance to figure it out. But if he didn't follow the women, if he didn't report them—

Then Lucifer would kill him for letting the opportunity pass. The Light-bearer would take one look into his eyes, into his soul, and know. And then he would kill him.

Slowly and with great finesse.

Samael rubbed the scar at the corner of his eye.

The vehicle pulled away from the curb. Indecision tore at him. Follow the car or his suspicions? All day, something about Mika'el's meeting with the Naphil had nagged at him. That Heaven wanted Seth to take back his powers had been stunning enough, but Samael was certain there was more to it. More that he needed to figure out before Lucifer completed his machinations and damned Hell itself to extinction.

The car's signal light flashed. Follow them or find out more about why the Naphil was so important? Lucifer's orders or his own instinct? Damn it, he needed more time.

Across the way, Aramael's head swiveled with uncanny accuracy in his direction. Samael drew farther back into the shadows. Now that the Archangels knew he watched the Naphil, they would be actively looking for him. He'd never get anywhere near her, especially not with her soulmate in attendance.

He snorted. The Naphil's soulmate guarding her. The Appointed had to love this turn of events. Except Seth wouldn't know about it yet, would he? Not if Mika'el was trying to recruit—

Samael's mind went still. Son of a bitch. That was it. That was the reason he'd hesitated. The answer had been staring him in the face all day. Mika'el hadn't told Seth, because the Appointed had already chosen the woman over Heaven. The Archangel needed the woman's help to convince Seth to take back his powers, needed her to convince him that some things were more important than their relationship. More important than his love for her. More important than him.

Talk about the ultimate déjà vu.

Taillights flashed at the end of the block, then rounded the corner and disappeared. With a smile, Samael stepped out from the sheltered doorway and stood in the pool of light beneath a streetlamp. He would not give up on the war. He would not give up on the possibility of returning to Heaven. And he sure as Creation itself would not risk losing Hell.

He turned his face upward. Atop the roof, Aramael's wings snapped open with a crack that shattered the quiet night, setting off a car alarm and sending a half dozen neighborhood dogs into hysterics.

That's right, Archangel, I'm here. Watch for me. Protect your precious Naphil. Because as long as you're with her, you won't get in the way of what I really want.

Sketching a mock salute, Samael pulled out of reach.

ONLY WHEN NIGHT had fallen silent again did Aramael slowly fold his wings together. So Mika'el had been right. Samael did watch Alex. Watched but did nothing more, even though he'd had ample opportunity to take her between Mika'el's departure and Aramael's own arrival: when she'd left work, or pulled her car into the parking lot, or walked to the building, or reached to unlock the door. Samael had almost certainly been present when she'd done all those things, and yet he'd made no move. Why not?

Aramael's wings gave an irritable twitch. The Fallen One's motives were Heaven's concern, not his. His problem was more immediate. The nature of Alex's job made her comings and goings irregular, unpredictable. With no reliable pattern of movement and no Guardian watching over her, he had no way of staying close enough without her noticing. In which case . . .

He grimaced down at the sidewalk vacated by Samael.

Mika'el was going to love this.

He preferred not to think what Alex's reaction would be.

NINETEEN

Alex twisted the dead bolt home. Never had she been so glad to see the back of her sister. Jen's icy silence had made those last few minutes downright torturous. And just think, Alex had agreed to do this all over again at dinner on Thursday. Leaning her forehead against the door, she let the quiet of the hallway wash over her. From the kitchen came a clatter of pots and pans as Seth cleared away the last of the dinner.

Seth.

Her shoulders sagged.

Seth—and the conversation she'd avoided all day. How the hell was she going to tell him about Michael? About the mother who'd decided she needed his help now that he'd survived her assassination order? She squeezed her eyes shut. Would life ever resemble anything close to normal again?

A throat cleared behind her. "I'm no expert on mortal relationships, but I'm guessing that wasn't the most successful evening."

"Not really, no." She sighed, facing him. "But it wasn't your fault. Things between me and Jen have been . . . strained for a long time."

"As strained as they are between me and her?".

She smiled in spite of herself. "Maybe not that strained, no."

"I never thought of myself as the invisible type."

"Trust me, you're not. And besides, she did thank you for saving Nina's life, remember?"

Seth snorted. "More like she thanked the wall." He leaned a shoulder against the doorpost beside him and slid his hands into his pockets, watching her. "You know the war will reach Earth eventually."

"I know."

"Will all mortals respond the way your sister does?"

"Pretending that it doesn't exist, you mean? Some will."

"And the others?"

Settling against the front door, she lifted a shoulder and let it drop. "Some will look for an explanation they can accept, others for a way to exploit things for their own purposes. Some will lash out in fear."

"And when the fear spreads? You can't protect humanity from itself forever."

She closed her eyes. "I know."

"I've decided to help."

Shock snapped her eyelids open again. "I thought you didn't want to get involved. You said this was between—Heaven and Hell."

She'd been about to say *your parents*, but her brain still tended to dance around the fact that she was living with the son of—well. It was just easier not to think about the idea, let alone voice it.

"Why the change of heart?"

His mouth twisted. "This isn't going to go away, is it? Your job, you trying to save the world . . ."

"No. It's not."

"Even if you know it's a hopeless cause."

"Even then."

"Then that's why. If this quest of yours is going to consume your days—and, frankly, many of your nights—I might as well help. At least it will let me be near you, that being the whole reason I chose to be here and all," he added dryly.

"You're sure."

"You want answers. I can help you get them. I'm sure."

The weight of Mika'el's visit grew heavier, pressing down on the relief she wanted to feel. The gratitude. She drew a breath. No more secrets. She had to tell him. "Seth—"

"Alex—"

They both stopped. She mustered a smile. "You first."

A muscle flickered in front of his ear. His dark eyes looked away. "There's just one thing. Did you mean what you told Jennifer? About Aramael?"

She searched her memory but came up blank on specifics. "I'm not sure what—"

Seth cut her off. "You called him the soulmate you can never have. Is that how you think of him?"

The roughness of his voice scraped across her heart. He'd overheard? Damn it. "No! Lord, no, Seth. I was angry and trying to make a point and—"

"Do you regret choosing me?"

She put a hand out to him. His arm, already rock-hard, contracted beneath her touch. She gripped harder. "I will never regret choosing you, Seth Benjamin. Ever."

"Then you do love me?"

She looked up into a pain that sliced to her very quick. Viciously, she pushed away the guilt that plagued her, the doubts that haunted her. She remembered the agony of standing in a Vancouver alley, certain she had lost him. Remembered how his name had been the first she'd thought of when she regained consciousness. Remembered and wanted—needed—to believe. In herself, in him, in them.

"With all my heart," she said.

For a moment, he didn't move. Then he folded her into his arms, his chin atop her head. "Me, too," he said.

Silence fell between them. Seth's hand moved rhythmically against her back, making slow, gentle circles. Closing her eyes, she focused on the steady rise and fall of his chest, the thud of his heartbeat, his warmth merging with hers. However badly the evening had ended with Jennifer, she preferred to focus on all the things that had gone right. Seth's attempt to bridge the gap between them, his efforts to belong, and this . . . one of those precious, priceless moments where the world seemed to fall away and leave the two of them suspended in a secure, protected bubble .

"It's your turn," his voice rumbled beneath her ear.

"What?"

"You wanted to tell me something."

Michael.

Her throat closed. She couldn't. Not now. Not after that.

"It can wait," she said. "It wasn't important."

His hand resumed its massage, but the bubble enclosing them had already begun to shrink.

TWENTY

"Any questions?" Alex shrugged into her coat and then reached for her scarf. Seth beat her to it, folding it in half, looping it around her neck, tucking the ends through the fold. Exactly the way she did it. She stretched up to kiss him.

"Apart from remaining skeptical about this whole Internet thing mortals have created, you mean?" He shook his head. "I still don't see the point in relying on a tool that contains so much misleading—or wrong—information."

"You just have to filter out the garbage. The real-time capacity is invaluable. It's the best way we have to figure out where the babies have disappeared to—and who took them, on the off-chance that it isn't the Fallen Ones after all. If humans are behind this, at least we can intervene."

"And if it is the Fallen?"

She took down the strongbox from the closet shelf, unlocked it, and took out her service pistol. Slipping its magazine into place, she glanced at Seth. "You're sure they'd still be here, in this world? Lucifer can't take them?"

"To Hell? I'm sure. He wouldn't even if he could. Their presence would sully his realm."

She blinked at the idea that Lucifer, of all beings, could consider humans—or half-humans—dirty. Thrusting aside the incongruity, she slid her weapon into its holster at her waist and replaced the box on the shelf.

"Call me if you find anything?"

Seth arched a black brow. "Will you answer if I call?"

Heat crawled across her cheeks. "I will," she promised.

Walking down the hall toward the elevator, she made another promise, this one to herself. Come Hell or high water, she would talk to someone today about her intimacy issues. She had no idea how she'd dance around the whole angel/demon thing in such a conversation, but she'd find a way. She had to. If Seth was willing to work at this, he deserved at least the same effort from her. They both did.

And maybe doing so would finally make telling him about Michael easier, too.

ALEX'S GOOD INTENTIONS lasted right up until she stepped out of the office elevator and into chaos.

She leapt out of the way as two of her fellow detectives pushed past her, boarding the elevator she'd just left, and dodged three others headed for the stairs. All were gone before she had a chance to formulate a single question. From behind the Homicide door, voices competed with the shrill of telephones.

Then, above all else, the roar of Staff Inspector Roberts. "Where the *hell* is Jarvis?"

She pulled open the door. "Here," she called, waving her hand for Roberts's attention. "I'm here."

Roberts's gaze met hers, relief warring with something dark and awful in its depths. "My office," he said. "Now."

She headed across the office, catching snippets of conversation as she passed by desks. Enough to know that there had been an incident in the Leaside neighborhood, not enough to figure out that incident had been. Joining her supervisor, she closed the door against the commotion. Roberts paced the tight space behind his desk. Filing cabinet to wall, window to desk.

"There's been a stoning."

His voice was so quiet, Alex didn't think she'd heard right. Was certain she couldn't have.

"Excuse me?"

"A stoning," Roberts repeated. He stopped to stare out the window, holding apart the slats of the horizontal blind covering it.

She shriveled inside. "A stoning. As in—?"

"As in an honest-to-God, straight-out-of-the-fucking-good-book stoning." Roberts released the blind with a metallic clatter and turned to her, his face ashen. "Two of them, actually. Women. Buried up to their necks in a playground in Leaside."

Alex's hands curled at her sides. Horror rose in her. Words to describe it didn't exist. Things like this just didn't happen here. Not in Toronto. Not in a civilized world.

"At least one of them was pregnant," Roberts

continued hoarsely. "They haven't pulled out the other one yet."

"Where do you want me?"

"Now that you have a partner again, on scene. Bastion has point, report to him when you get there."

Partner? What partner?

"Thank you for that, by the way," her staff inspector said. "I still don't know who he is exactly, and I would have preferred you give me a heads-up, but I'm happy to have him back. Bringing someone new into Homicide in the middle of all this"—he waved an encompassing hand—"would have been a nightmare."

A brick slid down her throat and landed with a sickening thud in her gut. She swallowed twice before she found a semblance of her voice.

"Him? Him, who?"

"Trent. He stopped by a few minutes ago—" Roberts broke off. "You didn't know."

He continued speaking, but the buzzing in her ears drowned him out. Trent. Jacob Trent, a.k.a. Aramael, angel of the Sixth Choir, the Powers. Aramael, who had killed his twin to save her and had endured exile for his sin; who had been sent to assassinate Seth and then, at the last minute, chosen to help her save him instead. The room tilted sideways.

"Jarvis."

She jolted back to the present and found her supervisor scowling at her.

"You caught all that, right?"

"Um . . ."

Get a grip, Alex.

"No," she said. "I mean yes, I caught it. But no, I didn't know he was back."

"And? Tell me you can do this, Detective. I know the

two of you don't see eye-to-eye, but I need you on the street and I can't put you out there without a partner."

Aramael, back as my partner.

Fuck.

She looked out the window into the main Homicide office, half empty now. The remaining faces were all familiar. Joly, Abrams, Penn, Smith.

No Aramael posing as Jacob Trent.

She unglued her tongue from the roof of her mouth. "Where is he?"

"He said he'd wait in the coffee room."

She straightened her shoulders, drawing on the strength she was learning she possessed. Wondered, briefly, how much longer that strength would hold out.

She strode toward the door.

"Detective."

Pausing, her hand on the doorknob, she looked over her shoulder.

"You can't fall apart," Roberts said. "Not now. We can't afford to lose you."

She went in search of an angel.

TWENTY-ONE

Alex tried to keep her stride purposeful, but placing one foot in front of the other on the way to the coffee room proved to be an all-consuming exercise in determination.

Aramael. Was he still in exile? Had he, by some miracle, been taken back into Heaven? Either way, what the hell was he doing here? She'd chosen Seth over him. Had made that choice clear. Hadn't seen so much as a feather from him since. So why now, and why like this? Why as her goddamn partner again?

She stopped for the office cleaning lady and her cart. The tiny woman's usual nod and smile hardly registered. Alex waited for her to pass, focused on the simple act of remaining upright and not taking shelter under her desk. It didn't matter why Aramael was here, only that he left. Roberts could be as pissed as he liked. She wouldn't work with him again. She couldn't.

And she'd tell him so as soon as she unglued her

feet from the floor.

Shit.

The cleaning lady moved out of her path. Alex looked through the coffee room window at the angel standing inside with his back to her. Her vision blurred, tunneled, narrowed. Everything around her faded into the background. Everything but him. She took in the dark, unruly hair, the breadth of the shoulders straining beneath the suit he wore, the familiar, balanced poise with which he carried himself. And the wings.

Her eyebrows twitched together.

Black wings.

Aramael's wings were golden.

Cold pooled in her belly, emerged on the palms of her hands. She thought of how easily Lucifer had fooled her once, taking on the visage of his own son. Remembered how Aramael's twin, Caim, had assumed the identity of the priest he had killed. She flicked a glance toward the door and the escape it offered. If she moved fast, and if she was very, very lucky, she might be able to get out before whoever this was—*whatever* it was—noticed.

And then what? Go home to Seth? Tell him she was being stalked by someone who had taken on Aramael's persona? That she'd neglected to tell him yesterday about Michael's visit? That she had once more become entangled with the ones he wanted so very much to leave behind?

She shifted her weight, held hostage by indecision tempered with the first stirrings of panic. Then she froze. The angel in the coffee room had turned. She knew without looking. Felt his attention on her, his will reaching out to her, his desire enveloping her. She fought against its pull.

This was no impostor, no other pretending to be her soulmate. It was him. It was Aramael.

Jaw set, she turned her head to meet the turbulent gray gaze, felt it reach inside to her most private places . . .

And coldly shut it down. No. Not this time. Not anymore.

She crossed the last few feet to the coffee room and stepped inside. Hands in pockets, her would-be partner regarded her warily.

"Alex."

Aramael, her heart whispered.

She ignored it. "What are you doing here?"

"You're being watched by one of the Fallen. Mika'el sent me."

So Heaven *had* taken him back. "Watched—why?"

"We're not sure, but the watcher is a former Archangel and Lucifer's top aide. He wouldn't be involved unless it was something important."

The very mention of Lucifer's name turned her mouth dry. Bitter. "All right, then try this. Why do you care? I'm hardly important in the grand scheme of things. What does it matter if Lu—" She pressed her lips together. Christ, she couldn't even bring herself to say the name. "What does it matter if this Fallen One does want me for some reason?"

"You know why it matters."

Alex's heart skidded sideways. She ruthlessly brought it to heel. That wasn't what he'd meant. This wasn't personal, not if Mika'el was behind it. No, it was about Seth. She lifted her chin.

"Then you're wasting your time, because I won't ask him to do it."

"Not even with all that's at stake?"

"Apart from Seth himself? I don't care."

Aramael frowned. "Your entire—"

"Today, Jarvis!" Roberts's bellow cut between them, a reminder of the job waiting for her.

She put a hand to the back of her neck, wrestling with this latest collision of her two realities. A Fallen One stalking her again. Aramael, shoulder to shoulder with her in the car. Roberts's obvious relief at her having a partner. Seth, oblivious to the machinations going on behind his back.

A stoning, not in some far-off country prone to religious fanaticism, but here in Toronto. Her city. Her home.

Eighty thousand Nephilim babies about to be born and molded into Lucifer's ultimate army against humankind.

A world teetering on the brink of chaos. Maybe even the brink of extinction.

All that, and she wanted to turn away the only angel volunteering to ride shotgun with her?

Yes.

No.

"Jarvis!" Roberts roared.

Damn it to hell and back.

Twice.

"Fine," she snarled. "I don't have time to argue. I drive, you shut up."

Aramael opened his mouth. She held up a hand.

"I'm not kidding. One word about Seth or Michael or whatever new disaster you claim is looming on the horizon, and I will dump your ass at the side of the road. Are we clear?"

It didn't matter that they both knew she had no

way to carry out her threat, it simply felt good to set the parameters. It felt even better to have him nod acquiescence. She turned on her heel and headed for the door.

TWENTY-TWO

"You're certain no one else saw you?" Samael slipped the slim, leather-bound book into the pocket of his coat.

Raziel, one of only a handful of female Fallen, arched an eyebrow at him. "A dozen or more saw me," she said. "As they always do when I take his tea things in or retrieve them."

"You know what I mean."

"He was nowhere in the area." Her eyes narrowed. "You still haven't told me why you want it."

"No, but I did tell you it was better that you didn't know."

The pert former Cherub smiled. "And you know I'm not very good at minding my own business. That's why you like me so much."

Samael stared down at the Fallen One. Raziel had remained in Heaven as his informant when he'd left to follow Lucifer, until it had become too dangerous for her. Uniquely unobtrusive, she had a way of blending into the background so that others failed to notice her, failed to realize she listened in on conversations meant to be private. It made her useful in the extreme, and she was right. He liked her a great deal for it. He didn't for an instant, however, consider her infallible.

"I'll let you know when I'm ready for the next one," he said. He started down the alley toward the street.

"What if I don't want to help again?"

He looked over his shoulder. Raziel watched him with a cool expression, her spikey-haired head tipped to the side. She was the first to look away.

"Same old Samael." She gave a quick laugh. "Fine. I'll be waiting."

"YOU LET HIM *WHAT*?"

Verchiel tried—but failed—to hide a flinch. Mika'el was an imposing figure at the best of times, even when seated, but Mika'el irritated? She took a tiny step away from the temper brewing.

"I let him take on the mortal persona of Jacob Trent," she repeated. "He was right. There was little chance he could follow her movements, let alone anticipate them, without being at her side. Her job is too unpredictable."

The Archangel glared at her. "And I wasn't consulted because . . . ?"

"Because you were otherwise occupied at the time, and because, frankly, this was an administrative matter." Verchiel drew herself up. "You cannot be everywhere at once, Mika'el. Not even the One can do that. Nor can you take responsibility for all the decisions that need to be made."

"I'm perfectly willing to leave certain decisions up

to others," he growled, "but allowing Aramael to make his presence known to the woman? Allowing him to *be* with her? You've seen their connection. Surely you see the risk this poses."

"I've also witnessed her rejection of him. She chose Seth, remember?"

"Has the Cleanse made you forget the strength of the soulmate bond? She can choose whomever she likes. It will never negate what was forged in Heaven itself."

"But you have overcome your—" She broke off. "Forgive me. I shouldn't have mentioned it."

Mika'el's jaw hardened. Emerald ice glinted in his eyes. He rose from behind his desk to prowl the room with long, restless strides. "I've learned to control my bond, Highest, not overcome it. Do not mistake the difference. With every beat of my heart, every breath I take, I feel the loss of her presence. The need—not the desire, the *need*—to seek her out again. To join with her. It takes all I possess to resist. No human, regardless of her bloodline, has that kind of strength."

Verchiel hesitated. He was right. She *had* forgotten the strength of the bond. And now that he'd reminded her, the decision to allow Aramael to return as Jacob Trent seemed a great deal less clear-cut. "My apologies. I didn't consider the risks."

"Or the consequences." Stopping, Mika'el faced her. "If, by some miracle, Aramael and the Naphil do resist the connection, his very presence in her life might prevent Seth from taking back his powers."

"Do you want me to recall him?"

Rubbing a hand across his eyes, Mika'el sighed. "I don't know what I want you to do. We still need her protected from Samael, and you're right that Aramael cannot do so if he can't follow her." He fell silent. Then he shook his head. "No. Leave him where he is. I'll talk to the Naphil again. Even if she's unwilling to speak to Seth on our behalf, perhaps she'll agree to stay quiet about Aramael."

"And Seth? When will you speak with him?"

Another sigh. "After I speak with the woman," he said. "For all the good it will do."

TWENTY-THREE

Alex's shoulders had climbed almost to her ears by the time she steered the car onto Cardno Avenue in the upscale Leaside neighborhood. From the moment Aramael slid into the seat beside her, the tension between them had ratcheted upward with every passing second, every kilometer, because his silence hadn't stopped her brain from dwelling on the reasons for his presence—or what Seth's reaction would be if he found out.

A headache throbbed in her temples.

She passed a lineup of news vehicles, waited for a uniformed officer to move the wooden barrier blocking the street, and pulled up beside the mobile command post. The familiar jolt of adrenaline kicked through her as she switched off the engine—every cop's reaction to facing a crime scene and the ensuing hunt for the perpetrator.

Stepping out of the car, she scanned the street. Not a single person was in sight, despite the mild fall day.

No toddlers on tricycles, no nannies with strollers, no one raking the thick, colorful layers of leaves from the lawns. Not so much as a mailman. One might have thought the neighborhood deserted if it weren't for the parted window coverings up and down the block.

On the other side of the car, Aramael slammed his door.

Alex ignored him, tallying the resources on hand. Two ambulances, crews standing to one side as they awaited their cargo; three marked cars and two unmarked; half a dozen uniforms; a forensics team clad in their head-to-toe bunny suits to prevent contaminating the scene; and the requisite yellow tape. Yards of it.

She hunched her shoulders. Even with all she'd seen on the job, she still had trouble wrapping her head around the idea of a stoning. It would be a long time before the neighborhood recovered from this. If it could.

Aiming for the marked motorhome housing the command post, she strode past the ambulance that had blocked her view of the full scene. Her step faltered. She stopped. A single black bag lay stretched out at the edge of the grass. Two more forensics members stood knee-deep in a gaping hole beside a swing set, sand piled beside them. They plunged their shovels into the ground around a bloodied object.

Long seconds ticked by before she recognized the object as a human head. Horror warred with disbelief until a voice hailed. She tore her gaze from the grisly remains and focused on the command post. Detective Sergeant Mark Bastion stood in the open doorway.

"I see you have your partner back."

"Looks like."

"You don't sound happy about it."

She shrugged. "It puts me back on the street."

And maybe if she said that often enough, she'd start to believe it. Nodding at the scene where Bastion's partner, Timmins, stood to one side scribbling in his notebook, she changed the subject. "So? What do we know?"

"Too much. Not enough." Bastion sighed. "Two victims, both female. Young, but there's too much facial damage to accurately determine ages. We'll have to wait for the autopsy."

"Do we know yet if the second was pregnant?"

Timmins called from across the playground before Bastion could answer. He held a hand out in a thumbs-up sign at odds with his grim expression: a confirmation rather than an indication of something gone right.

The second woman had also been pregnant.

Bastion made the sign of the cross over his chest. "Christ."

Alex squeezed her eyes shut until starbursts went off behind her lids. For the first time in her career, she wondered how much longer she would be able to continue. How much longer she could tolerate bearing witness to atrocities like this.

She fought a rising urge to simply leave. To be somewhere else, where people didn't kill one another in such horrific ways. Where she didn't have to see with her own eyes just how far downhill humanity had slid. Where women didn't die in childbirth three weeks after becoming pregnant, or have their babies ripped out of their bellies, or get brutally murdered simply because they were pregnant.

Somewhere safe.

Except safe didn't exist anymore. It never really had, and it never would again. Not as long as Heaven and Hell were at war over humanity's very existence.

Bastion's voice jolted her back to the present. "We'll canvass a six-block radius. There's not many people home this time of day, so I'll have the uniforms set up roadblocks to catch them on their way home later. We'll keep coming back until we've talked to every single household. If someone is away, track them down. I want a list of every woman who is or might be pregnant, and I want their well-being confirmed. In person."

"We should look at churches that serve the area, too," Alex said. "Places of worship."

The forensics duo laid aside their shovels and lifted the second body from its sandy killing ground.

The second very pregnant body.

"Christ," Bastion muttered again. He let out a gust of air. "Nicole is pregnant, you know. Four months. We had the first ultrasound on Monday."

Alex unlocked her teeth. "Congratulations. That's wonderful news."

"Is it?" He turned haggard eyes to her. "Apart from the fact she seems to have avoided this virus thing"—he waved a hand at the playground—"what the hell kind of world are we bringing a kid into?"

She had no answer. Could not, for the life of her, give the reassurance he sought. Bastion swallowed audibly.

"You and your partner—Trent, isn't it? You do the initial sweep of the immediate neighborhood," he said. "This street and the one that backs onto the park. The church idea is a good one. We should include cultural centers as well. I'll get more uniforms down here."

You and your partner.

Hugging her coat close, she started toward the car. Stopped. "Bastion? Tell Nicole I said congratulations. It's wonderful news. Really."

The forensics team laid the woman's body on a tarp beside the monkey bars.

TWENTY-FOUR

S eth stepped into the elevator, shifting the groceries
he carried to one arm and reaching with the
other for the eighth-floor button. Another man
slipped inside as the doors slid closed. Ignoring him,
Seth focused instead on his plans for the evening—the
next stage in his attempts to fit into Alex's world, to be
what she needed him to be.

Tipping his head back, he stared at the buzzing
fluorescent light panel in the ceiling and went over
the menu for the dinner he'd planned. He'd kept
his choices simple: grilled chicken with lemon and
rosemary, roasted vegetables with avocado and goat
cheese, and a tossed salad, all tied together with a
chilled Chardonnay and his determination to make
good on his word to try harder. If Alex was going to
work these insanely long hours, at least he could make
what little time they had together as pleasant as—

"I hope she's worth it."

He looked sideways at his elevator companion.

"Excuse me?"

A bland, golden gaze met his, then dropped to the grocery bag he clutched. "Whoever that's for. I hope she's worth the effort."

"Not that it's any of your business, but yes. She is." He went back to watching the light flicker. The elevator lurched past another floor.

"Because too many of them come with all kinds of baggage," the stranger continued. "Expectations. As if we could ever care about the things they do."

Seth's breath stilled. *We?* Carefully, without moving his head, he slanted another glance at his companion. At the gleam of light reflected on his dark, burnished face, the puckered scar at the corner of one eye . . . and, for just an instant, the hint of wing-shaped shadows behind him. Seth scowled.

"I told Mika'el—"

"I'm not with Mika'el." The other man leaned back against the elevator wall. "Just as you're not with *them.*"

Not with Mika'el? If he wasn't with the Archangel, then he was—

His uninvited companion smiled. Cold trickled through Seth's gut.

A Fallen One. Bloody Hell, he was trapped in an elevator with one of his father's minions.

In the time it took to inhale, his awareness of his lack of power skyrocketed from a dull, ill-defined ache to an acute sense of loss. He shifted his stance, standing tall and facing the Fallen One head-on. He curled his free hand into a fist. With or without powers, he wouldn't go down without a fight.

"I'm exactly where I choose to be," he told the intruder.

"Are you?" the Fallen One asked, nodding at the groceries. "You, the son of Lucifer and the Creator herself, this is where you choose to be?"

"I gave that up," Seth said through his teeth.

"And you can choose to have it back again."

The paper of the grocery bag crackled as Seth's grip went tight. His companion raised an eyebrow.

"You look surprised. You didn't know? Oh, my. How very awkward. I was so sure she'd have told you."

The cold solidified. Turned heavy. *Don't. Don't ask. You don't want to know. It doesn't matter...*

But it did matter. Seth's heart twisted. It mattered a great deal.

"Who?" he asked. "Who would have told me?"

The Fallen One eyed him pityingly. "You have to ask?"

No. No, he didn't because she had started to tell him last night.

"You wanted to tell me something."

She had started, and then she had changed her mind.

"It can wait."

She had chosen instead to hide it from him.

"It wasn't important."

To lie to him.

Seth shifted his grip on the grocery bag.

"What didn't she tell me?"

The Fallen One shrugged. "What I just said. You can have it back. The power, the immortality, all of it. It's all still yours."

The carton of milk in the bag gave way with a little pop beneath Seth's grip. Cold liquid bathed his hand and dripped onto his shoe. "I don't believe you."

"Yes, you do." The Fallen One straightened up from

the elevator wall as the doors slid open onto the eighth floor's empty hallway. "You can feel it. You know you can. Right where you left it, waiting for you to reclaim it as your own."

"You're wrong. You can't know—"

Seth found himself pinned against the wall before he registered that the other had moved. Fingers like steel clamped around his throat, lifting him until his toes barely grazed the floor.

"I *do* know," his father's henchman hissed. "Just as your Naphil knows. The Archangel Mika'el himself told her when he came to her asking for her help. Her soulmate has been returned to her, to ensure that she persuades you. The only one who's still in the dark about this is you. You might want to ask your Naphil why that is." His grip tightened another fraction. "She's not like you, Appointed. She is mortal. She cannot love you the way you do her, the way your father loves the One. Already she puts her own kind ahead of her feelings for you. Already she keeps secrets."

The Fallen One shook him and then, as suddenly as he'd attacked, released his grip. Seth dropped to one knee, gasping. His visitor stepped into the corridor.

"Look around you, Seth, son of Lucifer. See where you are, what you've become. What you've *chosen* to become."

Only when the doors began to slide shut did Seth rise to his feet. He jammed his foot into the opening, gathered the scattered groceries, and, clutching the sodden bag, followed in the Fallen One's wake. The corridor sat empty before him. His visitor's words echoed in his skull. Tangled in his chest.

"Her soulmate has been returned to her."

Her soulmate. Aramael. Returned.

Seth's gaze dropped to the groceries in his arms and, nestled among them, a plain, leather-bound book with the number one engraved on its spine.

TWENTY-FIVE

"Anything?"

Alex looked up from her notebook as she joined Aramael on the sidewalk. "Do you care?"

His mouth thinned. "It would go faster if you'd let me help."

"No."

"Alex—"

"We've been over this. Twice. You're not a cop."

"No, I'm a bloody Archangel," he snapped. "I think I can handle asking a few questions."

Archangel? Her gaze flicked to the massive black wings half unfolded behind him. Michael's wings had been black, too, and so had the other Archangels'. That must be what differentiated the choirs, the color of their wings. So. Aramael had not only been welcomed back into Heaven for his part in Seth's attempted assassination, he'd been promoted, too. Wasn't that just ducky.

She returned her attention to her notes. "I don't

care. You're not trained, you might miss something, and the answer is still no. Feel free to leave if that's a problem."

"Is this how it's going to be between us?" he asked quietly.

Scowling, she ignored the jab of pain beneath her ribs. "There is no *us*. There's me, and there's you following me." She stepped around him, coming up short as he moved to block her. "You're in my way."

"I didn't ask for this."

"Neither did I."

The slate gray gaze softened a fraction. His sigh stirred her hair. "I know. And for what it's worth, I wish it could be otherwise."

"It can. Leave."

He shook his head. "You're too important."

Her brain shied from all that stood behind the statement. "Fine. Then let someone else protect me."

"I can't do that, either."

"You're hardly the only angel in Heaven."

"None of the others would protect you as I can."

"Michael—"

"Mika'el is the one who assigned me to you. He knows the strength of my connection to you. Knows I would risk everything to keep you safe."

The pain beneath her ribs sharpened, taking away her breath. She clutched the notebook and pen tighter, felt their edges imprinted on her fingers.

"Don't," she snarled. "Don't you dare go there. You made your choice when you went after Seth, Aramael, and I made mine when I saved him. We're done."

"You know that isn't true."

"I. Made. My. Choice." She crossed her arms, settling into outright belligerence. "We're *done*."

"We're soulmated, Alex. We can never *be* done."

Even if she could have found her voice, she had no words. No argument. No rebuttal for the truth her soul recognized even as her mind rejected it. Sudden, infinite weariness pressed down on her. He was right. No matter how much she wanted it otherwise, no matter how certain she might have been—*was*—in her choice of Seth, Aramael was still right. The bond between them would never go away. She could love another with all her heart—and she did—and still she would feel that tie. That unbreakable connection.

Footsteps sounded along the sidewalk, slowing as they neared. Gritting her teeth, Alex gathered up the few scraps of coherence she still possessed and made herself look away from Aramael's stormy gray gaze . . . right into the hard emerald one belonging to Michael.

"We need to talk," he said.

TWENTY-SIX

M ichael.

Shock ricocheted through Alex's body. Flat-out antagonism followed. Before she could do more than open her mouth, however, Michael cut her off, directing a pointed look at Aramael.

"Leave us," he ordered.

The storm brewing in Aramael's expression seethed with a new level of turbulence, and for a moment, Alex thought he might refuse. Then he stalked across the street to the car and leaned against the front fender, hands shoved into his pockets. His wings, half unfurled, twitched with an irritation echoing her own.

She scowled at the Archangel towering over her. "Are you always this overbearing?"

He ignored her. "Have you reconsidered my request?"

"No. I told you—"

"Fine. I will speak to Seth. But not about this." He

jerked his chin toward Aramael. "And I don't want you to mention it, either."

"Excuse me?"

"If Seth knows Aramael has returned, it will skew his judgment. I need him to consider my request with a clear head, not one filled by unnecessary emotion."

"First of all, you don't get to tell me what to do. And second, I don't keep secrets from the *man* I love." Her emphasis on *man* was deliberate, a reminder to Michael of Seth's mortality, the choice he had already made. It went unnoticed.

"Have you told him about me?"

"Not yet, but—"

"Then you do keep secrets."

"I haven't had the chance to tell him," she growled.

"The chance or the courage?"

Alex bit back a *go to hell*. No matter how much she detested him and his high-handedness, he was still an Archangel. And he was right.

"Both," she said with quiet dignity. "I'm not going to pretend it will be an easy conversation, Michael. Not after what he's been through. But while I might not be looking forward to it, I will do it. And I will make it clear to him—just as I am to you right now—that I am and always will be on his side. That means no secrets. Not about you, and not about Aramael."

She drew herself up. "Now, if you'll excuse me, I have work to do."

Michael's hand caught her arm as she turned away.

"He will destroy your world, Naphil."

His words made her hesitate, but only for a single heartbeat. Whatever he meant, it didn't matter. Seth had saved her life, had chosen her over himself. She would not—could not—betray his trust. Not for a

Heaven that had already betrayed hers. She pulled away from his hold.

"Before or after Lucifer does?" she asked.

Leaving Michael on the sidewalk, she crossed the street to join Aramael by the car. She opened the door and leaned in to rummage through the glove compartment for a spare notebook and pen. She slammed the door shut and rested the notebook on the sedan's roof. Aramael glanced between her and Michael as she jotted down a series of questions.

"May I ask what that was about?"

"No." She slapped the notebook against his chest, holding it there until he raised a hand to take it. "The questions you need to ask are on the first page. Make sure you note the address of everyone you speak to, and keep a list of the houses where no one is home."

"I thought you didn't want my help."

"I changed my mind." She looked across the street to Michael. Met, without flinching, the hard green eyes. Knew he monitored her words. She turned her back on him.

"I want to finish this canvass," she told Aramael, her voice clear and steady, "and then I want to go home. I have things I need to tell Seth."

TWENTY-SEVEN

As much as Alex tried to tell herself otherwise, the conversation with Michael had rattled her. Deeply. By the time she finished with the last house backing onto the park, she was footsore, frustrated, and had never been more ready to pack in a canvass. She'd also been unable to stop the Archangel's parting words from replaying in her head with every single step she'd taken.

"He will destroy your world," he'd said—and still she'd walked away. She'd failed to demand an explanation because she'd let her own feelings get in the way. Across the street, Aramael descended from a porch and walked toward her. Her gut twisted into the special knot reserved for him. She scowled. She knew better—was better—than that. And if she was going to get the answers she needed to save even a portion of humanity, this knee-jerk reaction to all things angelic had to stop. Now.

Stepping onto the sidewalk, Aramael handed the

notebook to her. She flipped it open. His notes filled the pages in an impatient scrawl. Legible, but only just. She scanned them. At least he appeared to have asked all the questions and kept a list of addresses they'd need to return to.

"What now?" he asked.

"We write up the file in the office, and then we—*I*—go home."

"To tell Seth about me."

"And Michael. Yes."

"You really care enough about him to risk your own world."

Again with the world thing. She closed the notebook Aramael had given her and slid it into her pocket along with her own. "Explain."

"If he doesn't take back his powers, the imbalance he caused could destroy the entire—" Aramael stopped. "You didn't know."

She shook her head, partly in answer, partly in denial. Tiny crystals of ice formed in her veins, invaded her heart. "There must be some mistake."

Aramael's gaze held hers, the same flat gray as Lake Ontario on a sullen day. "You've seen the news. The increase in earthquakes and storms—"

"That's *Seth*?"

"The energy he released in giving up his powers."

No. There had to be a mistake. They had to be wrong. Alex realized her head continued to move from side to side. Through sheer force of will, she held it still and made herself face Aramael's words. Their truth.

"That's what Michael wanted to tell me."

"It's why he came to you for help, yes."

Dear God.

The cell phone at her waist vibrated. Fingers

shaking, she fumbled it from its clip.

"Jarvis."

Even to her own ears, her voice sounded strangled. It was no wonder Henderson picked up on it instantly.

"What's wrong?" he asked.

Her throat closed. *Everything*, she wanted to say. *Everything in my whole goddamn world is wrong.*

But she couldn't. Couldn't tell him. Not about this. Not before she'd talked to Seth and sorted out her own head. Not before she figured out what she was going to do. She cleared her throat.

"Just a case I caught this morning. Two pregnant women, stoned to death."

"I saw something about that on the news. You okay?"

"Fine."

"Of course." His voice was dry. "How could I think otherwise?"

Alex bit back an invitation for him to piss off and sought instead for words to distract him. Normal words that didn't reflect the agony that had taken up residence in her very soul. "Anything exciting at your end?"

"A whole lot of overtime. The demand for DNA testing is through the roof. Every pregnant woman in the city wants a test, regardless of how far along she is, and we've had multiple threats against labs that have refused. Some of them have hired armed guards to protect their staff, so we've had to step up patrols to keep tabs on things. Half our detectives are back in uniform to meet the demand. You can imagine how busy that makes the rest of us."

"And Father Marcus?"

"Not a word. I think we can count on the Church

to keep him and the scrolls under pretty tight wraps until they figure out what to do with their information. Worst case scenario, they go to governments with it—they're not interested in creating a worldwide panic."

Which is exactly what would happen if the general public learned of the scrolls' existence. And their contents. Alex held back a shudder at the thought of the world's reaction to knowing the reality of Heaven and Hell.

"I hope you're right. I just wish we could have confirmation on that."

"Hey, as long as it stays off the Internet and out of the hands of the nutcases, I'm happy. Which reminds me, I've had a look at the list of what the tech guys are monitoring for. It's pretty focused on end of the world and wrath of God stuff. I think we need to expand it to include"—his voice dropped to a murmur—"you know, the other."

"You mean angels?"

"And their offspring."

"You want to put the Nephilim on a list of watch words? You're a brave man. Have you decided how you'll explain where you came up with the idea?"

"I was hoping you might take care of that at your end. Your boss is a little more . . . tolerant of these ideas than mine."

"I'll talk to him."

"So how's the other stuff going? Any give from your other half with regard to helping us out?"

Alex's grip on the phone tightened until pain radiated from her knuckles through her wrist. "Some. He's looking into the babies that are disappearing. Trying to find out where they're being taken."

"The ones that haven't been taken by various

governments, you mean." Henderson grunted. "It's about bloody time he came around. Those superpowers of his would come in handy right now, wouldn't they?"

She choked on her inhale. "I should go. I'm still canvassing the neighborhood, and I'd like to finish before midnight."

Silence. Then, suspiciously, "What aren't you telling me, Jarvis?"

"Nothing."

"Bullshit. Spill."

A thousand demons hammered at the inside of her skull—a metaphor far too close to actuality for peace of mind. "I have a new partner. Well, a new *old* partner. Aramael is back. One of the Fallen has been watching me."

"What the hell, Jarvis?" Henderson growled. "I thought you were done."

"Trust me, so did I."

"When?"

"This morning."

"Does Seth know?"

Trust the Vancouver detective to get right to the heart of the matter. "Not yet."

"Are you going to tell him?"

"I have to." That, and a whole lot more.

"He's not going to like it."

"You called him the soulmate you can never have. Is that how you think of him?"

"No," she said. "No, he's not. And now I really do have to go, Hugh."

"All right. But you call me if you need me, Alex. Anytime. I mean it. I don't care if it's three in the morning, understand?"

She gave a nod the Vancouver detective couldn't see and ended the call.

TWENTY-EIGHT

S eth glowered at the Archangel standing stiffly in the doorway.

"Finally come to finish what you started?"

"To talk."

"I know what you want. The answer is no."

"The Naphil told you?" Surprise flickered across Mika'el's face.

"It's true, then. You did visit her."

Mika'el's eyes narrowed. "She didn't tell you. Then how do you know?"

"Like the rest of my life, that would be none of your bloody business." He moved to close the door again, but the Archangel's hand snaked between it and the frame, pushing back.

"We need your help."

Seth stared, torn between laughing at him and slamming the other's hand in the door. "After what you tried to do to me? Are you out of your mind?"

"I did what was necessary."

"You tried to have me killed, Archangel, and the One—my own mother—went along with you."

"It wasn't an easy decision for her. We'd run out of options."

"Cry me a fucking river."

A muscle in the Archangel's jaw twitched. "You're the one who reneged on his duty in the first place," he snapped. "None of this would have happened if you had done as you were supposed to do."

"Bullshit. At best I might have been able to delay the inevitable a little longer, but that was all. Because war is just that—inevitable. Whatever choice I made would have been ignored by both sides. Lucifer wouldn't have given up—won't give up—until every last mortal is wiped from the face of this planet. You know it, I know it, and she knows it. This battle will never end."

"There won't *be* a battle if you don't shut up and listen."

"I'm not interested."

Mika'el shoved the door wider. "This isn't about the One or Lucifer, damn it. It's about the survival of the mortal race."

"Not interested in them, either."

"In case you hadn't noticed, you live with them."

"I live with Alex."

"She's one of them."

Seth scowled. Samael had used the same words. Sought to make the same distinction that, despite Seth giving up his divinity, Alexandra was mortal in a way he could never be. He jutted out his chin.

"She's different."

"Because she's Nephilim?"

Because she's mine. "Maybe."

"That doesn't make her any less mortal."

"And if I take back the power? Will that make her any less mortal?"

"You know it won't."

"You're bloody right, it won't. I also won't get any more time with her than I have now—in fact, I won't get any time with her at all, will I? I'll have to give her up, return to Heaven, and watch her die with the rest of humanity without interfering because my mother's rules won't permit it. Isn't that what taking back my power will mean?"

"Damn it, Seth, the entire human race—"

"*Isn't* it?"

Mika'el said nothing.

"Then fuck the power, and fuck you," Seth said viciously. "I damn near died—twice!—to get to where I am now, Mika'el. Don't you get it? I love Alex as I have never loved anything or any*one* before. I will *not* give up what precious little time I have with her for the sake of an already dying world. Now get the Hell out of my life—and hers."

TWENTY-NINE

"You're late."

Alex hesitated for a bare breath of an instant, then secured the dead bolt on the door and turned to face Seth. "I left you a message earlier."

He leaned against the living room door frame, arms crossed, shoulders stiff. "And I left you three."

"I'm sorry. I know I said I'd answer, but there was an incident."

"The stoning? I saw it on the news."

"It's these pregnancies. People are terrified."

"And so they kill innocent pregnant women?"

She lifted her chin at the coldness in his voice—coldness, and a derisive note that made her spine stiffen. "No. A very small minority do things like that. The rest of us try to stay calm and stop things from getting out of hand."

Seth studied the floor between them. "You really care about them, don't you? These mortals."

"Of course I care. I'm one of them."

"You know I don't understand why."

"Give it time. Get to know us better. We're not all like the ones who killed those women."

"I'm not interested in getting to know the others."

She snaked a hand through her hair. "I thought we got past this last night," she said tightly. "When you said you'd try. That you'd help."

"And you said you'd answer your phone if I called. The lies simply abound, don't they?"

Struggling with irritation fueled by fatigue, Alex made herself take a deep breath. "I wasn't lying, but you're right, I should have made it clear that it's not always possible to answer right away. I'm sorry."

"That's it?"

"What more do you want me to say? We've been over this a hundred times, Seth. I'm a cop. This is my job."

"Fine. Then tell me about that job. About your day. All of it."

Alex's heart skidded to a stop. Restarted with a thud that jolted through her.

He knew.

She crossed her arms over herself. Her voice quiet, unlike the blood hammering in her ears, she said, "Michael came to see you."

The muscle in his jaw went tight again. Fury and hurt glittered in equal measure in his black eyes. "Why didn't you tell me?"

"I didn't know how. With all that's happened, I was afraid you'd be angry. I didn't want another fight."

"I am angry, but my fight isn't with you. Unless . . ."

"Unless what?"

"Unless you agree with them."

"He's going to destroy your world."

"Do you?" Seth asked.

"No. No, of course not. But—" She slumped against the door, shaking her head at the surreality of their conversation. At the two of them, standing in their apartment hallway, calmly discussing the fate of her entire race. "Are they right? About the power you released destroying the world?"

"The war between my parents will destroy the world, Alex. Lucifer's hatred for humanity will destroy the world. It began with your creation, and it won't end until every last one of you is wiped from existence."

"Even if—?"

"Taking back my powers might end an imbalance, but nothing more. The Nephilim will still be born, still become an army, and still annihilate your race. And I will still lose you. Without having had the briefest of lives with you, I will watch you die and then spend eternity living with your memory and the knowledge that, under my mother's rules for the universe, I could do nothing to save you. Is that what you want for us?"

Her chin jerked up. "That's not fair. This isn't about what I *want*, Seth, it's about what's right."

"Is it?"

"Of course it—"

"I know he's back."

Her teeth snapped shut. After all that, Michael had told him about Aramael? Without at least warning her? *Son of a bitch.* "I was going to tell you."

"Of course you were. As soon as you told me about Mika'el."

She ignored the shot, rubbing a weary hand over her eyes. There was no easy way to do this. "He was waiting for me at the office this morning. He'll be working with me as my partner again."

"And you're okay with that." Seth delivered the words in a tone so cold that it turned the air between them frigid.

There was no easy way to do this, either.

"Luci—" The name caught in her throat. She rubbed false warmth into her arms and tried another approach. "I'm being watched. By one of the Fallen. Michael thinks I need protection."

"Your soulmate's protection."

"The Fallen One is an Archangel. Aramael is the only one—" She stopped. Telling him that Aramael was the only one who would lay down his life for her would not help matters.

But Seth had already filled in the blanks, his features going so still they might have been carved from marble. Hard, unyielding marble. "The only one who would die to protect you," he said. "Because that's how powerful a soulmate connection is. I should have known."

"It doesn't change anything, Seth. I made my choice. I love you, not him."

Silence stretched between them, a vast emptiness that widened with every tick of the utilitarian clock on the living room wall. Until, without speaking, Seth walked down the hallway to the bedroom and closed the door. The lock clicked into place with a snap that found an echo the length of her spine. She waited for long seconds and then, with a sigh rooted in her toes, headed for the kitchen and the bottle of ibuprofen. She'd give him time to cool off, get her headache under control, and—

Her steps dragged to a halt. She stared at the dining room table, with its guttering candles and the hardened wax pooled at their bases. The cold, congealed food sitting on the plates. The bottle of wine, a corkscrew beside it. She forced her feet to carry her forward. With stiff, spare movements, she cleared Seth's dinner efforts, scraping the food into the kitchen garbage can, placing the tepid wine in the fridge, blowing out the candles, putting away the napkins and silverware.

When only the spilled wax remained on the table, she took down the bottle of Scotch from the cabinet beside the stove, collected a glass, and retreated to the living room for the night.

THIRTY

Alex's cell phone jolted her awake at four a.m. She swallowed the cotton that filled her mouth and answered on the fifth trill. "Jarvis."

"You sound about as enthusiastic as I feel," Joly observed. "Shall I make it worse?"

"If I say no, will it matter?"

"Some guy just shot up the emergency ward at the General. Three dead, fourteen injured, two critical. I'll see you there."

The line went dead. Alex set the phone on her stomach, crossed her arms beneath her head, and stared up at the shadow lines across the ceiling, cast there by the light of a streetlamp coming through the blinds. She listened to the quiet of the apartment. Had Seth heard the phone? Would he wake if she went into the bedroom for clean clothes? If he did, would the events of last night be forgotten, or would they carry over to this morning, poisoning her departure?

She turned her head to look at the Scotch bottle

on the coffee table. Despite being down by half, it had done nothing to make sleep any easier. By her generous estimate, she was lucky if she'd managed an hour.

Long seconds dragged into minutes. The bedroom door remained closed, the apartment silent.

With a sigh, Alex pushed aside the blanket. She reached for the shirt she'd draped across the sofa back, slid her arms into it, and buttoned it. Ten minutes later, teeth brushed to remove the stale remains of alcohol and a brief note left on the table for Seth, she let herself out.

A biting November wind greeted her as she stepped out of the building. Tucking her chin into her scarf, she pulled on gloves and rounded the corner to the parking lot. Her step faltered. Hell. She'd hoped . . . but supposed she should have known better.

Straightening her shoulders, she joined Aramael beside her car.

"How did you know I'd be leaving?"

"I told you. I'm watching you."

Heat gathered at the nape of her neck as she thought of her night on the sofa. "Not—"

Something unnameable flickered in his gray eyes. "Not when you're with Seth, no."

Thank Heaven for small mercies.

"Where do you watch from?"

"When you're in the apartment? The roof."

"And you'd still know if . . . ?"

"If Samael came for you? Yes. Or any other Fallen One, for that matter. In any form. My capacity as an Archangel is different from when I was a Power."

As if to emphasize his words, the wind ruffled the black wings rising behind him, so much larger than the ones he'd once had.

Alex looked away. "And you're absolutely sure this Samael is after me."

"I've seen him. Standing across the street."

A chill slipped through her. She hadn't thought much about the idea before now. Apart from not wanting to, there had been plenty to keep her distracted from it: work, Seth, meeting Michael, Seth, the turmoil of seeing Aramael again . . . and always Seth. Now, however . . .

She looked down the street, taking in the parked cars, darkened storefronts, lampposts, an overturned garbage can, a homeless man huddled in a doorway. Imaginary shadows.

She pushed a button on the key fob, and the sedan gave a chirp as its doors unlocked. "There's been a shooting," she said. "Same deal. I drive, you keep quiet."

"You can't ignore this forever, Alex."

"Watch me," she muttered, sliding into the car.

SETH LEANED HIS FOREHEAD against the cold window glass, staring down into the street after the departing taillights. In the car, Alex and *him*—her soulmate. Behind him, once again, the apartment. Silent, empty, hollow. His hand closed over the note she'd left him, crumpling it. He let it fall to the floor.

Damn it to Hell and back, were they not to be allowed *any* peace? A mortal lifetime was already so short, and now—now the machinations of others threatened even that. Others who played with the future of the entire universe and all its occupants. Others who would drag him back into their game.

Again.

And now they tried to use Alex herself against him. To make her doubt him. To make him doubt himself.

He scowled. Well, they'd be disappointed, because he wouldn't abandon her. Not now. Not ever. And certainly not for the sake of his mother's precious Earth. However long he might have with her, he intended to treasure every minute, every breath, every heartbeat.

He crossed to the dining room table and swept up the book the Fallen One had left in his grocery bag. The poison of its contents—its secrets—seeped through its very cover. How he wished he had never opened it. Never read the words now burned into his brain.

That I even consider such an act . . . I cannot find words to express the horror I feel at my treasonous thoughts. And yet, what choice do I have? She is my Creator. I, her helpmeet, the other half of the whole she once was. How she could allow these creatures to come between us is beyond comprehension. Beyond endurance. If this is what I must do to put things right again . . . so be it.

Seth shuddered. His father's words, filled with jealousy, hatred, and yes, the absolute and utter love that had driven him from the One's side. He'd grown up knowing the story behind Lucifer's departure, but seeing it written in the Light-bearer's own hand, his own words . . .

Damned if he hadn't felt a flicker of compassion.

Maybe even one of understanding.

But no more. He strode into the kitchen and lifted the lid on the garbage can. Soft leather caressed his fingertips as the journal slid from his grasp. His parents' history had no bearing on him. No bearing on any of this. He wasn't part of them anymore. He was mortal, and the Fallen One was wrong. Alex *was* like him, and she *did* return his love. And he'd be damned if he'd let anyone take that away from him.

Letting the lid drop, he turned away. He had offered his help, and now he would live up to his word. He would find where the Nephilim babies were being taken. He would give Alex a reason to work with him as she did with the others. With—

He stopped. Stared at the leather-covered book sitting on the table. At the carefully carved Roman numeral II on its spine. A resounding crash sounded behind him, and he whirled in time to see a half-rotten apple roll away from the garbage spilled across the floor. Vegetable scraps, empty packaging, the withered remains of the dinner he'd made for Alex the night before . . .

But no sign of the journal he had just placed there.

A black feather drifted through the air and settled on the floor beside his shoe.

THIRTY-ONE

Dropping keys and coat on her desk, Alex headed for the coffee room, shooting a black look at Aramael when it seemed he might follow. He settled onto the desk's edge, arms folded across his chest and expression neutral. She strongly suspected he humored her, but she couldn't summon the energy to feel annoyed. After the fight with Seth, her ensuing date with the whiskey bottle, and then the call-out to the hospital scene, she had nothing left.

Hell, if she were truthful, she hadn't even had it in her to react to the scene. Three bodies, a dozen shell-shocked medical staff, enough blood sprayed across chairs and floors and ceilings to have saved a dozen lives, and for all the response she'd felt, she might as well have been watching a movie. Bell would love to sink his teeth into that little detail.

The cell phone at her waist vibrated as she reached the coffee room door. She unclipped it, looked at the display, and sighed. Jen.

"Morning, sis."

"I'm surprised you answered," Jennifer replied. "I wasn't sure you'd be speaking to me."

Rolling her eyes, Alex drew a deep, calming breath. "Really, Jen? You think that little of me? We had minor difference of opinion the other night, and you seriously think I'd be petty enough not to speak to you?"

Silence.

"Jen?" Alex held the cell phone away to make sure the call was still connected. She put it back to her ear. "Are you still there?"

"I—you—" Jen paused. "You don't know."

"Know what?" Alex saw Roberts emerge from his office, scan the room, focus on her. He pointed, then jabbed his thumb over his shoulder. *You. In here. Now.* She nodded and held up a finger. *One minute.* She returned her attention to her sister, who hadn't answered. "Jennifer, what don't I know?"

"I thought—it's past ten. I thought you would have found out by now."

"I just got into the office. We had a shooting last night—" Alex broke off and shook her head. None of that mattered. Not to Jen, anyway. "Can we speed this up? Roberts wants to see me. What haven't I found out yet?"

"You know I love you, right?" Jen asked. "And I'd do anything for you. You know that."

The blood in Alex's veins turned cold. Slowed to a sluggish trickle. "What's going on, Jennifer Abbott? What have you done?"

A defensive note entered her sister's voice. "It's for your own good, Alex. You've been under so much pressure since—since the fire and everything. And

I'm not the only one who's worried."

"Jennifer."

"Jarvis!" Roberts still stood in the doorway. "Today!"

He turned and disappeared into his office, giving her a clear view of the desk within, the chairs in front it—and the gray-haired woman seated in one of those chairs. Alex lowered the phone from her ear and slid it closed on her sister's rambling explanation as the woman turned. Sharp blue eyes met hers.

What in *hell* was Elizabeth Riley doing in Toronto?

"YOU DON'T LOOK particularly pleased to see me." Elizabeth Riley stayed seated as Alex stepped into Roberts's office and closed the door. Her sharp blue eyes watched Alex from behind wire-framed glasses.

"I'm not. I mean, I am, but—" Alex paused, took a firmer grip on the thoughts milling through her brain, and tried again. "Did Henderson send you? Is he all right? What's wrong?"

"He was fine when he dropped me off at the airport last night, and nothing is wrong." Her lips pursed. "Well," she added, glancing at a stoic Roberts, "nothing more than usual, anyway."

"So you're here because . . . ?"

"Dr. Riley is here at the force's request," Roberts said, and her gaze flew to his. Or tried to, except he refused to meet it. "Please. Sit."

She remained standing, fingers locked over the back of the chair beside Riley. *The force's request?* Understanding gelled. Her sister's phone call. Jen had known about this. She'd been in on it. They'd all been in on it: Jen, Roberts, Riley, Henderson—it was a goddamn conspiracy. Alex scowled, but Roberts held up a hand, cutting her off.

"I'm going to get straight to the point, Detective. Dr. Bell went over my head to the chief. I've been told that you either voluntarily put yourself into therapy or I'm to suspend you."

She actually rocked back on her heels for an instant, so startled was she by the announcement. She gaped at her staff inspector. "You're serious. When did you find out?"

"The same day I returned you to duty."

Alex did a quick calculation and realized with a start that what seemed a lifetime ago had only been three days. So—the closer Armageddon got, the faster time passed? Great. And now she was to be saddled with Riley and "therapy" as well? She favored the psychiatrist with a baleful look but directed her words to Roberts. "You couldn't have told me then?"

"It wouldn't have made a difference. This was out of both our hands."

"Still—"

"Besides, given all that's going on, it might not be a bad idea."

All that's going on? Alex stood for a long moment without responding, going first cold, then hot. An iron band closed around her chest. Tightened. *You have no goddamn idea what's going on.*

Roberts continued. "Dr. Riley is here because you need the support. I know the signs of trouble, Alex, and I'm seeing them in you."

Aware of Riley's keen observation, Alex lifted her chin and stepped back from the chair's support. "I don't have time for this. I have files to—"

"Make time." Roberts's uncompromising voice

stopped her at the door. "I meant what I said about not wanting to lose you."

Then don't make me dredge up things that are best left buried.

"Staff—"

"It's an order, Detective."

Anger flared inside her. Sudden, icy, raw. The tiny little cracks that had begun forming in her facade over the last few days widened. Roberts and Riley wanted her to talk? To share her secrets? *Fine.* She spun to face them.

"Maybe you're right," she said. She flicked a look from her boss to the psychiatrist. "Maybe I do need to get some things off my chest. What do you suggest we start with, Dr. Riley? Oh, I know. How about the nightmares I keep having about eighty thousand Nephilim babies being turned into Lucifer's army against humankind? That has to be worth a session or two, don't you think? Or maybe we should talk about how my angel soulmate has been put in charge of protecting me from the Fallen One that's been following me. Too complicated? No problem, I have lots of other issues we can discuss instead. In fact, here's a real doozy. Why don't we talk about how I haven't been able to let the One's son touch me because I can't get past his father raping me?"

Roberts made an odd choking noise and went pale. Riley regarded her narrowly.

Shit. She hadn't intended to blurt out that last one.

"Alex—" Riley began.

"Don't," she grated, hating that the door at her back was all that held her upright. "You could have backed me up from the start, Riley. You could have told him everything he needed to know over the phone."

"No. I couldn't. Not in good conscience," the psychiatrist said, "and not when I agree with him. I told you in Vancouver that you can't keep pretending you can do this alone. You need to talk—"

"No," Alex snarled. The remainder of her facade shattered, raining across her psyche in shards and drifting dust. "I don't. In fact, you know what? I don't need to do any of this. Not anymore. I'm done. With you, with them, with everything. As far as I'm concerned, the entire goddamn world can go to Hell."

She wrenched open the door and stalked out of Roberts's office through the silence, past the stares, and away from Aramael.

THIRTY-TWO

*B*loody Hell. Aramael stared after Alex as the outer office door swung shut behind her. The shock of a dozen mortals lay like a weighted blanket over the room. Only a few had been close enough to Roberts's office to hear her actual words, but those words would spread faster than wildfire when people began talking. Murmurings had already started. *Bloody, bloody Hell.*

Aramael hesitated, torn between going after her or attempting some kind of mitigation in her wake. No. Like it or not, he would have to leave Alex unprotected for an instant. Heaven itself needed to get involved in this crisis. This—all of this, including Alex right now—was beyond his ability to contain. He strode toward the file room at the back of the office and, as soon as he was out of sight of prying eyes, pulled out of the mortal realm.

Verchiel, blessedly, was in her office and on her feet the instant she saw him.

"Aramael! The woman—what's wrong?"

"We have a problem." He filled her in on the past few mortal minutes. "We need to do some kind of damage control. The mortals—"

"You know we cannot interfere like that."

He scowled. "Excuse me?"

"What's done is done, Aramael. It is beyond our control."

"Verchiel, she just told half her colleagues about Armageddon. We cannot sit by and do nothing."

"We can." She held up a hand to forestall his words. a great deal if Lucifer's plan for the Nephilim comes to fruition. Perhaps it is for the best that they know."

"Then you'll lose her."

"I don't understand."

Clenching his hands, he shoved aside the ache in his chest. "Her relationship with Seth is in crisis," he said. "She's—"

"You haven't—"

"No," he snarled. "I haven't. May I finish?"

Lips pursed, Verchiel waved at him to continue.

"Alex is already dealing with more than any mortal has ever had to. Her outburst today won't necessarily be believed by her colleagues, but it will almost certainly ostracize her from them. If that happens, she's going to break."

A tiny frown appeared between the Highest's brows. "This is speculation on your part."

Aramael thought of the ravage he'd seen in Alex's eyes as she emerged from Roberts's office and realized her words had been overheard. The spark of something in her that he'd watched flicker, gutter, and then die.

"It's fact, Verchiel. If you don't fix this, you'll lose her." The wings at his back fought to unfurl against his next words. He held them—and his voice—rigidly in check. "And if you lose her, I guarantee you'll lose any chance at Seth."

Verchiel stared down at her desk. Then, with a sigh, she rose to her feet. "Go back. Watch her. I'll take care of the mortals who overheard. Mika'el will speak with the woman."

THIRTY-THREE

Alex slammed into the bathroom stall, sat on the closed lid of the toilet, and stared at the beige metal door. She tangled her fingers into her hair and held tight as a great shudder rolled through her. Then another. Damn, she'd handled that badly. The memory of her supervisor's shock surfaced. Hysteria bubbled inside her chest. *Handled it?* Who the hell was she trying to kid? She hadn't *handled* anything. She'd lost it. Totally and completely. Lost it, made an ass of herself, and let her supervisor and Riley in further than she'd ever intended. Further than she'd ever let anyone.

Further than she could afford.

She closed her eyes, recalling the collective shock that had greeted her as she'd stormed out of Roberts's office. She'd raised her voice as she'd struck out at Riley and Roberts—but how loud? How much had her colleagues overheard? She cringed from the memory of her words. Words filled with truths none of them should know, truths that would give Bell all the ammunition he needed to deep-six her career if he heard about them. When he heard. Because given the number of open mouths when she'd stormed out of Roberts's office just now, it wouldn't take long for the grapevine to do its damage.

Hell.

The exterior bathroom door opened. Closed. Footsteps crossed the tile floor.

"Alex, it's Elizabeth."

Her eyes flew open, and she glared at the beige stall door.

"I owe you an apology," Riley continued. "I should have anticipated that things would deteriorate after you left Vancouver. Springing my presence on you in that fashion was badly thought out. I'm sorry."

Badly thought out? It was a goddamn ambush.

"Poor judgment aside, however, circumstances remain unchanged. On Dr. Bell's recommendation, you're required to attend daily sessions with a therapist. Staff Roberts felt—and I agreed—that you might be more comfortable with me than with Dr. Bell. The decision, of course, is yours."

Only with the greatest effort did Alex remain seated and not barge out of the stall. She gaped at the door. After her outburst in Roberts's office, to hear Riley speaking with such calm, such reasonableness, as if Alex was just the run-of-the-mill, overstressed cop—

It was no bloody wonder the psychiatrist irritated her so much.

Riley sighed and her voice softened. "Damn it, Alex, I'm not the ogre you think I am. Talk to me. Give me a chance to help you."

Alex blinked away an unexpected haze.

Another sigh from outside the stall. Then Riley returned to her usual brisk, professional self. "Have it your way, then, but I'm not giving up and you're not getting out of this. Bell isn't the only one who thinks you need to talk, and your performance just now only makes me more certain. Staff Roberts has arranged the use of an office for me while I'm here. I'll leave the information on your desk. As there's never any time like the present, we'll start this afternoon. I'll expect you at two o'clock."

Hollow footsteps retreated, pausing at the door. "And, Alex, if you're considering skipping, don't. Not if you want to remain on the job."

Door open.

Door closed.

Alex sagged, body, mind, and soul. So that was it. She'd run out of time and escape routes. If she wanted to have any impact at all on this whole mess, then she truly had no choice. She was going to have to finally succumb to having someone poke around in her head and, worse, her heart. *And* she'd have to do so while facing the stares and murmurs behind her back from everyone in the office who'd heard her outburst.

Her brain snagged on one thought that stood out from the rest, and the more she circled it, the more ludicrous it became. She thought she could have an impact? By doing what, running around after a handful of human murderers in the midst of everything the world faced? Who the hell was she trying to kid? What difference would her efforts make in a war between supernatural beings that could—and would—wipe out the entire mortal race? What—the outer washroom door opened again.

"Naphil?"

She stared at the beige metal between her and Michael. Now what?

"Are you all right?"

Whatever had begun to give way inside her in Roberts's office snapped. She stood, slammed open the stall door, and glowered at the Archangel in the main doorway. "You have got to be joking."

Michael's dark brows meshed.

"No," she said. "No, Michael, I am not all right. I will never *be* all right. None of us will be. Your precious One has made certain of that."

Glancing over his shoulder, Michael stepped inside the washroom. He closed the door behind him, keeping one hand braced against it. "Humanity has played a role in this, too, Naphil. You've had free will since your creation. You've been responsible for your own decisions, your own choices, for millennia. Yet look where you are, at what you've accomplished."

"*Some* of us. Not all."

"Enough to jeopardize your race right now. And not for the first time."

"Oh, don't hand me that bullshit. We may not be perfect, but we're a long, *long* way from being responsible for our total demise. Lucifer and the Nephilim will take care of that when you and the others have finished battling it out on our turf, and the One won't raise a hand to stop them. Will she?"

"She has done everything—"

"*Will* she?" she demanded harshly.

"Let. Me. Finish." Michael said, his voice so hard that she had to fight an urge to step back. "First of all, we're not battling it out anywhere at present, least of all in your realm. What's happening to the planet is because of the powers Seth refuses to take back, not because of us. Second, the One has done everything she can. Your race has the capacity to save itself from the Nephilim or not. It's your choice. She cannot—and will not—make that decision for you. For any of you."

"Bullshit. She's already asking me to sacrifice everything I love with no guarantee that it will make any difference. That feels pretty decisive to me."

"You're right. She is."

Alex blinked her surprise. He agreed?

"But the decision is still yours, Naphil. You can refuse, and do what you were thinking of doing when I walked in on you now. Leave, turn your back on what might very well be a lost cause, take what happiness you can while it's possible."

Alex jutted out her chin. "But?"

"But you'll have to live with your choice."

An invisible fist buried itself in her gut. Her mouth opened, closed, and opened again. No sound emerged.

Michael looked down on her from across the few feet of tiled space between them. "We've arranged it so the words you spoke to your supervisor will be forgotten by those who overheard them. Try to be more circumspect in future."

"That's it? That's all I get? Do the right thing and try not to screw up again? That's the best you can give me?"

"What more is there?"

"Hope? Encouragement? A word of goddamn *apology*?"

"Apology." His eyes turned to emerald chips of ice, and his black wings began to slowly unfurl, as wide as the limited space would allow. "Apology," he repeated. "And just what would you have me apologize for, Naphil? My kin giving up their soulmates and their free will just to survive the war we fought on your behalf? Our Creator not sacrificing herself sooner for your benefit? Are you really that *arrogant*?"

The metal frame of the bathroom stall bit into her spine between her shoulder blades. Michael hadn't moved an inch, but his presence still pressed in on her, driving her back. Her stomach flip-flopped. When the hell would she learn that pissing off an Archangel was *not* a bright thing to do?

"That's not what I meant," she began.

He fixed her with a dagger-like stare. "I don't give a damn what you meant. I've told you what your choices are, now stop feeling sorry for yourself and make your decision."

And with that parting gem of warm fuzziness, Heaven's greatest warrior simply disappeared, leaving Alex staring yet again at the emptiness he left behind. Slowly her alarm gave way to renewed irritation, then to annoyance, and then to outright anger. She scowled. *Stop feeling sorry for yourself?* And he called *her* arrogant. The self-righteous, pompous—

The washroom door swung inward, and Joly stepped through the opening. "There you are."

Alex threw her arms wide. "What is this, goddamn Grand Central Station?"

Joly paused, looked around the room that was obviously empty but for them, and raised a brow. "You okay, Jarvis?"

Apart from wanting to kick something? "I'm fine. Did you want something, or can I get a little privacy?"

"There's a meeting," he said. "In the conference room. Staff Roberts sent me to get you."

Alex hesitated, her lips pressed together so tightly that numbness set in. Michael's words rang in her ears, reached deeper to resonate in her soul. He was right. She could walk away now and be done with it all. With the murders, the angels, the Fallen Ones, the Nephilim. Walk away and take the only chance at happiness she might ever have. But *could* she live with that choice?

She looked at her reflection in the mirror over the sink. Met the resignation in her own gaze. Closed her eyes against the weariness that seeped from her every pore.

"I'm coming," she told Joly. "Just give me a minute."

Not until the door swung shut again did it register that he'd behaved normally. As if he'd heard nothing, knew nothing, despite being planted directly outside Roberts's door when she'd emerged after her meltdown. As if it had never happened. That must have been what Michael meant. Heaven had wiped the memory from them. She tipped her head back against the stall.

Damn, what she wouldn't give to be in their shoes.

THIRTY-FOUR

" . . . on those files?"

In the silence that followed the question, Alex raised her head. She found all eyes in the room on her and looked over at her supervisor. Hell. That would teach her to tune out of a meeting.

"Sorry, were you talking to me?"

A flash of impatience crossed Roberts's features. "I asked where you were on the files I asked you to review."

You mean in my spare time? Alex bit back the retort. "I haven't had a chance to finish them yet," she said.

"I want them done by tomorrow." Roberts nodded at her notepad. "What's that?"

"A list. Additional terms I thought tech might want to watch for on the Internet."

He held out his hand.

She hesitated, then tore the sheet of paper from the notepad and passed it to Joly beside her. It moved from hand to hand around the table, each holder taking a second to skim the contents—*Nephilim, Satan, second coming, Lucifer, angels, demons, fallen angels*. Some of the terms were probably on tech's watch list already. Others, such as *Nephilim*, maybe not so much.

The paper reached their staff inspector. Apart from a few raised eyebrows among her colleagues—and Joly's narrowed, sidelong speculation—no one seemed overly perturbed. Alex relaxed a little. Michael's magic memory-wipe was holding.

Roberts scanned the list, and then, without so much as glancing her way, held it aloft.

"For those of you who didn't have the opportunity to sneak a peek, Jarvis has just added to our list of Internet watch terms. The terms she is suggesting tie in with what's going on out in Morinville and quite probably with yesterday's stoning. They are also religious in nature. Now, we all know what happens the moment the press gets wind that the police are investigating any kind of religious angle. So let me be clear: your answer to any question put to you by a journalist is 'no comment,' because if anything on this list makes the news, I will have someone's head. Now get to work. Jarvis, stay."

Again?

Alex subsided into her chair and watched the others file out. Roberts closed the door behind them, keeping his hand on the knob.

"I'll be brief. What happened in my office . . ."

She stiffened. He remembered?

"I'm sorry. I know I sprang Dr. Riley on you, but you would have objected if you'd known in advance."

"That's it?" she asked cautiously. Nothing about her information dump?

"I don't know what else you want me to say. My

hands are tied, Detective. I have my orders, and you have yours. You're to see Riley."

Alex looked down at her hands, folded in her lap. He didn't remember.

"Like I said, Detective, this one's out of my hands. Though if I ever catch a certain psychologist in a dark alley somewhere, I don't guarantee his continued well-being." He half smiled, not entirely in jest. "My question at the moment is, are you good to remain today, or do you need some time?"

"I'm good."

"You sure? You've been under one hell of a lot of pressure."

A significant portion of which waited for her at home.

"I'm sure."

"All right, then. Let's get back to work."

"Jarvis! You have company."

Alex looked up at the sound of her name and found Joly near the door, waving for her attention. Seth towered over him. Her stomach migrated to her toes. *Hell. Now what?* She flipped the file folder closed and stood, aware of the curious eyes following his progress across the office.

And the watchful ones.

Catching Aramael's eye, she scowled a warning at him. *Stay away.* She still hadn't forgiven him for siccing Mika'el on her instead of handling her meltdown on his own—and she had no intention of letting him anywhere near Seth. Returning her glare, Aramael stepped back into the coffee room from which he'd emerged. She met Seth halfway across the office.

"Is everything all right?" she asked. "Did I miss a call? Did you find something?"

A shadow crossed his eyes. "I didn't realize that was a prerequisite for seeing you."

She swallowed an automatic denial. He was right. When had she stopped feeling anticipation rather than dread at the sight of him? "It's not. You've just never come to the office before, and I thought—" She touched his hand. "Never mind. I'm happy to see you."

"I wanted to take you for lunch."

"Lunch?"

"I believe that's a customary activity for a couple."

"It is. It's just—" She snapped her teeth shut against the words that threatened. *So ordinary.* Too ordinary to fit with the context of what they were. What they knew. What they did. And certainly too ordinary to follow on the heels of their argument the night before. The shadows in his eyes deepened and guilt twinged in her heart.

Lunch *was* ordinary, but maybe that's what they needed. What *she* needed before she had to act on Michael's—

No. She wasn't going to think about Michael now. Seth was making an effort here and she was damned if she wouldn't meet him halfway. At least this once.

Roberts's files would have to wait for an hour.

And so would Armageddon.

""I'd love to go for lunch with you," she said. "I'll get my coat."

Outside on the sidewalk, she reached for Seth's hand. "Let's walk for a bit. I haven't been out of the office all morning. The fresh air is nice."

So was pretending, for a few minutes at least, that they were almost a normal couple.

Seth stared down at their linked fingers.

Almost.

"Also customary," she said lightly. She tipped her head to the left. "This way. There's a sandwich shop a couple of blocks over."

Seth fell into step beside her, and their silence—perhaps for the first time ever—was comfortable. It didn't last long.

"Must your bodyguard follow us?"

Alex glanced over her shoulder and saw Aramael a couple of dozen feet behind. Hell. She pulled her hand from Seth's grasp. "Wait here."

Doing an about-face, she walked back to Aramael. "Go away."

"I can't do that if I'm going to protect you."

"I don't care."

"Alex—"

"No. It's broad daylight. We're on a busy street. No one is coming after me here."

"You don't know that."

"I'm willing to take the chance." She dropped her voice. "Aramael, I need this. Please."

Aramael's gaze bored into hers, flicked to Seth, darkened, returned. "I'll pull back, but not all the way."

"Damn it!"

"I won't risk it. I can't."

Alex met the granite-hard inflexibility in his eyes, spun away, and went to rejoin Seth, skirting a homeless man picking through a garbage can. "Let's just go," she said wearily. To her relief, Seth made no objection.

This time, however, their hands stayed in their respective pockets.

THIRTY-FIVE

Mittron stared after the couple walking down the sidewalk, shock holding him immobile. The Naphil and the *Appointed*? How—? What—? He dropped a discarded sandwich back into the garbage can from which he'd pulled it and pressed his fingers against his skull. This newest drug might muffle the voices, but it did the same to his thoughts. Holding on to an idea for more than a few seconds took conscious effort . . . sorting through something as big as this seemed impossible.

Seth and the woman disappeared around a corner. Dropping his hands to his sides, he looked for the Archangel that had been following, but Aramael had vanished. Mittron shuffled after the couple, his pursuit of the woman automatic. *Follow, watch, wait for her to be alone.* Seth's presence changed nothing. Well, it did, but it didn't and—

He smacked his fists into the sides of his head, interrupting the thought-loop threatening to form. A woman walking toward him scurried off the curb, out of his way. He scowled. For an instant, he was tempted to step toward her, to see if he could drive her farther onto the street and into the traffic . . . *No. Focus.*

Follow, watch, wait for her to be alone. Follow, watch, wait—

Wait. She'd sent Aramael away, which meant she *was* alone. He looked over his shoulder to double-check. There was no sign of the Archangel. Hope flickered, and his heart rate kicked up. This was it. This was his chance. His gaze snapped back to the end of the block ahead of him. He sped up his shamble to a stagger and rounded the corner in the Naphil's wake, searching for her familiar blond head.

There—beside Seth.

Seth. How—?

He clutched at his hair, pulling until water streamed from his eyes. He couldn't take her in this state. The damned drugs were too fresh in his system. They had to wear off enough to think again. *Follow, watch, think.*

Half a block ahead, the Naphil disappeared into a building. The Appointed followed.

The Naphil and the Appointed? How—?
Damn it to Hell.

DESPITE ALEX'S BEST INTENTIONS, lunch was an endurance event filled with long silences, stilted conversation, and the ever-present specters of Michael and Aramael. With one elbow on the table and her fist resting against her mouth, she stared out the window, her sandwich untouched, lunchtime odors assailing her. Roasted chicken, mushroom-barley soup, coffee.

None stirred her appetite.

She watched a ragged man stagger past on the sidewalk, his hands clutching at his hair. Seth reached past her for the napkin dispenser. She drew back with a murmur of apology, then returned to her brooding.

Unclaimed powers, a world that might or might not survive events that went far beyond this current drama, their own struggling relationship . . . Where did they begin sorting through the chaos? Seth had lost everything because of her, and now they wanted him to lose her, too?

Expected her to push him away?

Christ.

Seth shoved the plate with his own sandwich to one side. "We need to talk."

A woman laughed at a table in the back corner, a bray of sound that caused other patrons to go quiet and look for the source. Alex shook her head.

"This might not be the right time—"

"It will never be the right time, Alex, and we can't continue like this. You and Heaven want me to take back my powers—"

"I never said that."

"Semantics. Whether you want it or not, you think I should. But has it ever occurred to you—to *any* of you—to question the need for me to do so?"

"What do you mean? Aramael said—"

Fury sparked in his black eyes. *Shit. Wrong name to drop right now.*

His forearms on the table, Seth leaned toward her. "Think about it, Alex. My mother is the One, the Creator of All, and she can't deal with this? She needs me to take back my powers because she's not strong enough to keep them from damaging the planet?

Does that even make sense? Or are you too blinded by your soulmate's presence to *see* sense?"

Alex rocked back in her seat, recoiling from his viciousness, stunned by his words. He really thought that of her? And wait—could he be right about the One? When he put it like that, he was right. It *didn't* make sense. The Creator of the entire universe *should* be able to manage this. But then why would Aramael and Michael say otherwise? What weren't they telling her?

Christ, she didn't know what to think anymore. If there was a shred of a chance that Seth might be onto something here, however—

"I'll talk to Aramael," she said. "See if I can find out—"

"What, more lies? Do you really think he'll tell you the truth?"

"Michael, then." She watched Seth's mouth compress. "Damn it, Seth, we need more information. You can't make a decision without—"

"*My* decision is already made." His voice was cold. "Apparently, however, yours is not."

THIRTY-SIX

S eth walked Alex back to the office in stubborn silence. With every step, the few inches between them seemed to grow wider. The chasm in his heart did likewise. Try as he might to justify her words, to understand why she felt the way she did about her world, her race, it all kept coming back to one thing. If it turned out that the planet really was in trouble, she expected him to save it. To take back his powers and give her up. Give them up.

As she would do. Willingly.

Pain squeezed through his chest. He breathed around it, tthe words of his father's journal burning in his memory: *"That she has allowed these creatures to come between us is beyond comprehension. Beyond endurance."* He shoved them away. No. Alex wasn't like his mother, and he was nothing like Lucifer. They could still figure their way through this. If she needed more information, he'd get it for her. He'd ask the questions of Mika'el himself, find a way to make the

Archangel admit he was wrong. Make him admit the One could—

Alex's hand on his forearm sent a rush of warmth through him, stopping his thoughts, freezing his step. He looked down, even now all too willing to let go of their argument, to put things right again. Needing to do so. But her attention wasn't on him. He peered into the alley beside which they stood, then looked askance at her.

She frowned. "I thought I heard—"

A moan. He heard it, too.

Alex dropped her hand from his arm and stepped into the narrow passage. Reining in his impatience, he followed. Yet again, another took precedence. Even if he managed to convince Alex that his decision to remain with her would do no harm—that it was the right one, the only one, to make—would they still grapple with this, her job? Would she always put others before herself? Before him? He looked down at her touch on his arm and saw her pointing with her other hand.

"There."

A figure slumped in the shadow of a Dumpster a dozen feet away, head resting in a dark pool. Seth drew back in distaste. "Is that blood?"

"Most likely." She pulled out her cell phone and moved forward again, simultaneously punching in a number and calling out to the man. "Sir? Are you all right? I'm a police officer, and I want to help. I'm going to have a look at—" She broke off and turned her attention to the phone as she went down on one knee beside the man. "Hi, yes, it's Detective Alexandra Jarvis from the homicide unit. I have an injured civilian in an alley off—"

The man lunged at her. The cell phone flew from her grasp and smashed into the Dumpster. Seth leapt forward, reaching to pull Alex away, but he was too slow. The man's hands closed around her throat and he rose to his feet, lifting her with him. Her breath became a harsh rasp beneath his hold and Seth seized his arm. He pulled. Pulled harder. Bellowed his fury. His fear.

The man paid no attention.

Abandoning his hold, Seth snaked his forearm around the man's neck and tightened it with all the strength he possessed. An elbow plowed into his ribs and he sailed through the air. His head cracked against a brick wall. For an awful instant, the world flickered, on the verge of turning black. He struggled to breathe, fought off the darkness.

Alex. I have to help Alex.

He rolled to his hands and knees. Pain shot through his chest, hammered in his skull. A cold, awful realization gripped him. *I can't help her. I'm mortal. I have no power.*

"Call him," the man snarled.

Seth tried to focus through the flashes of light going off in his eyes. Alex's attacker held her off the ground, hands still at her throat, shaking her as he might a doll.

"Call him!" he demanded again. "Call your soulmate, Naphil. Like you did for—"

A rush of wind swept through the alley, driving grit into Seth's eyes, sealing them shut. He scrubbed at them, forced them open. Aramael towered above him, black wings spread wide, menace written in his every line.

"Let her go, Mittron," he snarled.

Mittron?

The man shifted, spinning to hold her from behind. He replaced the hands at her throat with a knife. Alex gasped for air, a harsh, ragged sound that clawed at Seth's heart. He struggled to his feet, ignoring the pain streaking through his rib cage, focusing instead on the cold glint of metal. He tried not to think about the terrible fragility of a mortal life. The world spun and his stomach heaved. He sagged to the pavement.

"I knew you would come," the man breathed. "I knew she would call for you."

"Let her go," Aramael said again.

The man shook his head, his amber eyes glowing with an intensity that sent a shudder down Seth's spine. Amber eyes that, despite the mania that had taken hold in their depths, he recognized. Aramael was right. It was Mittron. Fresh fury snarled through Seth. Damn it to Hell, would Heaven's interference never end?

"It's not that easy," Mittron said. "We need to trade. You want her, and I want what you gave Caim."

Aramael scowled. "Caim!" he spat. "I gave him noth—"

"Death," rasped Seth. "He wants you to kill him."

He felt the Archangel's shock. His denial. He kept his own focus squarely on the wavering knife, willing it to stay still. A thin line of blood trickled down Alex's throat. Something inside him shriveled.

"Do it," he told Aramael.

"I cannot."

"Yes," he snapped, flashing the angel a venomous glare. "You *can*. And we all know it."

Icy rage gathered in the other's eyes. Glittered in them. "We all know what came of it, too," he growled back.

"A little late to have discovered your principles, don't you think?"

"At least I have them."

"Oh, for crying out loud," Alex's mutter broke between them.

Seth switched his attention back to her in time to see her become a blur of motion. In the space of a heartbeat, before Mittron could react, she planted an elbow in his gut, clamped fingers over his wrist, spun on one heel, and pinned the knife-wielding hand behind his back. Practiced moves calculated to disarm and control a human.

But not an angel. Not even an exiled one stripped of his divine powers. A warning formed in Seth's throat as Alex glowered over her shoulder.

"When you two are done with your pissing contest—" she began.

Mittron jerked free and whirled, his knife slicing toward her in a wide, graceful arc.

THIRTY-SEVEN

Even as Seth's shout rang through the alley, Aramael's wings shot open, driving between Alex and her attacker. The knife slammed into unyielding feathers and Mittron staggered backward. Before he recovered his footing, Aramael reached one hand for the weapon, the other for the former Seraph's throat. A vast ugliness rose in his soul as his fingers closed around both.

Manic joy lit the Seraph's eyes.

"Yes," he croaked. "Do it. I deserve nothing less after what I've done to you, to her. I deserve to die."

The ugliness in Aramael's core darkened. Seethed. About that, Mittron was right. No one was more deserving of death. All of this was the Seraph's fault. He was at the center of everything: the breaking of the pact between Heaven and Hell; the failure of the eleventh-hour agreement; Alex's near death—twice; Seth's abandonment of his place at his mother's side...

And Aramael's own bond to a soulmate he could

never hope to have.

Deep within him, the power of an Archangel began to build, mingling with the rage he thought he had left behind. He inhaled a ragged breath and crumpled the knife in his hand. He let it fall to the ground. Energy—fluid, glacial—coursed through his body.

Dangling from his hold, Mittron closed his eyes. His features went slack and almost peaceful. "Please," he whispered.

No other word could have reached Aramael.

No other word could have stopped him cold.

He stared at the Seraph. Saw for the first time the agony etched into the lines there. The anguish. Slow understanding unfurled in him. The One's intent hadn't been to let Mittron live; it had been to let him live like this. With the same torment that he had caused so many. Inescapable, awful torment.

Her Judgment had been so much more than Aramael had assumed.

More, and infinitely worse than death could ever be.

He shook his head. "No."

Mittron's eyes shot open. Panic warred with madness in their amber depths. He scrabbled at the hand locked around his throat. "You must. I should die for what I've done. I *need* to die."

"Which is why I won't kill you. You don't deserve to *die* for what you've done, Seraph. You deserve to suffer. I can do no worse to you than what our Creator has done, and I'm damned if I'll do better."

He released his hold. The Seraph dropped to the ground, sagged to his knees. He reached to pluck at Aramael's leg.

"By all that is merciful, Archangel—"

Aramael backhanded the Seraph across the cheek,

snapping Mittron's head to the side. The wrecked, wretched angel toppled and lay weeping on the filthy pavement. Aramael stared down at him.

"I have no mercy for you, Mittron," he said.

Turning his back on that which Heaven itself had already discarded, he found Alex still standing where she'd been when he blocked Mittron's attack. Her sky-blue eyes stood out against the pale of her skin. Shocked. Wary. Appalled. He studied her, marveling at the strength that held her upright, that had let her become embroiled in a war between angels.

"Are you all right?" he asked. A dozen tiny cuts marred her face, seeping crimson. "I've hurt you. I'm sorry. In battle, my wings—"

She deflected the hand he put out to her, and he followed her gaze to the figure propped against the wall a dozen strides from where they stood. Seth. Of course. How could he have forgotten?

"Go," he said wearily. "He's injured."

Alex went.

ALEX WALKED CAREFULLY away from Aramael and the keening man by his feet, willing her legs not to give out beneath her. Reinforcements were arriving en masse, heralded by feet pounding down the alleyway, the approach of a siren, the slam of car doors. She shut them out, crouching beside Seth and reaching to touch his cheek.

"Are you okay?"

For a long minute, he didn't answer. Then, one hand against his ribs and blood trickling down his forehead, he lifted pain-glazed eyes to hers. "I couldn't stop him. I wasn't strong en—"

"Shh." She placed her fingers over his mouth. "It doesn't matter. I'm fine."

He twisted his head away from her. Something darker than the pain clouded his face. "Because of him."

Alex shivered a little at the bitterness underlying the emphasis on him. "He only did what he's supposed to do."

"Because I chose to be weak."

She brushed his blood-matted hair away from the gash over his eyebrow. "You're not weak,. You're just mortal."

He scowled. "There seems little difference at the moment."

"Christ, Jarvis," Roberts's voice growled behind her. "What is it with you and alleys?"

She looked up at him, and his face went white.

"You're hurt."

She shook her head. "It's superficial. But Seth—"

"I'm fine." Seth made as if to rise, let out a hiss, and subsided, his glower deepening.

"The ambulance is on its way," said Roberts. "What the hell happened?"

In as few words as she could, Alex summed up finding what she thought had been an injured man, concocted what she hoped was a plausible story about an attack driven by the influence of drugs, and prayed that it would be enough to satisfy the questions she saw in her supervisor's eyes.

Silence followed her explanation.

"And your face?" Roberts asked at last.

Damn. She'd forgotten that part.

"Glass?" she hazarded. "It happened fast. I'm not sure."

Roberts looked pointedly around at what had to be the only alley in all of Toronto that didn't have at least one broken bottle in it. He looked at Seth, then back at her.

"I'll see where that ambulance is," he said.

Alex settled onto the dank ground beside Seth. She took his free hand in her own. Neither of them said anything more, and he returned none of her pressure on his fingers.

THIRTY-EIGHT

"Typical that one of Heaven would leave you in this condition."

Head throbbing, Seth forced open his eyes against the glare of fluorescent lights. He closed them again when he saw the Fallen One at the foot of his bed in the emergency ward.

"Go away. I'm not interested."

The Fallen One snorted. "Right. That's why you've been reading those journals so fast. What are you up to now? Four? Five?"

"You know damned well it's seven, because you deliver them as fast as I read them."

"Just trying to be helpful." The Fallen One dropped into the chair beside the bed. "So that was quite a performance our Aramael put on for his lady friend. Very impressive. Nothing like having a big, strong Archangel around to save you when your mere mortal partner is too weak to do so."

Seth's fingers clamped onto the bedcovers.

"Of course, it didn't have to be that way," the Fallen One added. "If you'd taken back your powers—"

"I could have saved her myself. I get that," Seth snarled, jerking his head around to look at his visitor. Pain shafted through his skull. He inhaled sharply, and another jolt streaked across his ribs. He let his breath out in a slow hiss. "I know I could protect her better if I had my powers. But for what? So I can give her up and return to Heaven? I told you, I'm not interested."

"Is that what you think?" The Fallen One propped his feet on the edge of the bed and tipped the chair back onto two legs. "Seth, Seth, Seth. You disappoint me. It's not Heaven I want you in, it's Hell."

"My father wants—?"

"Lucifer has nothing to do with this."

Seth stared at him, and then snorted. "You want to take on the Light-bearer? You're not anywhere near strong enough."

"No. But you are. Or could be."

Shuddering, Seth remembered his short-lived attempt to stand up to his father in a Vancouver alley, when Lucifer had knocked him aside with less effort than he might have expended on a fly. "You overestimate my ability—and underestimate his. Even if I were interested, which I'm not, I wouldn't stand a chance."

"You would with my help."

Seth stared at the booted feet beside him. The Fallen One's proposal was ludicrous. Seth didn't have so much as the slightest interest in it. And yet, instead of telling his visitor to go straight back to whence he'd come, he found himself asking another question.

"You and what army?" he asked. "The Fallen are

aligned with him."

"They wouldn't be if they knew he planned to sacrifice them." The Fallen One dropped his feet to the floor and leaned forward. His voice became grim. "Lucifer's obsession with wiping out humanity has taken over. He doesn't care if Hell and all its occupants are destroyed in the process. He doesn't care if *he* is destroyed in the process. If the Fallen knew—"

"Then why not tell them?"

"Because there would be a thousand would-be rulers vying for control. The infighting would destroy us as surely as Lucifer's lack of interest will."

"You could rule yourself."

"I might have been an Archangel at one time, Appointed, but even if I remained so, I know my limitations. I'm no ruler."

"And you think I am."

"I think you could be, yes."

"There's just one flaw in your plan. I already have what I want right here."

"You mean the Naphil?"

"Alex. Yes."

"The woman who is even now at Aramael's side instead of yours." The Fallen One smiled. "Of course you have her."

Seth glowered as his visitor rose from the chair, but before he could form a satisfactory retort, the Fallen One placed one hand over his forehead and the other over the ribs broken by Mittron's elbow. Seth froze.

"A reminder of that which you were once capable yourself," said the Fallen One. "And what another might have done for you if he so wished. Consider it my gift."

Agony seared through Seth. Arching against the

bed, he clutched at the covers. "Bloody fucking *Hell*!"

He grabbed for the Fallen One but connected with nothing but his own ribs. His hand clamped in place, he fought for breath—and to push back the darkness hovering at the edge of his brain. Slowly the pain ebbed, receded, disappeared. Eyes closed, he probed his injuries with cautious fingers, increasing the pressure until he was certain.

The Fallen One had healed him . . .

. . . whereas Aramael had not.

THIRTY-NINE

"This seems a rather extreme way of avoiding talking." Elizabeth Riley's voice contained a dry note. "Even for you."

Alex finished tugging the T-shirt over her head. She settled it into place around her midriff as she turned to face the psychiatrist. "And so you tracked me down here to make sure I didn't get away?"

"No. I tracked you down because I wanted to be sure you're all right." Riley indicated her face. "Those must sting."

"Less so now that they've finished poking at them." Alex peered at her reflection in the mirror over the examining room counter. She suppressed a shudder at the dozen or so cuts inflicted by Aramael's wings. What kind of feathers were as sharp as razors? She turned away. "They look worse than they feel."

"Are they from your attacker?"

"No."

Riley waited.

Alex shrugged into her blazer, lifted her hair free, and reached for her coat.

Riley sighed.

"You're not going to volunteer a thing, are you?"

Alex took her pistol from the coat pocket and slid it into the holster at her waist. "You really expected otherwise?"

"No, but I hoped once you—" Riley broke off and shook her head. "Damn it, Alex, you have to know that I'm not your enemy. I'm trying to help you."

"Then go home."

"I can't do that."

"Yes," Alex said. "You can. Your credentials far outweigh Bell's. Tell the captain you've met with me, done all your mumbo jumbo stuff, and decided that I'm fine. Sound of mind, sane, however you want to put it. And then *go home*."

"I would have already done that if I thought it was true."

Alex slid her arms into her coat. "Meaning what? You think I'm nuts?"

"I think you're under a tremendous amount of stress. I think it would help you to talk."

At last Alex stopped and gave Riley her full, undivided attention. The Vancouver psychiatrist stared back implacably. Alex shook her head, feeling oddly sad, weirdly compassionate. She'd been in Riley's shoes not that very long ago, she reminded herself. That place of knowing but not wanting to know, seeing but refusing to accept. A place most of the world would likely find itself in the days to come.

"Look, Riley, try to understand. The world as we know it is very quickly coming to a grinding, crashing halt. For reasons I can't begin to fathom, I'm in the middle of it. Yes, it's tremendously stressful. Yes, under other circumstances it might be helpful to talk. But right now, I can't. I don't dare. Because if I start looking too closely at my own mess—" Her voice caught, and she paused to swallow.

"If I start thinking about everything that's going on, everything that's already happened, and what's still to come, I might fold. And if I consider what it might be doing to me personally?" She shook her head slowly. Shrugged. "I don't think I'll survive. So please. There are a lot of people who are going to need your help through this. I'm not one of them. It's time to leave me alone."

Blue eyes regarded her through wire-framed glasses for a long minute. Then Riley opened the door and stepped aside. "He's in the waiting area."

"I don't want Ara—Trent, I want Seth."

"That's who I meant."

Alex paused in the doorway. "He can't be. Roberts said he had broken ribs and a concussion."

"He did. He doesn't anymore."

Alex stared out into the corridor. She watched two paramedics rolled an empty gurney back toward the ambulance bay. She inhaled carefully.

"Right," she said. "Thank you."

"Alex."

Again she met Riley's wire-framed gaze.

"I understand more than you realize," Riley said.

Alex walked away.

FORTY

" A h, for chrissakes," a voice above Mittron
muttered. "What have you done to yourself,
you idiot?"

Mittron twisted away from the hand cupping his
chin, the disgust in the voice. *No. Don't make me come
back.*

The cell guard grabbed him again, harder this
time, forcing his head one way, then the other, then
thrusting him away with a sigh.

"Christ, your head is a goddamn mess. Wait here.
I'll call the ambulance."

He tried not to listen to the man rise, or to hear
the metallic clang of the cell door or the retreating
footsteps. He wanted to stay in the dark place he'd
found, where the voices couldn't follow. But it was too
late.

The cold of the concrete penetrated first, hard
against body parts stiff from lying on it too long. The
pain of his battered skull came next, a deep, throbbing

ache where he'd beaten it against the bars of his cage as the drugs wore off and the voices returned. Beaten it rhythmically, mercilessly, until the dark finally claimed him. How long had he managed to escape? Not long enough. Nothing short of eternity would be long enough.

A whisper slid through his brain, heralding *their* return. All the souls lost so far to the Fallen, to be joined by billions more by the time Lucifer was done. And now, caged and without access to the drugs, he would have no choice but to endure. He lifted his head and smashed it down on the floor once, twice, again.

Strong hands seized his shoulders and hauled him to his feet, shoved him against the bars. "Would you stop that?" an irritated voice asked. "I can't talk to you if your brains are scrambled."

Fingertips tried unsuccessfully to pry open one of his eyes. Then the hand slapped his cheeks, once on each side, sharp enough to create a new pain that overrode the first. Forcing his arms up to ward off another blow, he mumbled an objection.

"Then open your eyes," the voice retorted. "Look at me."

He sagged to the floor.

"Bloody Heaven, Seraph." The voice's owner dragged him upright again. Sheer surprise at the address accomplished what pain could not. Mittron's eyes flew open. A hand patted his cheek. "That's better."

He stared at the burnished, mahogany-dark face inches from his own. "You—what—*Samael*?"

"You recognize me. Good. I wasn't sure you would in your current state." Samael drew back, wrinkling his nose. "For the record, you reek."

Footsteps thudded somewhere down the corridor.

Mittron's visitor shot an impatient look in their direction. "We need to make this quick."

More words issued forth from Samael's mouth, but they became lost in the growing volume of whispers. Mittron put his hands to his ears, trying in vain to block what originated within his soul. Trying to focus.

"What?"

Samael pulled his hands away.

"Limbo. You broke Caim out. Can you do so for others?"

The whispers—

"Damn it, Seraph. Can you or can't you get others out of Limbo?"

"How many?" he mumbled.

"All of them."

The voices dropped to murmurs.

A door clanged. The heavy footsteps drew nearer. More than one set. Cursing his own sluggishness, Mittron wrestled with Samael's question, seeking its purpose. Was such a thing possible?

"Why?" he asked.

"Suffice it to say I need to raise an army, and they're the most likely recruits. If I can get them out."

Mittron shook his head. His brain smashed against the inside of his skull. "Even if you could, there's no telling *what* you'd get. Some of them have been in there for millennia. Their minds—"

"I'm willing to take the chance. Can you do it?"

"Why should I?"

Samael held up a clear glass vial filled with an amber liquid. "Because I can stop the pain," he said. "Temporarily for now, with this. Permanently if my plan succeeds."

"Permanently—you'll kill me if I help?"

"If all goes well, I won't have to. But yes. If necessary, I will do what your enemy will not."

Mittron stared at the vial. He fought to still his tremble, to block the voices so that he could think for one moment more. What Samael wanted—opening Limbo and releasing the Fallen imprisoned there—it would be the ultimate betrayal of the One who had created him.

Another door clanged, closer this time, and the guard who had gone for help gave a shout.

"Hey! Who the hell are you? How did you get in—"

A betrayal of the One whom he had wanted nothing more than to serve for eternity.

Booted feet broke into a run. Samael glanced toward the approaching men. His wings spreading wide, filling the cell. He looked at Mittron. "Well? I need a decision, Seraph."

The One who had instead chosen to Judge him and sentence him to this.

Mittron reached to grasp Samael's arm.

FORTY-ONE

Mika'el looked around from his post at the window as the door opened without invitation. He raised an eyebrow at Verchiel. "Let me guess. Another problem?"

"Is there ever not?" The Highest Seraph slumped into one of the wingback chairs on the other side of the desk.

Mika'el's other eyebrow joined the first. Verchiel didn't slump. Ever. Nor did she chew on her lip the way a dog worried a bone. "I doubt the news will improve with waiting."

"There's been an attack on the woman."

"The Naphil?" He became alert. "Was she harmed? Was it Samael?"

"She's fine. And it was Mittron."

"Mitt—" He gaped. He couldn't help it. He paced the floor between window and desk, then turned and retraced his steps. "How in all of Hell did he find her? And why attack her?"

"As far as we can tell, he wanted to goad Aramael into putting him out of his misery. The One's Judgment has been most . . . effective."

"And Aramael?"

"Resisted temptation."

Thank the One for that. Mika'el traversed the floor again. "Where is everyone now?"

"Mittron was taken into human custody. Seth and the woman were taken to a hosp—"

"Seth! How does he fit into this?"

"He was with the woman. He was injured trying to defend her. Nothing serious, just broken ribs and a concussion. The woman sustained superficial lacerations."

"So everything is under control, then."

"Not quite. Mittron has disappeared."

"I thought you said he was taken into human custody."

"And locked in one of their holding cells," she agreed. "And now he's gone. The guard saw someone talking to him and then—in his words—*poof.*"

"*Poof*? As in he simply disappeared?"

"Apparently so."

"We're sure it wasn't one of ours?"

"They found a black feather in the cell."

Samael. First his interest in the Naphil and now Mittron. What in Hell was the former Archangel up to?

"I'll assign someone to look for him," he said. "Was that all?"

"Not quite." Verchiel pressed her fingertips to the crease between her brows. "Seth appears to have healed himself."

His eyes narrowed. "Healed himself how?"

"One minute he was injured, the next he was fine."

"Without taking back his powers? That's not possible. The doctors must have been wrong about their diagnosis."

"X-rays confirmed it."

"And Aramael didn't—?"

"No."

"Bloody Hell." He spun on his heel and crossed to the window again, turned, and started back.

Verchiel dropped her hand. "Will you *please* stop pacing!"

He halted mid-stride. Glared. Then dropped into his chair with an aggrieved sigh. "Maybe we're wrong. Maybe he's reclaimed a portion of his powers. Have you checked with the One? She would know better than we do."

"That would be the third thing I came to tell you. She refused to see me."

"She—" He stared at her. "She has never refused to see anyone. Ever."

"I know."

An eternity ticked by. At last Mika'el roused himself, pushing out of the chair again. "I'll speak with the One," he said, crossing to the door. "But, Verchiel, if this isn't the Appointed's own doing . . ."

Verchiel folded her hands into her robe. "If it's not Seth's doing," she finished his thought, "then we have a bigger problem than protecting the Naphil."

ARAMAEL STEPPED in front of the door, blocking Alex's exit to the waiting area.

"Move," she growled. "Or I will cause the biggest scene you have ever witnessed."

"Alex—"

"Now, Aramael."

He held his ground. "Something isn't right about this. We both know it."

She did. But she'd be damned if she'd discuss it with him. She squared her shoulders and met him stare for stare. "*Now*."

Gray fire flared in his eyes. Then, in stony-jawed silence, he moved aside. Alex brushed past. In the emergency ward waiting room, Seth stood, tall and impassive, beside windows still boarded over from the shooting the night before. Her step hitched. She stopped. He remained unmoving, waiting. With a steadying breath, she crossed the room. She didn't skirt the issue.

"How?" she asked simply.

"One of the Fallen. Not by request."

"Why?"

"I don't know."

His gaze didn't move from hers. Didn't so much as flicker. Yet she knew without a shadow of a doubt that he lied to her. Deliberately. Her throat contracted. She looked away. She ran a trembling hand through her hair. Tomorrow. Tomorrow they would sit down and figure things out. Look at their options. Make some decisions. Tomorrow, but not tonight.

Tonight—she closed the space between them, sliding her arms around his waist and resting her head against his chest—tonight they just needed to go home. Seth hesitated for half a heartbeat, and then folded her close. Held her fiercely.

"I'm glad you're okay," he whispered into her hair. "And I'm so sorry I couldn't stop him."

They stood that way until Alex extricated herself

and wove her fingers through his. Together, they left the hospital.

Aramael didn't suggest that he go with them.

FORTY-TWO

Alex slid her gun's lockbox back onto the closet shelf and, with the same care that had guided all her movements since she'd left the bed, quietly closed the door. Just her coat to put on now and she could leave, be gone before—

"Stay."

She jumped. Closed her eyes. Gathered herself. Then she reached for the coat she'd laid across the hall table. "You know I can't," she told Seth.

"I know you choose not to." His voice was flat. "I heard your supervisor tell you not to come in today."

She shrugged into the gray wool coat. "I have work to do."

"With your soulmate."

"Damn it, Seth, can we please get past this ridiculous jealousy? For the last time, I chose *you*, remember?" The cell phone at her waist vibrated. She glanced down, saw Jen's name on the display, and hit *Ignore*. One fight at a time was enough.

Buttoning her coat, she scowled at Seth. "Look, I'm sorry I need protection from a Fallen One I've never even met, and I'm sorry Aramael is the one who has to protect me. Hell, I'm sorry any of this is happening. Armageddon, your mother, the Nephilim—I'm sorry about it all. But I can't change it and I can't make it go away, and sooner or later we're just going to have to deal with it. You are going to have to deal with it."

"The way you're dealing with it?" he snapped, his expression turning as dark as his eyes. "You spend your days with the one being I know you still have feelings for, and even when you're with me we're not a real couple. Every time I touch you, you pull back. I know here"—he tapped his head for emphasis—"that it's because of Lucifer. But here?" His hand dropped to cover his heart. "Here, I know how strong the connection between you and Aramael is, and yes, I doubt. I chose you, too, Alex. But I sure as Hell didn't choose all of this."

Hot tears spilled over onto her cheeks, burning the tiny cuts inflicted by Aramael's wings the day before. She dashed them away with one hand and reached for the doorknob with the other.

"Neither did I," she told him.

SAMAEL SPRAWLED on the park bench beside Mittron, arms extended along the back, legs outstretched across the sidewalk so that pedestrians had to go around him. He sent a sidelong glance at the Seraph, who sat with hands wrapped around a Styrofoam cup of coffee. Eyes closed, Mittron inhaled deeply. He brought the mug to his lips and sipped at the scalding liquid. The tremble in his hands was half what it had been scant minutes before.

Mittron looked over. "Whatever you gave me, it's good."

"You expected otherwise?"

"I haven't been thinking clearly enough to expect much of anything lately. This makes a nice change." Mittron took another sip of coffee. "So. You want to take over Hell, do you?"

"I'd like there to be a Hell when all this"—Samael waggled the fingers of one hand—"is over."

"I don't understand."

"Lucifer isn't what he used to be, Seraph. The idea of wiping mortals from the planet consumes him to the exclusion of all else, including the survival of his followers."

"And this has changed how?" Mittron asked dryly.

Samael grunted. "Maybe you're right. Now that he's this close to achieving his goal, however, I'd rather like to know I'll survive."

"He's close? How close?"

In a few clipped words, Samael brought Heaven's former executive administrator up to date on what had happened in his drug-induced absence: Seth's choice of the Naphil, the Nephilim army waiting to be born, Lucifer's obsession with fathering a child to lead that army—and his complete lack of interest in whether any of them, including himself, survived the war yet to come.

Mittron was silent when he finished. Then, "Former Archangel or not, the Fallen will never follow you. You're not strong enough."

"Not me. Seth."

"Seth! But you just said—"

"I said he gave up his powers. I didn't say he couldn't

get them back."

"And why would he want to do that? He gave up everything to get rid of them, and he didn't make the decision lightly. He's right where he wanted to be. He has the woman."

"Not if I can convince him otherwise." Samael withdrew the next of Lucifer's journals destined for Seth's hands and laid it on the bench between them. Mittron's eyebrows went up.

"That's your plan? You're going to convince him with a book to take back his powers and overthrow Lucifer?"

Samael grinned at an elderly woman forced to maneuver her walker onto the rough grass to get around his feet. "Hasn't anyone ever told you not to judge a book by its cover?"

Mittron set down the coffee and picked up the leather-bound volume. He flipped through a half dozen pages, then looked up at Samael. "Lucifer's journal?"

"One of a thousand and eleven at last count. Six millennia of history as seen through the eyes of the Light-bearer himself. A rather ugly read, if you ask me."

"I still don't see—"

"A son should have the opportunity to know his father, don't you think? Especially when they have so much in common, such as an obsession with the females in their lives. Females who insist on choosing the good of an entire race over the ones who worship them."

Speculation narrowed Mittron's eyes. "You think you can turn Seth from the woman? After he gave up all that he did for her?"

"I know I can."

Mittron closed the journal. "Even if you succeed, we're talking about Lucifer. There's no guarantee Seth will be strong enough to take him on—with or without an army. Or that Hell will survive if he does."

"Perhaps not. But I can guarantee neither it *nor* we will survive if we don't at least try."

"So you're choosing between the lesser of two evils and you want me to join you?"

"Unless our fearless leader has a sudden change of heart—and I wouldn't hold my breath on that—yes. That's exactly what want." Samael raised an eyebrow. "So what will it be, Seraph? Take a chance on my plan, or return to your Judgment?"

Mittron took a swig of coffee, staring out across the little park.

"Tell me what you need."

ARAMAEL FROWNED as Alex joined him beside her sedan. "Are you—?"

"Don't." Her throat aching, Alex brushed past him and went around to the driver's side. Seth's gaze bored into her back from his vantage point in the apartment window, but she refused to turn. She didn't trust herself not to break down if she did. "Just get in."

"Alex, if there's—"

She rested a gloved hand on the car roof, holding on for dear life to the door handle with her other. Steeling herself, she looked across the car into Aramael's concern. His caring. Her knees trembled and she locked them so they couldn't fold beneath her.

"Can you leave?" she demanded.

Can you go away forever and take all of this with you?

The pain of having known you, the agony of still doing so, the heartache that you're inflicting on the man I'm trying so hard to love? Can you please—please—break this connection between us before it destroys me?

Aramael shook his head slowly, sadly, responding to all her questions, spoken and unspoken. "You know I can't."

Her breath slid down her throat like a thousand shards of glass. She wrenched open the car door. "Then no, Aramael. There's nothing you can do. So get in, shut up, and leave me the hell alone."

FORTY-THREE

Alex gathered up the scattering of messages. Two from the Internet techs looking to clarify the list Roberts had given them; one from Riley, giving her an office location in case she wanted to stop by—at least doing so was a suggestion now and not an order; and one from Roberts ordering her to his office.

She eyed the coffee room longingly, and then, suppressing a sigh, shed her coat and scarf and dropped them onto her chair.

Roberts's door stood open. She tapped on the door frame. "You wanted to see me?"

His back to her as he stared out the window, her supervisor waved her in. She took a seat and frowned. Hadn't Roberts been wearing that same suit yesterday? Had something else come up after they'd sent her and Seth home from the hospital?

She opened her mouth to ask. He spoke first.

"There's a press conference in Ottawa tomorrow afternoon." Roberts let the blinds fall back into place with a metallic clatter. Shoving his hands into his pockets, he turned and leaned back against the window ledge. "The federal health minister is announcing a country-wide implementation of the same measures we used here for the SARS scare in 2003."

"SARS! But we quarantined—" Alex broke off. "You've got to be kidding me. They want to quarantine pregnant women? *That's* their answer to this?"

"No. That's their attempt to contain things, at least for a while. It will apply only to women in their first trimester. Beyond that, there doesn't seem to be much danger. World Health is recommending the measures be taken globally as a precaution while they work to isolate the virus." Roberts held up a hand to ward off her pending outburst. "Our hospital incident night before last wasn't an isolated one, Alex. Demonstrations are springing up at clinics across the globe and ten more women—that we know of— have died giving birth to those babies. People need to believe we have a handle on this thing, or we're going to lose any chance at control."

"Quarantining pregnant women and handing out surgical masks does not constitute a *handle* on things."

"I know that, Detective. WHO knows it. We all know it, but what would you suggest we do? China has already imposed martial law because of the demonstrations there, and damned if I'm not half in agreement with them. People are scared. If these measures give people any peace at all, every member of this force will help to enforce them, including you. Do I make myself clear?"

She held his glare for a second and then subsided. "Of course. You're right. We need to keep people calm."

"Good, because we don't have time for disciplinary crap. You've been called to Ottawa."

"I—what? But why?"

"They didn't say. I got a call from CSIS half an hour after I sent your list to the techs. They want to see you tomorrow morning at ten. My guess is that someone started connecting the dots and discovered you're part of the picture." Roberts grimaced. "I shouldn't have mentioned your name in that memo to tech. I didn't stop to think."

CSIS—the Canadian Security Intelligence Service. With the number of connections she had to events— from Caim's killing spree in Toronto to the mess in Vancouver—it was inevitable that someone would flag her as a person of interest. She should have expected as much.

Alex shook her head. "It's okay, Staff. Really. I haven't exactly kept a low profile. Someone was bound to put it together eventually. Do you know how long I'm there for?"

"Just one night. Trent will go with you."

"Trent?" The name escaped before she could stop it.

"After yesterday?" His brows rose. "Not up for debate."

Shit. Overnight in Ottawa with Aramael after that row she'd had with Seth this morning?. She massaged at the ache forming behind her temple. Hell, maybe she'd skip coffee and just find a bar somewhere instead.

"Is that everything?"

"Just one more thing. I've been looking into the DNA reports you mentioned. The ones for the babies. They've been sealed. So has the one for the claw we found. All I could get out of anyone is what they've already released to the media and a promise to keep us apprised of the situation."

"They?"

"Government Operations Centre. They'll be at the meeting tomorrow, too."

FORTY-FOUR

Mika'el hesitated midstride as he passed the gaping hole in the greenhouse's side. A window, not yet repaired, shattered by pruning shears thrown by the One when their struggles with Seth had begun. He made a mental note to have it looked after by one of the Thrones, then looked beyond the broken glass to the riotous, unkempt growth within the building. The air of desertion was unmistakable, sending a whisper of cold down his spine. How long had it been since the One had tended her beloved plants?

He'd best have the Thrones tend to that task as well.

He continued walking. He had already been through the gardens without success. The only place left to look was the One's office. Pushing open the great oak door of a small stone building tucked behind the greenhouse, he stepped inside. The coolness of the interior reached out to wrap around him, dim, silent, empty. No Principality standing guard over the outer office, no light other than what filtered through the deep-set windows. Mika'el paused. Was the One not—?

"I'm here, my Archangel," came a quiet voice through the open door behind the Principality's desk.

He found her seated in one of the wing chairs by the window overlooking her rose garden. A shadow among the room's shadows but for the pale glint of light off silver hair. He moved closer, his footsteps absorbed by the carpet. Looking up at his approach, the One held out a hand to him. He took it in his own and crouched at her side. He studied her face, his heart recoiling.

"You look tired," he said. The understatement of his existence. The Creator's pale skin had become almost translucent, giving her a fragile, ethereal air, as if she had lost a portion of her very substance.

"I'm not surprised." She turned her face to the window again. Sadness clouded her silver eyes. "My son's powers have proved greater than I anticipated, Mika'el."

His breath snared in his chest. This was why she'd refused to see Verchiel. How long had she been like this, without anyone telling him? Without him paying attention? How in *Heaven* had he not known?

"How bad is it?" His voice was gruff.

Ignoring his question, the One closed her eyes. "Have you made any progress with the woman? Will she help us?"

"I don't know. She's very loyal to your son."

A sad smile tugged at the corner of his Creator's mouth. "She loves him. She thinks I have failed him, and she is right. What kind of mother uses her son's life as currency for bartering with her helpmeet?"

"You did what you—"

"I did wrong, Mika'el. I should have ended this matter with Lucifer when it began. When you wanted me to." Her voice dropped. "When I could."

The chill returned to crawl along his skin. "But you still can."

Had her hand always been this tiny? This fragile?

"One—"

"Oh, never mind me," she said brusquely. "I'm just feeling maudlin today. I'll be fine, and you have enough to look after without worrying about me. You wanted to know about Seth's healing." She raised a brow at the surprise he failed to hide. "You didn't think I knew why you were here? I am still the Creator, you know."

"Of course. I just—"

"It wasn't one of Heaven who healed him." The One's gaze drifted away to the window and became distant. "Nor was it Seth himself."

Mika'el let his head hang. Damn. He'd really hoped he'd been wrong about this. "And the Naphil's attacker—"

"Mittron. I know." She shook her head slightly. "I hadn't anticipated that, either. The woman is unharmed?"

"Her injuries were minor. She's fine."

"Is she?"

He opened his mouth to reassure her, then snapped it closed again. "Hell," he muttered. "I don't know. I feel like I'm beating my wings against the Hellfire itself where talking to her is concerned. Whatever words she needs to hear to convince her, I don't have them." He grimaced. "And I might have made it worse this morning."

He heaved a sigh and recounted his latest conversation—if it could be called such—with the

Naphil, ending on an embarrassed mutter: "I told her to stop feeling sorry for herself and make a decision."

To his surprise, the One chuckled. "You never were one to mince words, my Archangel." Withdrawing her hand from his grasp, she rose to her feet. "But I think perhaps the reason you haven't found the right ones for the Naphil is because they're mine to speak rather than yours."

Mika'el stood, towering over the One. "I beg your pardon?"

"You asked how bad it is?" She gave him another tiny, infinitely sad smile. "It's bad, Mika'el. We're running out of time. If Seth doesn't take back his powers soon, I won't have enough left in me to join with Lucifer. You've done what you can, and now I must do my part. Perhaps I might find the words to convince her."

"LUCIFER!" Samael stepped back, hitting the edge of a garbage can. The metal lid slid off, landing with a crash that echoed the length of the street. "You—I wasn't expecting you here."

The Light-bearer regarded him without word. Then he nodded at the building across the street. "She's there?"

"The Naphil? Of course. Eighth floor, corner apartment, overlooking the parking lot." Samael pointed at the lighted window of the Naphil's residence, surreptitiously studying his companion. "She and your son, both."

Lucifer gave an impatient wave, dismissing the mention of Seth. "And the Archangel who protects her?"

Samael pointed upward again, this time at the rooftop of the building towering above the first— and the barely discernible outline of the brooding, omnipresent Archangel who watched over the woman. "There."

The Light-bearer jammed his hands into the pockets of his dark overcoat. "So he really is there. Does he ever leave?"

He really is there? Samael scowled.

"You're checking up on me."

Lucifer slanted him an unpleasant look. "That surprises you? Answer the question."

Samael swallowed the acerbic retort hovering on his tongue. The time to take on the Light-bearer would come, but this wasn't it. Not yet. "No. Not without her."

"And does he know you're here?"

"He saw me once. I've been more careful since."

The Light-bearer stared up at Aramael. "Well, I'm not going to wait forever. We'll need a distraction. Something big enough to draw him away so you can capture her."

Samael tensed. "But—"

"Not now, of course. After the infants are born. Get them safely to this place you've prepared—this . . ."

"Pripyat."

"Whatever. And then, as soon as they're looked after, do whatever you must to draw the Archangel— all of the Archangels—away from the Naphil. I want her sister and niece."

"Of course."

"And Samael, for the record, I'm glad you passed."

Samael stood rooted to the spot for long, agonizing minutes after Lucifer's departure. Part of him—a quivering, jelly-like mass deep in his core—waited for the Light-bearer to reappear and strike him down, to tell him that he knew Samael hadn't been watching the woman as ordered, that he would pay the price of failure. But Lucifer didn't return, and slowly the cold cramp of fear in Samael's gut relaxed. He sagged back against the wall and wiped the sweat from his forehead. Bloody Heaven, that had been close. Too close. He'd only just returned to his surveillance— another minute or two and Lucifer would have known of his absence. And he wouldn't have bothered to ask questions.

Samael lifted a hand and stared at the tremble in his fingers. He'd have to be more careful—and he needed to speed up the agenda, too. He'd start by speaking to Mittron about opening Limbo sooner rather than later....

He shot another look at his surroundings.

As soon as he was certain Lucifer wasn't still watching.

FORTY-FIVE

Alex froze, her hand on the kitchen light switch, blinking against the glare at the woman pouring water into the teapot at the counter. Despite the darkness in which the stranger had been working, she had laid out matching china cups and saucers, sugar, milk . . . *Wait. Cups and saucers? I don't own cups and—*

The woman turned, teapot in hand, and gestured toward the chairs. "Please. Sit."

It didn't occur to Alex until after she'd obeyed that she might object—that she *should* object, given that this was her kitchen. By then her midnight visitor had set down the teapot and taken the other seat at the tiny bistro-style table, making protest seem petty to say the least. She waited.

Her visitor pushed a plate of muffins toward her. "Eat. If you keep losing weight the way you are, you'll make yourself ill."

Alex curled her hands into fists on her lap. "You—"

Silver eyes met hers. Calm, radiant, crystalline in their clarity.

She tried again. "Who—?"

"You know who I am, Alexandra."

Oh, fuck. Hastily she tried to erase that last thought from her mind. A corner of the woman's mouth tilted upward as if she knew exactly what passed through her brain. Alex added a silent but heartfelt *shit* to her list of mental transgressions.

"Tea?" the woman asked, reaching for the pot.

Tea? She had the One, the Almighty Creator herself, sitting in her kitchen offering tea? She had to be kidding. Alex's gaze sought the cupboard over the fridge where the more appropriate beverages were stored. The One slid a filled cup toward her in its saucer.

"Tea," she said. "I need you alert and sober."

Alex looked at the kitchen doorway and the darkened hallway beyond. Seth slept at the end of that hallway. Would he wake? Hear voices? Come to investigate? She shivered at the thought. She could just imagine his reaction at finding her having a midnight tea party with his mother. She pushed cup, saucer, and muffin-laden plate away.

"What do you want?"

"Your help."

"With Seth."

"Yes."

"I already told Michael—"

"I know how much you love him, Alexandra. And I know why. But he's not your responsibility."

Alex, she wanted to correct, *my name is Alex.* But the words stuck in her throat, held captive by the utter gentleness of the One's voice. Her chest went tight. The One reached out and covered her hand with a tiny one of her own, fingers barely capping Alex's fist. Alex focused on the touch. Warm and dry, it held none of the power she had expected. Not so much as a tingle, never mind a surge. In fact, there seemed a remarkable lack of anything about her that she would have termed godly, or even remotely divine. Alex drew away, defiance sparking in her.

"No, he was *your* responsibility," she said, "and you failed him. Just as you failed us."

The One's mouth tightened for a fleeting instant. "I might have failed in a great number of my responsibilities, child, but Seth is not one of them. Choices have consequences. My son should never have made the one he did."

"He should never have chosen you."

Even unspoken, the words were a like a fist driven into Alex's belly.

"You know I'm right," the One said. "You've thought the same thing yourself. It is that which stands between you, not Lucifer."

Alex shook her head, but her objection refused to be voiced. The One's hand covered hers again.

"Not even I can save everyone, Alexandra. Seth is responsible for his own decisions, just as you are. When he chose you, he did so over the fate of all humanity. And he did it knowingly."

You're wrong. I can't believe that of him. I won't survive knowing that. I'm not strong enough.

"You're stronger than you think."

No, I'm not. I'm tired, and I'm hurt, and—

The tiny hand on hers squeezed with a fierce, surprising strength. "I know, child. And I'm sorry I must ask this of you when you have already given so much. But you *are* strong and you *can* do this."

Alex ripped her voice free of its bonds. "And us?" she grated. "What about us? If he does take back his powers and he becomes like you again, what happens then? To him and me, to the rest of the world?"

The One didn't answer. She didn't need to.

"So that's it." Alex looked down at the hand covering hers. She pulled away. "Your little marital spat nearly ended my life—twice—and it will destroy humanity, and this is your answer? You really expect me to turn my back on the son that you and all of Heaven already abandoned? Do you have any idea what that will do to him? And for what? You can't even promise it will do any good."

"No, but I can guarantee the outcome if you *don't* help."

"That's the best you have? A guilt trip?"

"The truth."

Alex shoved back from the table. Scowling, she towered over the One, the Creator of All, and said, very clearly, "Get out. Take your little schemes and plots and get out of my kitchen. Get out of my life. Get out of Seth's life."

"I can't."

"Fine. Then sit here and drink tea by yourself. I'm going back to bed."

She made it two stomps across the floor, her bare feet slapping painfully against the linoleum, before the quiet voice stopped her.

"Alexandra."

Nothing else. Just her name—and an unspeakably compelling, impossible-to-ignore demand that she turn. She resisted until her entire body vibrated with the effort. Then, clutching the door frame for support, she glared over her shoulder.

The One's crystalline gaze lifted from the table and fastened on hers, seeming to reach inside to the very core of her soul. In the space of a heartbeat, Alex felt herself weighed, measured, and wrung dry of her every awareness and every intention, conscious or otherwise. Her heart turned cold. Panic licked through her. Wait . . . what about Seth? If anything happened to her, what would he think? How would he cope? What would he—?

The One closed her eyes and took a slow, deep breath. "Sit," said the One.

"We're done—"

"I. Said. Sit."

The words, and the tone in which they were spoken, rang with the divinity Alex had previously deemed lacking.

Absolute divinity.

She returned to the table and sat.

The Creator's eyes opened, glittering diamond-hard. "You're right, Alexandra. I have failed. Many times and on many levels. I created Lucifer as my companion, as the yang to my yin. In my arrogance, I believed I had created the perfect creature and that, because he was perfect, he could do no wrong. I believed in him. I trusted him. I loved him with every fiber of my being. But I remained a creator. It is what I do. What I am. And so I continued to create. The stars, the planets, the galaxies and universes . . . all the skies that you see and infinite others beyond those. And then I created Earth and seeded it with the potential for humanity."

The One stood, pacing the cramped kitchen: table to sink, sink to fridge, fridge back to table. "I loved watching your planet's evolution, the birth of humanity, your discoveries, your growth. I wanted to believe Lucifer shared my joy, but in truth, your every success drove another wedge between us. He resented the time I spent watching your world unfold, hated that I could find happiness in anything but him. I ignored the warning signs, found ways to justify his outbursts, tried to soothe his jealousy. I gave him a"— she paused in both step and sentence, straightened her shoulders, and continued. "I gave him a son, thinking a child of his own would assure him of my love for him. But he wanted nothing to do with Seth, and before I had recovered from the birth, he turned the Grigori against me. Against you, my mortal children."

Alex wanted to run from the One's confession, from a story that, surely, she had no right to hear. But she stayed seated, held in place by the tale of betrayal and the Creator's raw, unspoken grief.

"He gave me an ultimatum," the One continued at last. "Him or humanity. The rest of the story you know . . . except for this. When part of the host followed Lucifer and we went to war to defend your world, I did try to stop him. To destroy the monster I had created. And I failed."

FORTY-SIX

Resting an elbow on the arm of his chair, Lucifer idly rubbed a forefinger over his eyebrow. He stared at the journal on his desk, a pen laid across its blank page. Each of the entries he'd made over the last month had been progressively more difficult to write, and now this. Nothing. No words, no inspiration, no desire.

No need.

It was as if he had emptied himself. As if he found himself in Limbo, where nothing existed anymore. Where nothing mattered.

Oh, he still cared—his whole existence was about caring, for all the good it had done him. He'd just run out of reasons to write about it.

And this interminable *waiting* didn't help.

He snatched up the pen and pitched it across the room, scowling when it stuck point-first and quivering in one of the fireplace stones. What in bloody Heaven was taking Samael so long? Finding the Naphil's sister was such a simple task, the last piece in his plan, and the goddamn Archangel couldn't get his act together long enough to complete it.

The dish of peppermints on his desk followed in the pen's wake, shattering against the mantel and sending a shower of glass shards and candies across the room.

Lucifer pushed out of his chair. He wouldn't put it past his aide to be focused on the whole Mika'el and Seth issue rather than on his orders. Samael's ability to think strategically might be his greatest asset, but it could also be his most annoying one. The Archangel was forever searching for hidden motives where none existed. Or worse, where they might exist but didn't matter.

He closed the journal on his desk and turned to slide the volume back into place in the bookcase. Then he paused, staring at the top row of books, the ones at eye level. He inspected the Roman numerals on their spines, neatly lined up in ascending order. Except they weren't. Not entirely.

They couldn't be, because the fourteenth journal was missing from its place.

His gaze swept the row, then the room, then returned to the shelf. He released his hold on the journal he'd replaced. Sliding his hand between volumes XIII and XV, he pushed them apart and scowled. Not just missing from its place. Missing, period. As in gone. As in someone had entered his domain and taken his private property. Had dared trespass against him.

Disbelief unfurled in his gut. A snarl of fury—cold and visceral—drove it out. He whirled and stalked around his desk. If he had to rip apart the whole of Hell, he would—

The door opened as he reached it. A diminutive

Cherub stood in the opening holding a tray, eyes wide and startled. "Light-bearer!"

Lucifer stopped short of plowing over her. He glowered down. "You're in my way."

"I'm s-sorry," the Cherub squeaked. The dishes on the tray rattled as she held it out to him. "I have your tea."

Lifting his arm to brush both the tray and the Cherub from his path, he saw her gaze dart past him. The pupils of her eyes widened almost imperceptibly. He went still, resisting the impulse to turn and look at what he already knew she'd seen. The gap between the books on the shelf. His own eyes narrowed as the Cherub's dropped. Her breathing quickened, and the pulse at the base of her throat hammered. Lucifer stepped back and aside, turning his raised arm into a sweeping invitation to enter.

"Raziel, isn't it?" he murmured.

Shocked blue eyes lifted to his. "Yes, sir."

Raziel, favored informant of Samael for several hundred years after the Fallen had departed Heaven. His nostrils flared. Bloody Heaven, he'd rip the Archangel apart with his bare hands.

"You can leave that on the desk." He smiled and, hands in his pockets, wandered toward the fireplace. "Thank you."

Thank you for solving my mystery for me.

Raziel hesitated for a second more and then scurried forward to set the tray, now jangling in a most irritating manner, on his desk. She slanted a glance at him. "Weren't you going somewhere?"

"Hm? Oh. It can wait. I think I'll have tea first."

She hovered, biting her lip, and for a moment, he wondered if she might not confess on the spot and save him the trouble of digging for the details. But with a quick last glance at the bookshelves, she sidled toward the door. It slammed shut as she came within reach of it. She stopped in her tracks, a hiss of air escaping her.

"Stay," Lucifer said. "We've never had a chance to chat. I'm sure you have much to tell me."

The Cherub turned to face him. Her gaze, hollow with the knowledge of what was to come, met his. He smiled, and with a soft mewl, she crumpled to the floor.

FORTY-SEVEN

Alex waited for the burn in her throat to subside, then poured a second, generous portion of whiskey. Swirling the amber liquid in a slow circle, she stared at her reflection in the dark kitchen window.

"So you're not really all-powerful." Even now, with one drink already warming her belly, her brain kept dancing around the idea. The blasphemy behind it. Except the One herself had said it, so was it really blasphemy? She slugged back the second shot of whiskey.

"I have limits," the One agreed.

"How? How can you have made all of this"—she waved an encompassing hand—"and still have limits?"

"Everything I've made is a part of me, a tiny bit of my essence. My power, if you will. That holds true of Lucifer as well, only he is more of me than my other creations. A great deal more. I wanted a helpmeet in him. A partner. I wanted him to be my equal, or very close to it."

The liquor in Alex's stomach gave an uneasy roll. Lucifer, equal to the One? That didn't sound good.

"The real problem," continued the One, "lies with the part of myself I used to create him. Whether because of instinct or a need to retain at least an illusion of control, I wanted him to be just slightly less than what I was. I didn't want him to feel lesser to me, however, so I compensated by giving him the illusion of equal power . . . more of my yang than my yin, I suppose you could say."

"I don't understand."

"At one time, I was the All, the everything. I was balance itself, both Creator and Destroyer, both light and dark. When I made Lucifer, I gave him more of that darker side of me. Now, while I create, he is more prone to destroy. I love, while he holds my capacity to hate. I am the champion of good. He . . . is not. All that he is, I no longer am. And what I am, he can never be. It isn't that I don't *want* to rise against him or his Fallen followers, it's that I can't. I don't have the strength—and I gave him my will."

"So how in Hell," Alex grated, "did he get the name of Light-bearer?"

"In the beginning, he was the light of my existence. Now he is the light of truth—the truth about me. My failure, my arrogance, my ultimate demise."

"De—" The empty glass dropped from Alex's grip, floated above the floor for an instant, and rose to settle gently on the counter. She stared at it, then at the One. "What *demise*?"

"It's how I will stop him, Alexandra. The only way that I can. It's the reason I ask you to do the unbearable and convince Seth to take back what only he can possess. Holding this world together against my son's discarded power is taking everything I have. If Lucifer turns to open warfare—and it's only a matter of time until he does—I cannot stand against him as long as Seth remains mortal."

Alex wrapped her arms around herself and hung on for dear life as what little remained of reality shuddered, splintered, and crumbled to dust. She opened her mouth to speak but found no voice. Swallowing twice, she tried again, managing a bare whisper. "What about the angels? Michael and—the others?"

"They can stop the Fallen from destroying you outright, but not from inflicting great damage. Should Lucifer himself decide to get involved, things will not go well."

"And the Nephilim?"

"They, I'm afraid, will remain humanity's burden."

"So if I don't convince Seth, humanity will absolutely be wiped from existence, and if I do convince him, you'll die and we'll still have the Nephilim to deal with."

"Not die. Become other. I will bind my energy to Lucifer's to become what I used to be a very long time ago, before I took a form."

"There will be no one left?"

"My angels will remain to watch over you, and there will be Seth."

Seth. Many times damaged Seth, asleep in the other room. Asleep, waiting for her, with no idea of the treachery taking place in his own kitchen. She thought about the cool politeness to which they had resorted in their dance around what neither wanted to discuss. Her job. Aramael. The unsettling question of why he had allowed a Fallen One into his life. The continued, looming presence of Lucifer between them. The lack of his concern for anyone but her among humanity.

And now, Heaven's request that she, too, betray his trust.

Silence settled between them. Alex tried to imagine a world without its Creator. Her world without the man she loved if he stepped back into his immortal birthright. She tried, too, to be angry with a deity that could have let things go this far, get this out of hand, become this hopeless.

But all she could manage was emptiness. Sadness. A single question. "How soon?"

The One rose from the table. "As soon as you can," she said. "And, Alex . . . for what it's worth, I'm sorry."

FORTY-EIGHT

Alex slipped back into bed and lay beside Seth, listening to his deep, steady breathing. Light and shadow played across the ceiling as cars passed by in the street below. Pain stabbed beneath her ribs with every beat of her heart.

Sliding an arm under her head, she glanced sideways at the glow of the digital clock. Four a.m. Another hour and she had to be up. The effort of trying to go back to sleep almost wasn't worth it. Except facing the day would be harder. She closed her eyes. Heaved a shaky sigh. How in all of Heaven and Hell and Earth combined was she going to find the strength to do what the One asked? It didn't matter that she understood now why Seth needed to go back, she was still going to lose him. She was still going to hurt him.

Warm fingers threaded with hers beneath the sheet. A thumb caressed the inside of her wrist.

"I'm sorry," Seth's quiet voice rumbled. "About today, and before. I haven't been fair to you."

She squeezed her eyes tighter. "Seth—"

"Shh. Let me finish. I know you're doing your best, Alex. You're in an impossible place, knowing what you do about what's coming, trying to protect your world against forces beyond your control. Part of me wants you to give up because I don't believe you can win, part of me can't help but admire you for standing up for what you think is right. For not giving in. But another part of me—most of me, I think—can't get past the guilt of not being able to do anything. I've never felt helpless before. It's not a pleasant sensation." His hand moved to caress her arm. "But I'm still trying. Even if I can't stop Armageddon or the Nephilim, I want to be here for you. Without the hysterics of jealousy or feeling sorry for myself."

Hell and damnation. He wasn't making this any easier.

"Seth—"

He placed his fingers over her lips. "I don't think you understand how much I love you, Alexandra Jarvis. You are my entire existence, and I do not—*will* not—let anyone make me regret having chosen you."

He shifted his weight toward her, and his mouth replaced his hand. She resisted, guilt swamping her. She should have stopped him, should have interrupted and told him about his mother's visit, about how he needed to go. Should do so even now, because delaying would only make it worse.

The tip of his tongue touched her bottom lip. Traced it. She shuddered.

A tear slid from the corner of her eye. Losing him might be necessary, but it was also wrong. They hadn't had enough time to get to know each other. They'd never, from the very beginning, had a chance to be anything near normal or ordinary, to just *be*. Christ, they hadn't begun to explore the possibilities—*their* possibilities. She buried her face against Seth's neck. If she had to give him up, it wouldn't be like this. He deserved better. *They* deserved better.

She kissed the hollow at the base of his throat, tasting his skin. Sliding a hand beneath the T-shirt he wore to bed, she drew her fingers, feather light, over the hard muscles of his back. Seth went still. An image of Lucifer flashed into her mind and merged with one of Seth.

"He should never have made the choice he did. You've thought the same thing yourself. It is that which stands between you, not Lucifer."

Was the One right? Was that the reason—? Her stomach clenched, and her skin dampened, chilled. *No.* She wouldn't believe that. She couldn't believe it. Gritting her teeth, she forced her touch lower and let it travel the curve of Seth's buttock. His breath hitched.

It had been Lucifer between them all along. She was certain of it. She needed to be certain of it. And she'd be damned if she'd let the Light-bearer's presence remain any longer. Shifting sideways, she lifted herself. Straddled Seth. Felt him surge against her, suddenly, fully aware.

"Alex?" A whisper, startled, filled with the ache of longing. Of need. Deep inside her, a fierce response snarled to life. Another tear slid down her cheek, hidden from him in the dark.

"I love you, Seth Benjamin," she whispered. "Always."

FORTY-NINE

S weet Jesus, what in hell had she been thinking?

The November morning light filtered into the apartment, as pale and cold as Alex felt as she stood in Seth's embrace, her every fiber screaming at her to pull away. She prayed that he didn't feel her stiffness, her resistance. Her regret.

She drew a deep, shuddering breath. Seth's hold tightened.

"I'll miss you, too," he murmured into her hair, misinterpreting her sigh. His hands slid down her back, kneading, caressing.

Her stomach gave a liquid roll. The moment she'd cracked open her eyes in the cold, watery light of the November dawn, she'd known her mistake. Known that she hadn't made anything better, not for either of them. She hadn't made it easier to let go of him, or for him to let go of her.

She'd made a monumental error.

And it had become a goddamn disaster in the

making.

She pulled out of Seth's grasp. "I should go. Traffic—I don't want to miss my flight."

"I still don't want you to leave."

"I'll be back tomorrow." She stretched her mouth into what she hoped would pass for a smile. "You won't even have time to miss me."

He framed her face with his broad, strong hands and kissed her forehead. "I already do."

Alex picked up her keys from the hall table and shouldered her overnight bag. She turned to the door.

"Alex."

She looked back, into eyes as dark as night itself and the steady warmth that glowed in them.

"I love you."

She spun around and stepped into his embrace, burying her face against his chest. Memorizing his smell, his warmth, the sound of his heartbeat. "I love you, too, Seth Benjamin," she whispered. "With all my heart."

Then, tears blurring her vision, she fumbled for the doorknob.

ARAMAEL KNEW.

She didn't know how, but he did.

She saw it in the rigid set of his shoulders, the almost imperceptible sagging of his black wings . . . the bleak agony etched into his face. Her step slowed, and only with grim effort did she keep moving toward the vehicle.

She went around to the driver's door and unlocked it. He remained still. Staring across the roof at his back, she tried—and failed—to come up with words to

. . . what? Apologize? Explain? Ease his pain? None of those things were possible; none of them should have been necessary. He knew Seth was her choice. She'd made it clear to him time and again. Abundantly so. He couldn't claim he hadn't expected this, damn it.

Clamping her mouth shut, she climbed into the sedan. Aramael followed suit. Silence hung over them like a toxic cloud for the duration of the drive to the airport, making every breath burn in the back of her throat. Not until she parked the car, switched it off, and opened her door to get out did Aramael finally speak.

"You're making it more difficult for both of you."

She went still, then leveled a cold look over her shoulder. "This is the only time you get to mention it," she said, "and the only time I will tell you that it's none of your business. Are we clear?"

The tiny muscle in his jaw flexed. "Crystal."

"Good. We have a flight to catch."

FIFTY

"Detective Jarvis? They'll see you now," a male voice said.

Alex looked up from the magazine she'd been pretending to read and dug up a smile for the admin assistant who had previously offered coffee to her and Aramael.

Aramael, who glowered out the window, his palpable hostility giving her ample reason to feign interest in the future of motocross in Canada. He'd been like this ever since the apartment, making the past few hours—at the airport, in the plane, in the taxi they'd shared—the most uncomfortable of her life. Bar none.

She set aside the magazine and stood.

Aramael straightened.

"No," she said. "We've been over it a dozen times, Ara—Trent. You're not coming in with me."

His voice stopped her at the door. "Just—be careful."

Be careful what you say, what you tell them. Protect

our secrets.

All valid warnings, but if they'd called her to Ottawa, it was almost certainly too late for careful. And far too late for secrets.

She followed the young man down the hallway. Her cell phone vibrated with another call from Jen—the fourth one this morning. Thumb poised over the buttons, Alex hesitated. Then, as the admin assistant stopped in front of a door and looked askance at her, she smothered her guilt and touched the button to ignore the call. Jen hadn't left a voice message with any of her other calls, so it wasn't urgent. It would wait until tonight.

Stepping past the admin assistant, she entered the room and scanned its occupants. Three men, one woman, all seated at a small, circular table; all wearing suits and the vaguely harried expressions of those who carried too much responsibility. She recognized none of them.

But she did recognize the logo of the Toronto coroner's office on the DNA report laid out on the table.

One of the men, middle-aged and balding, with the lean look of a habitual runner, stood. "Detective Jarvis, I didn't realize you'd been injured. I hope the trip wasn't too much for you."

She touched fingertips to the healing cuts on her face. "It's nothing," she said. "Superficial."

He nodded. "Well, thank you for coming. I'm Stephane Boileau, aide to the minister of public security. This is Frank Allan from CSIS, Vic Hamilton from the RCMP, and Madeleine Renault from the GOC."

The Canadian Security Intelligence Service, the

national police force, and the Government Operations Centre responsible for coordinating the country's emergency response management. Oh, yeah. The time for secrets had definitely passed.

Alex shook hands with everyone and then took the only empty seat.

Stephane Boileau slid a pair of wire-framed glasses onto his nose and pulled a notebook toward him. Turning to a clean page, he jotted down a note. Alex waited. At last he looked up.

"Detective, I trust you understand that what we're about to discuss here is highly sensitive."

"I'm fairly adept at keeping secrets, Mr. Boileau."

He peered at her over the glasses, then nodded. "*Bon*," he said in French. *Good.* "Then we begin. You know why you are here, of course?"

Because I know things you don't. "Not exactly, no."

"There have been a number of unusual occurrences across the country. The serial killer in Toronto, an amnesiac man who disappeared from a Vancouver hospital, the DNA match between the children born of these pregnancies and a"—Boileau looked down at the papers before him—"a claw. These things, along with the freak earthquake that hit Vancouver . . ." His voice trailed off and he raised his eyes back up to hers. "Detective, your name seems to be the one common thread between these incidents. We'd like to know why."

"You forgot to add the scrolls to your list."

Boileau and the others exchanged a flurry of glances. For a shot in the dark, her accuracy was impressive. Boileau cleared his throat.

"You know about the scrolls."

She nodded.

"And did you know they're missing?"

"Missing?"

"The Church reported the theft to Interpol yesterday, but they've been missing for more than a week."

Hell. She'd known it was just a matter of time before those damn things bit them on the ass.

Resting his elbows on the table, Boileau folded his hands and leaned forward. "I'll be blunt, Detective Jarvis. We're dealing with a highly nervous population. That makes us nervous, too. We know what's in the scrolls and what the DNA evidence tells us, and we know that—somehow—you're connected to everything that's happening. If we're going to keep a lid on this, however, we need to know more. We need to know everything."

Alex stared out the window. The drizzle that had started while they were in the taxi from the airport had settled into a steady, miserable downpour. She grimaced, picturing her umbrella on the closet shelf at home.

"Well?" Boileau prompted.

"You must have theories," she said, knowing full well she attempted to sidestep the inevitable. Maybe she should have let Aramael come into the meeting with her after all. Maybe he could have done one of those memory-wipe tricks and made all of this just go the hell away.

"Detective—"

She shoved back the chair and stood. Arms crossed, sheaced the width of the meeting room. "What if I told you it was true?"

"The information in the scrolls?"

"Yes."

Boileau tapped his pen against the table. "What if I

told you we already believed it?"

Tension she hadn't known she held in her shoulders slipped away with a suddenness that made them sag. She stopped pacing and stared at the others. "Seriously?"

"Not exactly as written, of course. The scrolls are thousands of years old, after all, written when humans had little to no understanding of possibilities such as extraterrestrials, and—"

"Extraterrestrials?"

"Of course. That is your explanation for this, isn't it? We've been studying the possibility for years. Decades, even. It would be arrogant in the extreme to believe ourselves the only life in the universe, after all. And now that the children born of these pregnancies are exhibiting such unusual traits—"

"Wait," she interrupted. "Unusual how?"

The minister's aide leaned back with a sigh. He exchanged another look with one of his companions, the woman from the GOC, who shrugged in response. *Your call*, the gesture said.

"Inhumanly so," Boileau said. "They're continuing to mature at a phenomenal rate, their IQs are off the charts . . ."

She waited, certain he hadn't finished.

But it was the woman who continued. "There's evidence of other traits as well," she said. "Violent ones. And . . ."

Alex stared at them, but the four gazes that had so willingly held hers a moment before had settled with steadfast focus on the table before them. "And?" she prompted.

"And they've disappeared," Boileau said. "Two days ago."

FIFTY-ONE

"You wanted to see me?"

Lucifer looked up at the owner of the rumbling voice, a former Virtue whose massive form filled the doorway. "Qemuel. Come in."

Qemuel's gaze flicked to the bloodied bundle of rags in front of the fireplace. Then, with a shrug, he strolled over to stand before Lucifer's desk, his hands folded loosely before him. Every inch a thug, he had always done what was asked of him without question. Unlike certain other Fallen Ones.

"I have a task for you." Lucifer tipped back in his swivel chair. "The Naphil you were tracking for Samael a few days ago—do you remember her? Where she lives?"

"And where she works."

"Excellent. I want her sister."

"Dead?"

"Alive. Find her, then come and get me."

"I thought Samael was watching her now."

"So did I. If you run across him, make sure he doesn't see you."

The former Virtue raised an eyebrow, glanced again at the rags, and unfolded his hands. "Done," he said. "Should I send someone in to clean that up for you?"

Lucifer looked over at what remained of Raziel. "Thank you, but no. I'm not done with it yet."

With a last shrug, Qemuel ambled back out the way he'd come in.

SETH STOOD UP from the computer and stretched tall to rid his back and shoulders of their kinks. How mortals put in entire days sitting at one of these was beyond him. Why they did it, even more so. He glanced at the clock. Ten fifteen. Alex would be in Ottawa by now.

With Aramael.

He shoved away the insidious thought. He wasn't going there anymore. Not after last night. Just as he wasn't reading any more of the trash his father had written. His gaze fell on the journal lying on the dining room table where he'd placed it after Alex's departure. It hadn't been replaced, hadn't moved.

"Wherever you are," he said to the empty room, "you were wrong about her, so you might as well come and get your damned book. I'm through playing your little game."

The doorbell rang.

He stared down the hall. The Fallen—? Giving himself a mental shake, he started for the door. Of course it wasn't the Fallen One. The too-polite Mika'el, maybe, but not his supremely confident visitor. He pulled open the door.

"Jennifer?"

Alex's sister studied the door frame. "Is she here?"

"She's in Ottawa—did she not call you?"

Jennifer's looked up and then away again. "No. She's not answering my calls or my texts."

"She's been—"

"Oh, don't you start, too." She glared at him. "I've seen the news. I get that she's busy, and I get that she's angry with me. She has a right to be. But she has no right to take it out on my daughter. She could have at least called to tell Nina she couldn't make it last night."

"I'm sorry, but I have no idea what you're talking about."

Jennifer puffed up like an angry Cherub. "It was my daughter's seventeenth birthday dinner last night, Seth. Alex promised her she'd be there. You were both supposed to be there."

"I'm sure she just forgot."

"That's the point. Oh, never mind." Jennifer threw up her arms in disgust. "Just tell her she owes Nina a massive apology for this. Assuming she can spare her family two minutes away from saving the world."

Seth watched Alex's indignant sibling march down the corridor and around the corner to the elevators. He'd never imagined connecting with Jennifer on any level. Odd how he actually found it comforting to know he wasn't the only one struggling with Alex's heroic tendencies. About to close the door, he paused as a movement near the end of the hallway caught his attention. He narrowed his eyes. The Fallen One, come to retrieve the journal?

But the man stepping out of the shadows and pushing open the door to the stairwell was a stranger to him. A great, hulking stranger, perhaps, but

unknown nonetheless. Seth shoved away the last
threads of paranoia and closed the door.

FIFTY-TWO

S amael scuffed a toe against the crumbling stone
path. What was taking Raziel so long? He shivered
in the damp chill. Lucifer never had managed to get
the temperature right in this godforsaken place. Or
much else, for that matter. The only creature comfort
to be found in all of Hell was in front of one of its
many fireplaces. Perhaps Seth would have more luck.

And more interest.

He peered down the path. Raziel's message had said
urgent, but if she didn't show up in the next five—

A wad of rags sailed out of the trees and landed at
his feet. Samael stepped back, wrinkling his nose at
the stench of urine and feces rising from the pile. And
was that blood he smelled? What the—

"I believe that's yours," a voice said, its very
neutrality making it sound deadly.

Lucifer.

Ice shot through Samael's bowels. *How—?*

"You really should choose your help with more

care, my friend." Polished black shoes came into view beside the bundle "She didn't even try to hold back."

One of the shoes prodded at the pile. A pale, slender arm flopped out of the folds and onto the path. Samael closed his eyes. Bloody Heaven. Raziel. Samael was as good as dead. Footsteps circled him. He went rigid, waiting for the first blow. Lucifer chuckled.

"You think I'd make it that easy for you, Archangel?" His voice had gone soft. "Oh, no. I want to know things first. Such as what it is you're up to, who else is in on it, whether you've managed to disrupt my plan—"

"Your precious plan," Samael snarled, his eyes snapping open.

Lucifer went still. Marble still. He tipped his head to one side, purple eyes curious. "Have you always had such an inordinate desire for pain, or is this relatively new?"

A bead of sweat trickled down Samael's temple, trailing cold in its wake. "I only meant—"

"I know what you meant." Lucifer resumed his slow circling. "We haven't seen eye to eye for quite some time now. In and of itself, that's not such a bad thing, really. I think it's quite healthy for two intelligent beings to disagree on occasion. My problem—" The footsteps stopped directly behind Samael, and warm breath stirred against his ear. "My problem lies with your continued inability to recall which one of us is in command here, Samael. Especially after I've already reminded you. Twice."

Cruel hands clamped down on his shoulders. "Now, why don't we—"

"Lucifer," a new voice rumbled.

Lucifer's hands squeezed, sending pain streaking through Samael and felling him to his knees. "This had better be—" The hands dropped away. "Qemuel. You found her already?"

"It wasn't difficult."

"You hear that, Sam?" Lucifer grabbed Samael's chin and twisted it up and around until he looked him in the eye. "It wasn't difficult. That makes me wonder what your problem was all this time, you know." He released him again with a pat on the cheek that snapped Samael's head sideways. "We'll take this up again later, Archangel. And if you were thinking of running, please, be my guest. It will make this much more interesting—and we both know I'll find you."

Terror—utter, paralyzing terror—robbed Samael of the capacity to stand after Lucifer's departure. Long minutes dragged by, more than he cared to acknowledge, before he felt the blood return to his veins, the tone to his muscles. He dragged himself upright. He'd expected Lucifer to find out eventually, but not this soon. He wasn't ready—Seth wasn't ready. Another few days . . .

He stared at what was left of Raziel. He didn't have a few days. A few hours, maybe—or as long as he could stay ahead of Lucifer—but that was all. If he was going to pull this off, somehow he had to find the words to tip Seth over the edge *now*.

He stepped over the fouled clothing, past the pale arm. He'd speak with Mittron first. The Seraph's plan to cause Armageddon in the first place had more than demonstrated his ability for scheming. Maybe he could be of more use than just unlocking the gates of Limbo.

Assuming the drugs hadn't fried all his brain cells by now.

FIFTY-THREE

Alex closed the meeting room door behind her and headed for the elevator. Aramael fell into step at her side as she passed the waiting area. She felt his gaze on her, but he remained quiet. Blessedly so, because she was in no way ready to share all that she had learned in that meeting. She still hadn't processed it herself.

The elevator doors slid open at the touch of a button, and they stepped inside. She took her cell phone from its holster and dialed her voice mail. Four messages. One from Roberts, reminding her he expected a call; three from Jen the previous day. At each sound of her sister's voice, Alex pressed the button to skip the message, swallowing her guilt at doing so. She just couldn't deal with Jen on top of everything else right now.

Alex returned the cell phone to its case and closed her eyes, letting her head drop back against the wall.

Aramael's voice broke into her attempt to stop

thinking. "Are you going to tell me what happened?"

"Ask your Guardians."

"I could, but it would save time if you told me yourself."

She remained stubbornly silent. Aramael's clothing rustled as he shifted position. The elevator continued its descent, bumping past another floor.

Lifting her head, she regarded him. "Why are we bothering with this?"

"Bothering with what?"

"Any of it. Tracking down the Nephilim, convincing Seth to take back his powers."

Sudden interest gleamed in Aramael's eyes. "You've decided to help with that?"

Trust him to zero in on that rather than the question. She scowled. "I'm serious, Aramael. What's the point of any of it? Humanity has never been so far advanced and so far behind all at the same time. We're consuming more than the Earth can produce. We've created enough weaponry to destroy ourselves several times over. We're pushing the limits of our very existence—hell, the whole goddamn planet's existence—past the point of no return, and we know it, but we're too goddamn arrogant to care. What, in all of that, is worth saving?"

"Not all of you are like that."

She snorted. "There are more than seven billion of us, Aramael. Expecting a handful to be able to sway the masses is like asking us to empty the Atlantic with a teaspoon."

The number three over the elevator doors glowed red, then the two, then the letters *RC* for *rez-de-chausée*. Ground floor. The elevator jolted to a stop.

"Maybe this entire war is too late," she said wearily.

"Maybe Lucifer has already won."

"You wouldn't be doing what you do if you believed that."

"Being a cop, you mean?" She snorted. "Most days that only makes me wonder more."

The elevator doors slid open, and she stepped out, Aramael close behind.

Alex turned up the collar on her coat against the frigid wind and pulled gloves from her pockets as they emerged onto the street. At least the rain had stopped. Turning right, she headed toward Parliament Hill.

"The Nephilim children that have already been born are missing," she said. She stopped at the intersection and gazed across the street at a majestic stone building rising from an expanse of lawn, flanked on either side by similar buildings, together forming the seat of the Canadian government.

Her companion's stride faltered. "You're sure?"

"Only the governments that will admit to having held them for study in the first place are confirming, but yes, we're pretty sure. I'm assuming it's not Heaven rounding them up."

"You know we won't interfere like that. It's most likely Lucifer. He'll want to control their upbringing."

"Hard to say which would be the lesser of two evils," she muttered. At Aramael's raised eyebrow, she elaborated, "Between Lucifer controlling them or humans. The end result would be pretty much the same, I expect."

"Then the children . . . ?"

"Were exhibiting unusual traits. Superhuman, violent ones. My fellow mortals wanted to control their abilities, with an eye to weaponizing them. Only because other governments were doing so as well, of course." Sarcasm laced her words. "Self-defense, you know."

The crossing signal changed, and she stepped off the sidewalk. "The entire globe is coming apart at the seams, and we're still worried about one-upping one another. Right now, however, the question is where the hell is Lucifer taking them? There's another eighty thousand on the way. Where's he going to put them all?" She threaded through the oncoming pedestrians. Maybe Seth would come through with some information for her before he—well. Before.

Leading the way past the barriers, she entered the grounds of Parliament and skirted the crowd gathered on the frost-whitened grass. Atop the Peace Tower, the Westminster chimes tolled from the clock, marking the hour as 1:45. Fifteen minutes until speech time.

"Did you tell them about the other babies?" Aramael asked. "The eighty thousand?"

"Yes, though I'm not sure they believed me. They wanted to know where I got my information. I declined to tell them it was from Lucifer. They want me back for another meeting this afternoon, after they've tried to figure out whether I'm right. They also want to discuss what to do about you."

"Me?"

"*You* as in the angels and the Fallen."

Aramael caught her arm and drew her up short. "You told them about us?"

"They already knew. Did you really think they wouldn't? They have DNA tying the babies to Caim's claw, children being born who have powers no human has ever had, and six-thousand-year-old scrolls documenting precedence. The Nephilim have happened before, remember?" She jerked free and continued toward the sweep of driveway between Parliament and the lawn, the elevation of which would give her the best vantage point. "If it's any consolation, however, they're calling you extraterrestrial beings—angels not being real and all. I didn't correct them."

"Thank the One for small miracles," Aramael muttered. "And what are we doing now?"

"The federal minister of health is giving a speech. They've decided the best public explanation for the pregnancies is still an unknown virus and that putting visible measures in place will reassure people. They're announcing a Canada-wide prevention program today, including quarantine for pregnant women in their first trimester. I want to gauge public response."

She held out her badge to the uniformed RCMP officer standing at a wooden barricade. He nodded and allowed her to pass, but held a hand out in front of Aramael. For a moment, temptation beckoned, then Alex sighed.

"He's with me," she told the other cop tersely, and without waiting to see whether or not he believed her and let Aramael through, she stomped up the driveway's incline.

FIFTY-FOUR

"This is it." Standing on the sidewalk, hands in his pockets, Qemuel nodded at the house on the other side of a manicured lawn. "The car's in the driveway, so she's home."

Lucifer inhaled deeply and shook the remaining tension of dealing with Samael from his shoulders. He pushed his irritation with the Archangel to the back of his mind. He wanted to savor this moment: the final nail in humanity's collective coffin, six thousand years in the making. His lips curved. How ironic that one of their own would be so instrumental to their demise.

"Well done, Qemuel. Thank you."

"I'm done, then?"

Lucifer hesitated. He hadn't thought about what he would do with the Naphil afterward. He couldn't risk sending her to Pripyat with the Nephilim babies. She was too human, her bloodline too weak. There was no telling what exposure to the radiation there might do to her health.

"No," he said. "Wait here. When I'm done, I want you to take her somewhere. Watch her, provide for her, and bring me the child when it is born."

From the corner of his eye, he saw the Virtue raise an eyebrow. Seeming to understand his curiosity wouldn't be satisfied, however, Qemuel shrugged and wandered across the lawn to lean against a tree. Lucifer grimaced. If only certain others among the Fallen could be so inclined to cooperate.

He strolled up the drive and climbed the stairs. A single effortless shove shattered the frame and sent the door, hinges and all, crashing to the floor. At the foot of the staircase inside, a woman whirled to face him. Her wide eyes went from the door to him. From startled to terrified. Then, showing what he considered remarkable presence of mind for a mortal, she threw the filled laundry basket at him and scrambled up the stairs.

He met her at the top.

Shoving her against a wall, he blocked the blow she aimed at his head and deflected her knee. "Don't waste your energy, Naphil. You haven't a chance."

She'd opened her mouth to scream, but at the word *Naphil*, the attempt became a strangled gasp in her throat. The terror in her eyes became horror, and her entire body flailed in his grasp.

Holding her fast with one hand, he reached for her forehead with the other. He had no need of her awareness, and no desire for a struggle. Best that she— he paused, hand hovering near enough to feel the heat of her skin. The fear radiating from her in undulating waves. Something was wrong. He frowned. Lowering his hand, he jammed it hard against her belly.

Bloody fucking Heaven. She was sterile.

In a split second, his entire plan crumbled around his feet. He stood amid its ruins, staring in disbelief at his hand resting against white cotton. He'd been so focused, so determined—the possibility of failure had never occurred to him. Cold anger rippled through him. He curled his fingers against the woman's stomach. Heard her inhale, felt pain join her fear. Defeat sat bitter on his tongue. She had cheated him, just as her sister had done. For that alone, she would—

"Mom? Mom, where are you?" Another female voice, younger, filled with uncertainty and a note of panic, drawing closer with every shout. "Mom!"

The woman surged against his hold. "Run! Nina, ru—"

Lucifer threw her against the opposite wall, cutting her scream short. She slumped to the floor, unconscious or dead—it didn't matter which. The female at the bottom of the stairs stared up at him, then turned and bolted for the space where the front door had been. He blocked her escape with the same ease he had her mother's. She skidded to a stop and swayed on her feet, her hands dropping to her sides. Her eyes glazed over, becoming unfocused. Sanity itself seemed to drain from her. He scowled. She was his last chance to sire a Nephilim leader, but what if she was too fragile?

Ignoring her whimper, he grasped her chin and turned her face up to his, staring into her damaged soul. No, not fragile. Incredibly strong. She had seen—and survived—things that would have demolished most mortals. If her mind didn't survive this newest assault, well, it wasn't her mind he needed.

He pushed her to the side, then lifted the door from the floor and stood it against its shattered frame. No interruptions. Nothing more to stand in his way. He turned back to the female. Humanity's final days began here. Now.

"Amen," he whispered.

FIFTY-FIVE

Alex shoved gloved hands into her pockets and huddled deeper into her coat at the foot of the stairs to Parliament's main building. Beside her, a silent Aramael blocked the wind. She shifted away from the warmth radiating from him and scanned the crowd below. Despite the cold, at least a thousand had gathered, maybe more. The rain had started again, and the number was hard to judge with all the umbrellas. Many held up signs inscribed with demands in English to *Save Our Babies and Women; sauvez nos enfants et nos femmes* in French. A thousand citizens, representing billions more across the planet who shared in the growing alarm at the number of women dying in childbirth.

Television crews gathered at the crowd's edge, cameras and microphones pointed at reporters who would be talking about the growing unrest, the unanswered questions, the imminent speech from the minister of health. The fruitless, useless efforts of government to explain the inexplicable and solve the unsolvable.

Just wait until the eighty thousand were born.

A flurry of interest in the crowd below made Alex look over her shoulder. The massive oak doors had swung open behind her, and Canada's health minister emerged, surrounded by an entourage of aides and dark-suited RCMP officers. Alex grimaced at the show of security, normally reserved for the prime minister or top-ranking dignitaries. One more indication of how tightly wound nerves had become.

The very pregnant Lilliane Benoit waddled down the stairs, across the driveway, down the next set of stairs, and across the lawn to the podium that had been set up for her. The government couldn't have had a better spokesperson for the situation. A mother-to-be reassuring other women in her condition, counseling the public to remain calm, to trust their leaders. On the lawn below, the crowd drew closer to the podium, faces pinched with cold and anxiety but still patient. So far, so good.

Glancing up at the rooftop of the east block, Alex picked out the police sniper and two watchers posted there. To the west, more figures stood on top of the building that flanked the opposite side of the lawn. Still others would stand guard on the center block's roof, she knew. Right above where she stood. Their presence was a standard precaution, but one that had an ominous feel to it under the circumstances. She stamped her feet, attempting to restore circulation to her freezing toes.

On the podium now, Benoit switched on the microphone and leaned forward. "Good morning." Her voice rang out across the frost-whitened lawn.

"*Bonjour.*"

Alex tuned out the speech. Her gaze strayed restlessly across the crowd again. Equal numbers of men and women, some with children in tow. Benoit's voice droned on, switching from English to French and back again. From behind Alex came the impatient rustle of feathers, audible only to her.

She looked past Benoit and the security detail, to a stroller parked near the podium. She wondered idly how old the baby it contained would be. How relieved its parents must be to know their child was fully human. Then she frowned. Speaking of parents . . .

Straightening, she surveyed the people standing nearby—none of them near enough. Disquiet coiled like a serpent in her belly. She turned to Aramael. "Something's not right."

His wings instantly unfurled part way, brushing against a parliamentary page who glanced around, saw nothing, and gave a puzzled shrug. Scowling, Aramael folded the wings close again.

"What?" he asked. "I feel no Fallen—"

"No." Alex shot him a warning look. "That stroller down there." She nodded her head toward the lawn. "I don't see anyone with it. I want to have a look."

"I'm coming with you."

Striding across the driveway, she headed down the stairs, Aramael at her back. One of the plainclothes RCMP officers beside the podium looked toward her, eyes hidden behind sunglasses. Alex turned the lapel of her coat over to expose her badge and gave a jerk of her head to the right. The woman frowned and leaned forward to murmur something to her burly colleague, who also looked toward Alex. With a nod, he returned to his crowd surveillance.

The female officer stepped away from her position and crossed the grass, intercepting Alex halfway between the podium and the stroller. "You are—?"

"Alexandra Jarvis, Toronto Homicide. This is my partner, Jacob Trent."

Barely glancing at Aramael, the woman responded, "Julia Greer, RCMP. What's up?"

"That stroller." Alex nodded past her. "No one's with it."

Greer swiveled and did a quick reconnaissance. "You're right."

Alex fell into step beside her. Greer lifted her left hand to her face.

"We have what appears to be an unattended stroller on the west side of the podium," she murmured into the microphone clipped inside her sleeve. "I'm taking a look."

A half dozen pairs of sunglasses swiveled in their direction, tracking their progress. Fifteen feet, ten. At the center of a group clustered nearby, a man raised a cell phone as if to take a photo. Alex's steps slowed. She frowned at the words on the sign he held aloft in his other hand. *Luke 21:23.*

Luke, chapter twenty-one, verse twenty-three. A biblical reference.

Son of a—

The man moved his thumb.

Alex looked back to the RCMP officer, too far away to reach.

"Greer!" she yelled.

From the depths of the stroller, a cell phone rang.

The world exploded.

FIFTY-SIX

"So that's it, then. It's all over."

Whirling, Samael pinned Mittron against the graffiti-scrawled brick wall of the long abandoned factory. Snow, blown in through the broken window, swirled around their ankles. Pripyat was bloody cold at this time of year. It was a damned good thing the Nephilim children were stronger than their pathetic human half-kin.

"It's *not* over," he hissed. "I just need to accelerate things. If I can find a way to sway Seth . . ."

Mittron's shaggy brows ascended. "You're kidding, right? Lucifer has informed you that you're his personal target. You think you can—what, pretend he was kidding? You're a marked Fallen One, Samael. There's nothing to accelerate."

Rage snarled through Samael, sharpened by fear. He glared at Mittron for a second more, then released him and swung away. He paced the rotted wooden floor. "There has to be a way I can spin this," he muttered. "If I can convince him that I was only trying to help—"

"You really think he's that gullible? You've been passing his journals on to the son he all but disowned. He's not going to care one way or the other about Seth."

Samael stopped at a window. Mittron was right. He was as good as dead. Would be dead as soon as Lucifer tracked him down. The Light-bearer wouldn't give a—

"Unless . . ." Mittron murmured.

"Unless what? The One herself intervenes with a miracle? Not going to happen."

"Unless you go to him first."

Samael sent a scowl in his direction. "It must be time for your next dose, because you just became delusional. Why in bloody Heaven would I go looking for someone who just threatened to kill me—and who's capable of following through on that threat?"

"Because it might convince him you're telling the truth about trying to sway his son to his cause."

"I suggested something along those lines already. He wasn't interested."

"Not even to ensure that the balance of power lies with Hell when the war begins?"

"Let me think. I believe his exact words were *I don't care*," Samael said sourly. "I'm fairly sure that indicated a certain level of disinterest, yes."

"Then how about to ensure the survival of his army?"

Samuel shot the Seraph a sharp look. He crossed his arms and leaned against the window ledge. "Keep talking."

"He's not going to survive this time, Samael. He's gone too far. The One can't—and won't—allow him to continue. And once he's gone, who will look after his army? Who will make certain his legacy is carried out? One of the rabble that followed him or you, his trusted aide—with the help of his own son?" Mittron strolled across the warehouse floor to stop in front of him, just out of reach. "Don't wait for him to come to you. Seek him out. Convince him everything you've done has been in his best interests."

"And how do you propose I do that?"

"Look around you, Samael. Look at what you've accomplished here. You've done everything he asked you to do and more. You've given him the base he needed for his Nephilim army. You've rebuilt it, equipped it, protected it. Not even the Archangels know it's here, and that's no small success. You just need to make him aware of your hard work. Make him believe in your loyalty to the cause."

Samael stared through the broken glass at the derelict lot below. The Seraph might be on to something with the idea. Already his thoughts were aligning, mustering the words to frame his arguments, his defense. If he played this right, he just might pull it off.

"You really think the One will destroy him?"

"I don't think he's left her a choice."

"That still doesn't solve my Seth problem. Without him on board, there's no point to anything else."

The former Seraph's yellow eyes gleamed. "As to that, I think I know how to tip the Appointed in our favor."

FIFTY-SEVEN

A fireball consumed Alex's world.

Heat—intense, scorching, blistering—swept over her.

Burning shrapnel embedded itself in her skin.

And then—

Wings. Folding around her, cutting her off from the assault, the pain . . .

For a heartbeat that seemed an eternity—a thousand eternities—she stood with her soulmate. Protected, safe, apart. And then she jolted back to the here and now. To the screams. The panic.

Chaos.

Mayhem.

Shoving against Aramael's powerful chest, she fought her way out of the feathers surrounding her. Stood, swaying, in the midst of a devastation unlike any she had ever witnessed. Scorched, smoldering bodies strewn across the lawn. Parts of bodies. Unrecognizable fragments of shattered lives. Julia

Greer, who had stood between her and the stroller, gone. Obliterated.

Hands gripped her shoulders. Shook her. She stared into Aramael's face, into his stormy gray eyes clouded with worry. Made herself focus on his lips and the words they were forming.

"Damn it, Alex, answer me! Are you all right?"

She nodded. Inhaled. Gagged on the stench of burnt human flesh. Then she nodded again, this time with more certainty. She struggled to bring her brain back online. She was a cop. People were hurt. She needed to help.

She scanned the scene. People milled everywhere. Some sat or lay on the ground, others tended the injured. Screams ripped through the air. Beside her, the wooden podium burned fiercely, its flames unimpeded by the few small fire extinguishers aimed in their direction. Sirens wailed their approach.

She saw no trace of the pregnant minister of health—or her security entourage.

She snagged the arm of a passing security guard. "Find some crime scene tape," she ordered, her voice hoarse, throat raw. Her eyes watered. Goddamn, that hurt. "I want this area, the blast zone, secured. That"—she pointed at the crater where the stroller had stood—"is ground zero."

The guard hesitated, full of questions. Alex reached for her lapel to show her badge, but found only ragged cloth, crisp with char at its edges. Her gaze locked with Aramael's over the guard's head. *That close?* His eyes hardened. She turned back to the security guard.

"I'm a homicide detective," she told him. "And I need your help to protect the scene. Can you do that for me?"

His hesitation evaporated. "Crime scene tape," he repeated, and with a nod, he headed off at a trot.

"I'm going to help with triage," Alex said to Aramael. "No one is to come through this area. When the guard gets back, help him with the tape."

"Alex."

His voice stopped her midturn.

"You're injured."

She looked down at herself in surprise. At the wool coat half burned away, the scattered bits of gore—not her own—plastered across its remains, and the fresh blood seeping from beneath her blouse and both pant legs. *Hell.*

She met Aramael's gaze again.

Then she collapsed at his feet.

LUCIFER STOPPED in front of Qemuel.

"She's inside," he said. "The Naphil will look for her, so leave the city. When she gives birth, take the baby to join the others."

Qemuel nodded. "Will anyone else look for her?"

"Unlikely, but stay alert."

Another nod. Then, when he said nothing more, the bulky Fallen One strolled up the sidewalk and mounted the stairs. Lucifer watched him disappear into the house.

So. He'd succeeded at last. Fathered the perfect child to lead his army against the mortals. He'd expected more from the victory—pleasure or excitement of some kind—but there was nothing. No sense of accomplishment or satisfaction. Not even contentment. It was as if none of what he'd done had mattered after all, leaving him . . .

Empty.

Used up.

Tired.

He seized on the last thought. Tired. That was it. He was just tired, and after six millennia of waiting and building up to this moment, was it any wonder? A little rest and reflection—and perhaps dealing with Samael once and for all—and his outlook was bound to improve.

It had to, because otherwise—

Otherwise wasn't an option.

FIFTY-EIGHT

"Detective Jarvis, it wasn't a request. I need you to remain in Ottawa as part of our team," Stephane Boileau said. "After what you told us today—"

"Screw what I told you today." Alex abandoned her attempts to button the coat someone had dug out of the lost and found for her. She pulled the garment tight around her instead and folded her arms over it to hold it in place. And to still the violent tremors that she couldn't seem to stop.

Shock, the doctor had told her as he'd stitched up a slice along her thigh. She'd held back a "*duh*" only with great effort. She had no intention of making any similar effort for Boileau.

"That explosion had nothing to do with angels or Nephilim—" she broke off at his flinch and rolled her eyes toward the ceiling. "Fine. With *extraterrestrials*. Better? The point is that it triggered by nothing more than one thousand percent human stupidity. If we can't contain *that*, Mr. Boileau, the entire world is screwed—with or without E.T."

A dull flush crept up Boileau's neck from beneath his shirt. "May I remind you that it's your duty—"

"My duty is to keep the peace, not help you poke your nose into something bigger than you can begin to imagine."

"If that something is a matter of national security," he spat back, "then it goddamned well *is* your duty to help me poke my nose into it."

Her fingers twisted into the coat's fabric. The urge to fold inward and collapse onto the floor beckoned. How much easier it would be to let the doctors take over. Let them give her the sedative they'd offered, let herself slip away from Boileau and the stench of blood and burnt flesh that clung to her skin and hair. Easier...

And with Michael's words about choice sitting heavy on her conscience, equally impossible.

She shook her head, as much at herself as Boileau, and then scooped up her cell phone from the counter, marveling anew that it had survived the blast. "I've told you everything I can about the explosion and the Neph—the babies that are going to be born," she said. "And now I'm going to my hotel room, and I'm going to try very hard to sleep. In the morning, I'm going home as planned. I will assist—long-distance—with any security plan you put together that focuses on humans. Beyond that, you're on your own."

Especially where your testing of the Nephilim children is concerned.

Boileau put a hand on the door to hold it closed. "I could have you seconded to the task force here."

"You could. And I could refuse to comply. And

we could go back and forth through disciplinary committees and hearings and waste a whole lot of everyone's time while the situation just keeps getting worse. The choice is yours." Hell. Now she was starting to sound like Michael. "I get that you're worried, but this, the part you're most concerned about? Let it go. It's bigger than you are. Bigger than all of us. Focus on keeping our own world glued together. *That's* how we'll survive."

Boileau stared at her through his glasses.

"You know more than you've told us, don't you?"

"I know things no one should ever *have* to know. Trust me when I say you wouldn't want to be me."

"Not even if it meant I could walk away, virtually unscathed, from an explosion no one else anywhere near me survived?"

She froze, her hand on the doorknob.

"One of the news crews caught you on tape," Boileau said quietly. "You're being replayed every fifteen minutes across the entire country. Right alongside footage from the two latest earthquakes and the volcanic eruption."

Alex rested her forehead against the door frame. From out in the corridor came the muffled squeak of wheels rolling by. The news? Christ Almighty, how much had they caught? Had they seen Aramael? Seen her collapse? Watched him lift her from the grass and heal the more serious wounds he hadn't been able to protect her from?

Boileau's voice persisted. "That fireball rolled thirty feet past you, Detective. It incinerated everything in its path. They're still picking bits out of the grass. People on the opposite side of the podium were injured, some critically. And yet here you are. Walking out of the hospital with—what—a couple of dozen stitches? How is that possible?"

Alex waited for her stomach to stop churning at the reminder of the gore she'd witnessed, then she turned. Crossing her arms, she leaned against the door. "We both know it's not possible," she said. "So you might as well get to the point."

Boileau rubbed a hand over the bald spot on his head and glowered at her. "I have the best interests of this country at heart, Detective Jarvis. I'm not sure the same can be said of you. Give me one good reason I shouldn't have you detained."

"I'll give you two. One, because you're wrong about what you're thinking. You can test my DNA all you like; I'm as human as you or anyone else. And two, because this isn't about the best interests of this country. It's about the survival of humanity."

Before Boileau could respond or she could reach again for the door knob, the door swung inward and a nurse held out a cell phone to her.

"A Staff Inspector Roberts for you," the nurse said.

Alex's hand automatically to the hip where she normally carried her own cell phone, and then she remembered that it hadn't survived the explosion. She took the one from the nurse.

"You can return it to the triage desk when you're done," said the woman. She stepped out of the room again. Turning her back on Boileau, Alex put the phone to her ear. "Hey, Staff," she said.

"Is Trent with you?" Roberts's voice demanded without preamble.

She raised an eyebrow. "I'm fine, thank you."

"I'm serious, Alex. Where is Trent?"

"He's in the waiting room outside emergency. I was

on my way there now. What's going on?"

"Just get to him. Tell me when you're there."

Something very small and cold took root in her center. "Staff—"

"*Now*, Detective. That's an order."

Without another word, she left the examining room, hurried down the corridor, and pushed through the doors into the waiting area. Was it just her, or was this getting to be a habit? She searched the room for Aramael, and in an extension of her déjà vu moment, located him beside the exit doors. He raised an eyebrow as she joined him. *Roberts*, she mouthed.

"He's right in front of me," she told her supervisor. "Now what's going on?"

"Your sister's been taken to the hospital, Alex. She's unconscious. They're doing a CT scan now."

In an instant, the world narrowed to the phone in her hand and the row of buttons on Aramael's shirt. *Jen.*

"*Alex.*" Roberts's voice turned sharp. "Don't you dare pass out on me."

"I'm okay," she said. *Breathe in. Breathe out.* "What happened? An accident? Was Nina with her?"

"Her house was broken into. The incident report says home invasion."

Even through the chaos in her brain, his phrasing caught her attention.

"The incident report says," she echoed. "What does that mean?"

"Her door was broken in. Frame, hinges, and all. No explosion, no other signs of damage, nothing."

The cold in her center began a slow, sinuous uncoiling. "Nina. Where is Nina?"

"They found her backpack. And her coat."

But not her. Not Nina. The world tipped out from beneath Alex's feet. Iron hands clamped around her arms and steered her toward a chair, pushed her down. It took three tries for her to fill her lungs.

"When?" she croaked. *When did it happen? How long has she been missing?*

"We're trying to determine that now. The 911 call came in at five thirty. If Nina was in school today, then it would have been between then and the time she got home."

"Who called it in? Did they see anything?"

"One of the neighbors noticed the door coming home from work and found your sister inside. That's all we have for now. Dr. Riley is staying with Jennifer at the hospital. She'll call me with the results of the scan. I'm heading over to the house now."

She nodded. Remembered he couldn't see her. Made herself find words. "I'll catch the first flight out that I—"

Aramael plucked the phone from her hand. He held up a finger to ward off her fierce objection. "It's Trent," he said to Roberts. "How long does it take to get from the airport to Jennifer's house?" He listened a moment, then said, "She'll see you then."

He slid the phone shut, gave it back to her, and held out a hand. She stared at it, then lifted her gaze to the cold gray of his.

"But you're not allowed," she said.

"Call it extenuating circumstances. I have a bad feeling about this, Alex. We need to be there."

"Detective Jarvis!"

Alex looked around to see Boileau, cell phone to his ear, framed in the doorway through which she'd come a moment before. He shoved his wire-framed glasses up on his nose and stalked in their direction. She didn't wait. Didn't question Aramael about his feeling.

Wasn't sure she wanted to know.

"Outside," she told him. "It's quieter."

They headed away from Boileau, out into the chill of the night, handing the cell phone off to a security guard at the entrance as they passed. Within seconds they'd rounded the corner of the building and reached a quiet parking lot away from the main traffic area. Aramael stopped where the shadows were deepest.

"Ready?"

She shuddered as she thought back to the time when Michael had transported her this way. One could never be ready for that. But she nodded anyway, because it was Jen and Nina, and she needed to be there. With them. For them.

Aramael drew her tight against his chest. His wings enfolded her. A distant part of her noted that this was only the third embrace she had ever shared with him—if she counted having him protect her from the explosion—and then his body turned liquid with a molten energy that infused her, enshrouded her, became her.

The world fell away in a rush of vibration and heat.

FIFTY-NINE

When they arrived at the car in the Toronto airport parking lot, Alex held out the keys to Aramael. He took them without a word. They both understood she was in no condition to drive.

He offered to stop by the hospital first to see Jen, but Alex shook her head. Jen was in good hands. They could do nothing for her. Nothing except find her daughter. Find one small, seventeen-year-old girl somewhere out there, in that vast expanse of city.

She stared out at the passing lights as Aramael maneuvered through traffic. At the storefronts, cars, apartments, and houses; at the people coming and going about their ordinary lives, oblivious to the drama playing out on their very doorsteps. Even if they knew about Nina, to them she would be just another of the city's casualties. Another teen girl missing from her home. News today, forgotten tomorrow in the rush to get to work, to school, to yoga, to hockey practice. It was the same story in every city around the globe.

Except maybe for the part where an Archangel from Heaven had a bad feeling about the disappearance.

Strong fingers closed over hers. Squeezed. Withdrew.

It will be all right, the touch said.

She didn't believe it. She still didn't ask about the feeling.

"Do you want to call Seth?" Aramael asked. "He should know you're back."

Seth, who would have seen the newscasts by now and would be out of his mind with worry. Seth, who would be frantically trying to reach her on a cell phone that no longer existed.

Seth, son of the One, and source of a thousand complications that she just couldn't deal with right now.

"Later," she said.

Aramael shot her a quick look but didn't comment. He turned onto Jen's street and Alex's heart gave a shuddering thud on its way to her toes. They pulled up behind a half dozen police cars parked along the curb in front of her sister's house. Yellow police tape stretched across the bottom of the porch stairs, and the front door stood open. No, not open. Missing.

Aramael put the vehicle into park and switched off the engine. Gathering herself, Alex made a monumental effort to switch from aunt to cop. To shove anguish to one side. At least for now.

Her supervisor met her in the shattered doorway. While a disappearance wasn't within Homicide's purview—not as long as the victim was assumed to be alive, anyway—the incident involved one of their own. He and the others would be keeping close tabs on it.

Roberts glanced past her shoulder to Aramael. She ignored his silent question and asked her own.

"What do we have so far?"

"We got hold of her school principal and confirmed she made roll call this morning, but we're still trying to reach the individual teachers for period attendance. We're canvassing the neighborhood now. Forensics is sweeping for prints."

"You know they won't find anything."

"It's what we do, Alex." He shrugged. "And maybe we'll get lucky."

She didn't have it in her to argue.

Taking her arm, her staff inspector drew her to the side of the staircase. "I wanted to give you a heads-up about something."

"The video," she said. She looked around at the team sweeping for evidence, at the uniform in the doorway. So far no one had paid any more attention to her than they would at any other scene. "How bad is it?"

"Anyone who knows you will recognize you."

Shit. "Has everyone seen it?"

"In the office? Most. I've asked them to keep quiet, but—"

She waved him silent. It didn't matter. "There was a man at the scene, the one who pushed the button. He was holding up a sign that said Luke 21:23. I think it might be—"

"Luke, chapter twenty-one, verse twenty-three," Joly's voice intruded. He came down the stairs to join them. *"But woe unto them that are with child, and to them that give suck, in those days! For there shall be great distress in the land and wrath upon the people."*

Alex and Roberts stared at him. He shrugged.

"Catholic school," he said. "The brothers thought

having me memorize the Book of Luke would put the fear of God into me. I never for the life of me thought it would come in handy."

Roberts glanced down at Alex. "Did you tell Ottawa about the sign?"

She nodded. "They're looking into it. I wanted to see if tech had run across anything."

Her supervisor nodded. "I'll check with them when I go back to the office. Are you okay if I leave you here? Joly can stay with you if you want."

Alex shook her head. "I'm fine."

"Then I'll start checking the incident reports for anyone matching Nina's description," Joly said. He hesitated, then slung an arm around her shoulders in a quick squeeze. "We'll find her, Alex. I—"

Aramael's voice, a veritable growl, interrupted. "Alex."

She turned, took one look at the scowl stamped on his brow, and extricated herself from Joly's hold with a mutter of thanks and a good-bye.

Aramael waited for her by the front window. The same window Nina had shattered almost two months ago, using one of the shards of glass to slice herself open after she witnessed the atrocities committed by Caim. Alex clamped her teeth against a shudder as she reached him.

"It was Lucifer," Aramael said without preamble.

She groped for the back of a chair and waited for her stomach to climb up from the floor. "You're sure."

"There are traces left—" He broke off, his eyes growing grim. "I'm positive."

"But why—" She stopped dead. Stared at Aramael. And knew. The room went hazy around its edges as she struggled to ward off the impossibility. The horror.

She closed her eyes, standing again in a damp, dark alley between Seth and six silent Archangels, facing down Lucifer himself. Lucifer, who had raped her and impregnated her with his child, who had caused her to pick up Seth's discarded knife and slice into her own belly to end that child's life.

Lucifer, whose gloating words were indelibly etched in her memory. *"With her extraordinary Nephilim blood—and it is extraordinary, you know—mixed with mine, the child she carries will be a leader among his kind."*

Her Nephilim blood.

The same blood that ran through her sister's veins.

And her niece's.

Her stomach cramped, twisted, rolled. The Fallen One had never been after her. He'd wanted her family. The family she hadn't been here to protect. A touch on her elbow made her open her eyes again. Roberts, his forehead wrinkled with worry, held out his phone to her.

"It's Elizabeth Riley," he said. "Your sister has regained consciousness."

SIXTY

Samael stood rigid in the center of Lucifer's office as the Light-bearer prowled around him in silence. He had delivered his explanation to Hell's ruler just the way he'd rehearsed it with Mittron, relaxed, confident, without excuses or apologies—

Hadn't he?

He stared at the dark blotch on the carpet near the fireplace, so out of keeping with Lucifer's usual fastidiousness. Was it because Lucifer no longer cared about such details? Or because he intended it as an intimidation tactic? If the latter, it was working.

The Light-bearer circled closer. Samael went rigid.

"You look tense." Lucifer stopped in front of him, hands in his pockets, the picture of calm.

He made his fingers uncurl, saw the Light-bearer's gaze drop to them. *He's waiting for me to lie. He'll take it as a sign of guilt.*

"I have reason to be tense," he responded. "My life is on the line if you don't believe me."

Cool purple eyes watched him. Weighed him.

"I *don't* believe you, Samael."

Cold trickled through Samael. Run, a voice whispered in his head. His feet, cemented to the floor, disagreed.

"But you have a point." Lucifer swung away from him and crossed to the sideboard. Lifting a decanter of port, he raised an eyebrow in Samael's direction.

Samael shook his head. Fought to control the quiver coursing through him. "I don't understand."

Lucifer poured a glass of deep ruby-red liquid, replaced the crystal stopper in the decanter, and wandered over to the fireplace. Flames crackled to life in the stone recess. He rested a shoulder against the mantel. "I don't believe for a second you've had my best interests at heart, Archangel. I do, however, think you make a valid point about my army needing to be looked after should anything happen to me. Or to you."

Undecided on quite how to reply to grudging praise and a distinct threat delivered in the same breath, Samael decided that remaining silent was his wisest course of action.

Lucifer swirled his glass. Clockwise. Counter. "You're certain you can convince Seth to take back his powers *and* change sides."

"He's almost there now. A couple of nudges will tip him over the edge."

"And you're willing to stake your life on this?"

That one was a little more difficult to answer, but Samael managed a nod.

"All right."

All right? Samael made a conscious effort not to gape at the Light-bearer. Mittron's idea had worked?

He would never have believed it possible, let alone this eas—

"You have twenty-four hours."

"Twenty-four—but, Lucifer—"

"My army will be born at that time, Samael. If my son is not at my side, ready and willing to take over my cause if necessary, you die."

"Be reasonable. This is—" He ducked as Lucifer's glass sailed past his head and shattered in a spray of crystal shards and port against the bookcase behind him.

"Twenty-four hours," the Light-bearer repeated. "Less an hour for every objection you make."

Clenching his teeth, Samael turned on his heel and left. The Light-bearer wanted to be replaced twenty-four hours from now?

That was fucking fine by him.

SIXTY-ONE

A ramael drove her to the hospital. He didn't walk her in.

"Mika'el wants to see me," he said, holding out the keys to her as they stood at the rear of her sedan in the parking garage.

She stared at them for a moment before taking them. "Will you be back?"

"I don't know."

Of course. Now that Heaven knew Jen and Nina had been the targets, her own protection no longer mattered. She studied her soulmate, the Archangel who would have given his own life to protect hers. A few days ago, she had wanted nothing to do with him, wanted nothing more than for him to get out of her life.

Now she couldn't imagine her life without him in it.

She turned to walk away. Swung back. "Aramael."

Tall and strong and silent, he waited. Quiet fire burned in his gray eyes. For an instant, she wondered what he would do if she crossed the space between them. If she burrowed against that powerful chest and wrapped her arms around him and—

No. She wouldn't do that to him. Or to herself. Even before all of this had happened, even before Seth had happened, *together* had never been an option. Aramael had been right all along. They were a mistake.

It was up to her to put that mistake behind them once and for all.

"Thank you," she said. "For everything."

For getting me here, for saving me, for watching over me, for caring even after I chose another. Thank you—and good-bye.

The fire in Aramael's eyes dimmed, flickered, died. His gaze traveled over her, lingering on her face as if he would commit every detail to memory. Then he spread his wings wide—his magnificent, coal-black, mighty wings—and gave her a rare, small smile.

"Go," he said. "Your sister is waiting."

She walked away, her footsteps echoing in the cavernous space. When she looked back from halfway down the aisle of cars, he was gone.

Minutes later, Alex stepped into a hospital emergency ward yet again. The television in the waiting area was tuned to the news. She flinched from the image of herself emerging virtually unscathed from the fireball of the explosion. A few people seated nearby looked around as she walked past, but no recognition sparked and she made herself relax again.

Reaching the desk, she flashed her badge at the triage nurse, who nodded and buzzed her through the doors separating the waiting room from the ward.

"Jennifer Abbott?" she asked.

The nurse glanced at his computer screen. "Bed

number six."

Following the point of his finger, she skirted a
gurney wheeled by paramedics, a woman pacing the
corridor with a fractious baby in arms, a young girl
about Nina's age on crutches. The girl offered a smile
as she passed. Alex had none to return.

Elizabeth Riley emerged from the curtained cubicle
as Alex arrived, compassion softening her usually
sharp features. Her blue eyes brightened with relief.

"It's good to see you," she said, folding Alex into an
unexpected embrace. "The explosion is all over the
news. How are you?"

Alex stepped back from the contact and swallowed
the lump it had triggered. "I'm fine," she said. "Just a
few stitches." She motioned at the curtain. "Jen?"

"Sedated . . . and restrained." Riley put out a hand
to stop Alex's instinctive step toward her sister. "Wait.
Hear me out first. We had no choice, Alex. One minute
she was unconscious, and the next, her eyes were open
and she was shrieking nonstop. She gave one of the
nurses a broken nose before we pinned her down."

Alex didn't pull back this time. Instead, staring at
the beige fabric before her, she made herself focus on
Riley's touch. Let it be her anchor while the world
slowly righted itself again. She cleared her throat.

"Can she talk?" she asked.

"It's unlikely, but you're welcome to try."

Riley stepped into the cubicle and held the curtain
aside for her. Alex steeled herself, then moved to the
bedside. Jen lay against the pillow, her face pale and
hair awry. A four-point restraint system was visible at
the edges of the blanket covering her. Compassionate,
beautiful, too-serious Jennifer . . . tied to a hospital
bed. Reaching out, Alex brushed the hair back from

her sister's face. Brown eyes stared up at the ceiling without flickering.

Alex blinked back tears. She cleared the thickening in her throat. "Hey, Jenny-girl."

No response.

She tried again, this time gently turning her sister's head toward her. "Jen? It's Alex. I came to see how you're doing."

Jen's gaze drifted past her, unfocused, uncaring.

Alex drew a shuddering breath. Christ. She stared down at the woman who had raised her after their parents had died, the woman she had once thought to be the strongest person she knew. If Jen had caved under the pressure, what chance did Alex stand?

Riley's hand covered hers on the bed rail. "It's not unusual for a person's mind to temporarily close off after a trauma. Give her time. It's possible this is just the effects of the sedative."

The sedative. Alex watched the even rise and fall of her sister's chest. For the second time that evening, she wondered what it might be like to be drugged, restrained, no longer able—or expected—to take part in the world's disintegration. The idea held such seductive allure, especially when compared with the alternative.

Alex's hand curled beneath Riley's. She withdrew it and stepped away from the bed. "If she saw what I think she saw, she might be better off staying where she is."

"You know what happened to your niece?"

She shoved her hands into her coat pockets. "Lucifer happened to her. The same way he happened to me. Except Nina's only—" she broke off. "Oh, God."

Riley pushed Alex into the chair beside the bed.

"You look like you're going to pass out. Is it your head? Do you want a doctor?"

"What day is it?" Alex whispered. She hunched over, protecting herself from what the psychiatrist would tell her. What she already knew.

"Alex, if you're experiencing confusion—" Riley tipped up her chin with one hand and peered into her eyes.

"What day is it?"

"It's Friday."

"Christ. I missed it."

"Missed what? Look at this and follow it." Riley held up a finger. "Was there any blow to your head? It was hard to tell from that video. We should have you checked out, just in case."

Alex pushed away the psychiatrist's hand. "Her birthday, Riley. I missed Nina's birthday. It was yesterday, and I forgot it. She turned seventeen."

All those calls from Jen, all those texts she'd ignored because she hadn't wanted to deal with another confrontation—and all her sister had wanted to do was remind her. And now Nina was gone. Son of a *bitch*.

"Oh . . ." The word drew out into a sigh.

Alex braced herself for the words of comfort, the false reassurance, but Riley merely reached out and stroked back her hair, as if she understood the enormity of the failure. Tears clawed at Alex's throat, burned behind her eyes. A phone call. She could have at least made a phone call, or sent an e-mail, or texted . . .

Happy birthday, Nina. I love you.
Shit.

A hundred recriminations stabbed at Alex's soul.

She'd failed the two people who mattered most to her in the world. Opened them up to monsters beyond their understanding and then left them to fend for themselves. And three weeks from now, Nina would die giving birth to Lucifer's baby.

Sweet, sweet Nina, little more than a child herself.

Alex levered herself up from the chair. She motioned to her sister. "Will you stay?" she asked Riley. "Will you look after her for me?"

Riley rose to her feet. "Of course. You're going to look for Nina?"

"Not look, *find*," Alex said fiercely. "I might not be able to save her, but I'll be damned if I'll let her die alone."

SIXTY-TWO

"What do you mean, no?" Aramael towered over the desk, glaring down at the Archangel Mika'el.

Mika'el glowered back. "I *mean*," he enunciated between his teeth, "no. I need you here, and the Naphil doesn't need your protection anymore. You're done with her."

"And her niece? Are we done with her, too?"

"There are more than seven billion mortal souls on a planet that is about to implode. Do you really think we can drop everything and go running after a Naphil who is going to die whether we find her or not?"

"Protecting mortal souls from the Fallen is our *job*, Mika'el. It's what we do."

"No. What we do is stand between Earth and Hell so that mortals can live their lives independently, according to their own choices. We maintain balance, Aramael. *That* is our job."

"But she carries the child of *Lucifer*."

"Which changes nothing. With or without a leader born of the Light-bearer, the Nephilim are not our concern. You know this, Aramael."

Short, angry strides carried Aramael across the room. Mika'el was right. He did know it—had always known it. But somehow it had become muddled during his time with Alex. Less clear-cut. Infinitely more difficult. He spun to face Mika'el.

"This was easier when I was a Power," he growled.

"When you were a Power, you had no free will of your own. No reason to question your path."

"What about you? You left before the Cleanse. You didn't give up your free will when the rest of us did. Does that mean you've always lived with this level of conflict going on inside you?"

"Or worse," Mika'el agreed.

"So deciding to leave when you did . . ."

The Archangel's jaw flexed. "Wasn't easy. Just as this isn't easy for you. I get that. But I ask nothing of you or any of the others that I wouldn't do—that I haven't already done—myself. I need you here, Aramael. With us."

Hands shoved into his pockets, Aramael stalked over to the suit of armor, identical to his, standing in the corner. He scowled at it, his back to Mika'el. "You hold me to an awfully high standard."

"Because I know you're capable."

He thought of Alex, left alone to face her own impossible choices. How much more could she take? How long before Heaven's demands broke her? He closed his eyes as the ache in his chest spread to engulf his soul. And how long would he be able to stay away, knowing her pain?

Bleakly, he turned back to the other Archangel. "I

hope you're right."

ALEX PRESSED the lock button on the key fob and then stood by her vehicle, staring up at the light shining from the apartment she shared with Seth. She didn't want to go up there. Didn't want to face him. Didn't want to do this. Especially not now, with Jennifer and Nina—

She breathed in raggedly, exhaling a plume of steam. She didn't want to, but she had to. She'd already avoided it long enough, and he deserved better from her. Hell, she hadn't even called him after the explosion on the Hill this afternoon to reassure him she was all right, never mind let him know she'd come back to Toronto. It was time to stop being a coward.

She let herself into the building and crossed the foyer to the elevator, her bootrf heels thudding hollowly on the ceramic tiles. Her internal voice kept up a running monologue of instructions, without which she might not have moved. *Push button. Wait. Step inside. Stare at numbers. Press six. Lean against wall. Stare at ceiling.*

Breathe.

She drew a lungful of air. For something that was supposed to be an autonomic body function, she'd had to remind herself to do that a lot since leaving the hospital. Several times in the car while she'd waited for Aramael, before admitting to herself he wasn't coming back after all. Several more times before she managed to insert the key into the ignition and get herself out of the parking lot. Many more on the way home. She closed her eyes.

Breathe.

She'd wanted him gone, and now he was. The Fallen hadn't been after her, and so there was no need for him to continue watching her. No reason for him to stay. He was gone, Nina was gone, Jen was as good as gone, and Alex had no choice but to send Seth away.

The elevator door slid open onto a hallway as empty as her world had become.

Breathe.

SIXTY-THREE

"Going somewhere?"

Seth looked up from throwing things into the overnight bag on the bed. Samael lounged in the doorway, his expression one of mild interest. Seth took a pair of socks from a drawer.

"Beat it," he said. "I'm not interested."

Ignoring him, Samael strolled into the room. "There's remarkably little personality to this abode. Have you noticed? None of the clutter mortals are so prone to collect. It has such an impermanent feel to it."

Seth clutched the edges of the overnight bag. He didn't want to answer, but the words were torn from him—much as a groan would be torn from a man whose open wound had just been poked with a hot knife. "She's been a little busy trying to stop your kind from destroying her world."

"Of course. I wasn't being critical, Appointed. Just making an observation."

"Yes, well you can take your observations straight back to Hell with you." Seth zipped up the bag. "Because I'm done. No more journals, no more innuendo. Not interested. Get out."

"So things are better between you two. I'm glad."

"Like Hell you are." Seth slung the bag over one shoulder, switched off the bedside lamp, and headed for the door.

Samael tagged along behind him. "I am, believe me. Still, that performance Aramael put on this afternoon must have irked just a little. Flaunting his connection to her that way."

Seth's fingers gripped the bag's strap a little harder. "He saved her life."

"Raising questions about how she survived in the process." Samael's tone took on a chiding note. "You and I both know no other angel would have done that. Not in a million years. His instinct to protect her goes far deeper than mere orders."

Seth doggedly continued his tour of the apartment, turning out lights.

Samael persisted. "The soulmate connection—"

Seth rounded on the Fallen One. "She chose *me*," he snarled. "Not him, me. That's all that matters."

"Is it? Then explain to me why you're heading out the door to go to her when she has already returned. It's all very sweet of you, of course, wanting to be certain of her well-being, but—"

"Alex is back?"

"She didn't call? How remiss of her. She returned hours ago—safely wrapped in Aramael's arms."

The breath in Seth's lungs turned thick. "You're lying. She would have let me know."

"One would think so, given the relationship you're

supposed to have with her," Samael agreed. "But in this instance, one would be wrong."

The Fallen One circled behind him in the cramped hallway. Tutted. "Look around you, Appointed. See where you are, what you've become. You're the son of the two greatest powers in the universe, and yet you subject yourself to this, a few rooms shared with a mortal woman who has no appreciation for what you truly are? For what she has in you?"

"She loves me."

"Your mother loved your father, and look where it got him. This is like watching history repeat itself all over again. It's pathetic."

Seth scowled. "You're wrong. I've read the journals, and this is different. I'm not my father, Alex is nothing like my mother, and I'm *not* giving her up. What we have—"

Samael stopped in front of him, inches away, and returned his scowl. "What you *have*, Appointed, is a woman who devotes her time—her *life*—to a dying race rather than to the man who gave up everything for her."

"You're wrong," Seth repeated, but even to his own ears, the words lacked conviction. He reached inside himself for the confidence he'd woken up with that morning, the certainty he and Alex had at last found the connection that could see them through anything. Alex had told him she loved him and—

"You keep telling yourself that. Let me know when you start believing it."

The rattle of keys outside the door drew both their gazes.

"The prodigal Naphil returns." Samael drew back into the living room. "My cue to go—for now. There's just one last thing."

"You haven't delivered enough poison already?"

The Fallen One shrugged. "Consider this an antidote. Because I'd hate to leave you thinking it has to be like this. Not when you could change everything if you take back your birthright."

"I told you, I'm not giving up Alex."

"But don't you see, Seth, son of Lucifer? Take back your powers, and you don't have to. Not ever."

Samael disappeared, the front door opened, and a pale, haggard Alex stepped into the apartment.

"We need to talk," she said.

SIXTY-FOUR

"So it's true," Seth said. "You're back."

Alex hesitated in the doorway. "How did you—?"

"Does it matter? I didn't find out from you."

"I'm sorry. Things were insane. I didn't have time
. . ." *And I didn't think about calling, and when I did
think about it, I couldn't face talking to you and—*

Her gaze dropped to the overnight bag slung over
his shoulder. "Are you going somewhere?"

"I was coming to Ottawa to see you. I was worried
when I didn't hear from you."

Guilt slithered through her. "I'm sorry. I should
have called. You saw the news?"

"I saw what Aramael did for you."

Innocuous words. A flat delivery. And powder keg
to which she preferred not to put a match. She closed
the door and twisted the dead bolt home. Seth set the
overnight bag on the living room floor.

"I'm okay," she said. "But Jen's in the hospital and
Nina—Nina's missing. Lucifer has her."

He took his coat off and dropped it on top of the bag, slid his hands into his pockets. "I'm sorry to hear that. I know you cared about her."

She blinked back sudden tears. "*Care*, Seth. Present tense. She's not dead."

Yet.

The word hung between them. Seth cleared his throat.

"Don't," she said. "Don't say it."

"You know there's nothing you can do."

"I can find her."

"Why? So you can watch her die?"

She shrank from the bluntness but made herself square her shoulders. "If that's all I can do, then yes. And hold her when she does. She's just a child, Seth. She needs me."

"Someone always needs you, Alex." He sighed, taking a hand from his pocket and rubbing it over his eyes, then along his jaw. "How are you even going to find her? If Lucifer has her, she could be anywhere on the planet."

Alex looked down at the floor between them. This was it. Her moment of decision. Speak the words and destroy the man she loved, or swallow them and condemn the planet. She crossed her arms over herself, knowing the gesture was defensive, needing the protection.

"You could help."

Time itself stood still as a hundred different emotions flashed across Seth's dark eyes. Sadness. Betrayal. Bitterness. Bottomless hurt. But not surprise.

"I see." He didn't pretend not to understand. "So you would give it all up. Everything we have, for the sake of a single girl whose life you can't even save?"

"Not just for her." She lifted a hand to the ache in her heart. "Your mother came to see me last night. She said—"

He cut her off. "Last night."

Shit. "It wasn't like that—"

"So you'd already decided to do this before you came to me. Before we made love." Cold anger displaced all else in the black depths. "I waited for you, Alex. I was patient and understanding, I respected your need for time and space, and when you finally let me touch you it was because you felt *sorry* for me?"

"I didn't feel sorry for you—at least, not any more so than for myself."

"But you'd decided."

"I tried to tell you. I—" She stopped. He deserved truth, not excuses. "Love isn't supposed to be like this, Seth. It's not supposed to come with the responsibility for billions of lives tied into it. Last night—" Her voice broke, and she paused for a steadying breath. "Last night was about you and me, and having something to remember between us that wasn't weighed down by choices and decisions and the future of an entire world."

Leaving the support of the door, she crossed over to him, putting her hand out to his arm. "I know this is difficult, but—"

"Difficult?" Wheeling away, he stalked into the living room, smacking his open-palmed hand against the door frame on the way. "*Difficult?* Fucking Hell, Alex, you're asking me to sacrifice everything I want, everything I am, for souls I will never know or care for. Souls that don't have a chance of survival in the first place! That's not just difficult, it's pointless."

Everything I want? Everything I am? A shiver rippled

down her spine. Was that really how he defined himself, by their relationship? She remained in the doorway, wariness holding her in place. He swung back to her, his face hidden in the shadows of the unlit room.

"Tell me what she said."

She didn't have to ask who he meant. "She said the angels can hold back the Fallen, but if Lucifer comes after humanity, she can't stop him as long as she has to contain your powers. Keeping them in check is making her weak. She doesn't know how much longer she can hold out."

"What else?"

She hesitated. Should she tell him about the One's plans to bind with Lucifer? To become *other*? She shook her head. The same caution that held her in place made her hold her tongue. "Isn't that enough? Earthquakes, volcanoes, flooding, tornadoes—your powers are ripping the planet apart at the seams. People are *dying*."

"They're also deliberately killing each other—wars, shootings, bombings. Look at what happened to you today. My powers have nothing to do with any of that, and taking them back won't make a bloody bit of difference."

"It will make a difference to the ones who aren't like that. The ones who deserve a chance to fix things. To make things right."

"War between the angels and the Fallen is coming. There are eighty thousand Nephilim about to be born. You can't *fix* those, Alex. And you sure as Hell can't survive them."

"You don't know that."

Two strides brought him towering over her. "I

do know that," he snarled. "And it's about time the rest of you—my mother included—admit it. She's been fighting a losing battle on your behalf for six millennia. She's lost her helpmeet, a third of her angel host, her son—and now I'm supposed to sacrifice my own chance at happiness for the cause?"

A frisson of uneasiness threaded through her. "I know you're angry—"

"Don't tell me how I feel!"

"—and hurt," she continued, the cop in her striving to keep her voice level and not escalate the situation. "But try to understand—"

"Understand *what*? That you choose mortals over me? Oh, believe me, you've made that crystal clear."

"It's not that simple!" she exploded. "This isn't about you and me, it's about what's right. I won't give up on all of humanity—I *can't*."

"And I won't give up on us," he growled.

It took everything she had not to step away from him. Away from the cold that had reached out to wrap around her heart, brush against her soul. She shook her head. "There is no us. Not anymore. We're done, Seth. We have to be."

Anger wrestled with something else on his face. Something uglier. She saw him shift, saw his hands curl into fists. Her already damaged heart faltered. He wouldn't—

He didn't. Instead, he pushed past her and stalked to the door. He pulled it open. Then his vicious black gaze met hers over his shoulder. "You're wrong. We're nowhere near done, Alexandra Jarvis."

The door slammed behind him.

SIXTY-FIVE

"It's time."

Lucifer watched a withered leaf drop from the tree outside the window.

"Did you hear me?" Samael asked. "I said it's time. The births are beginning."

"I heard you."

"I thought you'd like to come to Pripyat for their arrival. It's what we've been waiting for—what you wanted."

What he wanted. Another leaf drifted down to join the growing pile at the tree's base. A Nephilim army to finally do what he could not. Because pacts and agreements aside, Heaven would have always found a way to stand between him and the mortals, to prevent him from destroying them as he had wanted to do since their very beginnings. The One had never hesitated to pit angel against Fallen, might against might. But the Nephilim were different. They could not stand against the divine, and so she would not interfere with them. She would let them do as they might, let her precious nature run its course.

An army of untouchables. The certain extermination of humanity. Everything he'd wanted for millennia, and he felt the same nothing he had when he'd finally fathered the child that would lead them. No triumph. No exhilaration.

Just that yawning emptiness that seemed to take a little more of his soul with every passing day.

He closed his eyes. "Has Seth agreed to your idea?"

"I'm on my way to him now. I believe he has made his decision."

"Then let him take my place at Pripyat."

"But—"

"Samael."

His aide fell silent.

"Just leave," Lucifer said. "Please."

SETH STALKED the streets with long, vicious strides. He'd left the apartment hours before and had covered miles of the city. With every step he took, a little more of him unraveled, a little more fell away. Alex had been everything to him—no. She was everything. His anchor, his reason for being, his entire identity.

From the moment he had given back her life when Aramael failed to save her, from the moment he had touched her soul to do so, she had become part of him, as vital to his existence as breath itself. Twice he had brought her back from where no other could. Twice he had connected with her on a level so deep, so profound, that they were inextricably, eternally entwined. Without her—

The air hissed from him.

Without her, he would cease. End. Become nothing.

Just as his father had become nothing without his mother.

Leaving the paved streets, he crossed the dark, sweeping lawns of a park and halted on the shores of the massive lake bordering the city. He braced himself against the biting buffet of the November wind, its chill against his skin nothing compared to the one at his core. In his head, Alex's voice settled into the same, endless rhythm as the waves crashing onto the rocks. *"There is no us. Not anymore. We're done, Seth . . . We're done . . ."*

He closed his eyes. Anguish warred with fury in his chest. All he had done for her, all he had given of himself, and this—*this* was how she repaid him.

"We're done . . ."

"Now are you ready to listen?" a familiar voice asked.

Seth's eyes opened onto the dark stretch of water before him. At the corner of his vision, a shadow moved, barely discernible in the night. He considered the question. Alex would be horrified to know he'd been speaking with one of the Fallen, but he'd tried to do things her way. To follow her lead. Hell, even to see what it was about her fellow mortals that inspired such loyalty in her. And now he stood alone in the cold, without her, crumbling from the inside out.

"You said I wouldn't have to give her up if I took back my powers."

The shadow beside him inclined its head.

With careful precision, Seth detached himself from any remaining doubt. Any lingering conscience. He'd tried it Alex's way. Now it was his turn.

"I'm listening," he said.

SIXTY-SIX

Mika'el was in his office when the seismic wave hit Heaven. A heartbeat later, before it had trembled to a finish, he was at the top of the stairs overlooking the great library. His gaze swept the toppled shelves, the books strewn across the stone floor, and the two dozen angels standing amid the chaos, staring at one another in stunned silence.

Bloody Hell. Only two events could cause such an effect in Heaven. Either Seth had taken back his powers or—

Cold gripped his gut, and he had to force himself to finish the thought. Either Seth had taken back his powers or the One had lost her grip on them. He had to find out which. Now. But before he could swing away from the banister, the massive oak doors on the far side of the hall crashed open. A Virtue in full armor burst through, white wings spread wide. She cast a frantic look around the room and stopped in her tracks when she saw him.

"The Hellfire," she gasped. "We can see the other side!"

Mika'el's fingers splintered the wooden rail in his grip. Despair paralyzed his lungs. The One— he slammed a door against the possibility. No. He wouldn't go there. Not before he'd made sure. He felt the eyes of all present turn to him. Sensed them waiting. He spoke to the Virtue.

"Find the Archangels," he ordered. "I want every inch of the border inspected. I'll meet them on the lookout mound."

That would give him just enough time to check on the One.

He turned away from the gallery below and then swiveled back. "Virtue."

The angel, already halfway out the door again, looked around.

"Send someone to see that the armory is ready," he said.

A second's hesitation, then a nod. Mika'el cast a last glance around the room, meeting the shock in the others' eyes. The resignation. He didn't say anything. He didn't need to. They knew.

They just didn't know everything.

He found the One in the rose garden, seated on the bench where they'd conversed so many times before, face turned up to the sun, eyes closed, hands folded in her lap. His steps didn't falter as he crossed the lawn this time. He didn't slow down. The time for being concerned about disturbing her had long since passed.

He stopped before her and cleared his throat.

Her eyes remained closed. "I know you're there,

Mika'el."

"The Hellfire fails. I wasn't sure—"

"My son took me by surprise, but I'm fine now."

"You're certain?"

She gave a soft snort. "Well, I'm as fine as I can be given the circumstances. How's that?"

He smiled even though she couldn't see him. Even though his heart ached with a ferocity that made him want to put a hand to his own chest. "I suppose it will do."

The One exhaled a fluttery sigh. "He's not coming back, is he?" she asked sadly.

He considered lying. Weighed the possibility of telling her that they couldn't be sure yet. Then he shook his head.

"No. No, he's not coming back."

"I'm sorry, Mika'el. I hoped I would be wrong."

We all did.

"Rest," he said. "Get your strength back. I'll have one of the Virtues bring you tea."

His Creator didn't reply.

SIXTY-SEVEN

Alex steeled herself, opened Homicide's door, and stepped inside. A dozen heads swiveled instantly in her direction. Shit. With it being Saturday, she'd hoped fewer people would be in. But given the state of affairs in the city, she supposed she shouldn't be surprised. Roberts had warned everyone there would be ample overtime. A woman emerged from the file room at the back of the office. Even, apparently, for the civilian staff.

Steeling herself for the fourteenth time since entering the elevator in the parkade, she forced her feet to carry her into the room. She stopped at the edge of a gathering and nodded at the television they'd been focused on before her arrival.

"Anything important?" *Please, please, please don't let it be a rerun of me surviving the explosion in Ottawa.* She'd watched the newscast a dozen times last night after Seth left. It had become more damning with every viewing. Anyone who knew her would recognize her, and judging by the silence that greeted her just now, everyone here had.

Her colleagues exchanged glances, and then Joly spoke up. "You haven't heard this morning's news?"

She shook her head. She usually listened to the radio on the way into work, but not today. She hadn't been able to tolerate the noise. Not with so much already going on in her brain.

"The better part of New York State's shoreline was hit by a freak wave sometime around two a.m. Up to fifteen feet in some places. There are dozens missing, including a Boy Scout troop."

Alex blinked, trying to process his words. "New York City, you mean?" she asked. "The coast?"

Joly shook his head. "Lake Ontario."

"A freak wave. In Lake Ontario."

"From Irondequoit to Lost Nation State Forest. That's where the scout troop was camping. They're calling it a . . ." Joly looked to his partner for help.

"A meteotsunami," Abrams supplied. "A tsunami caused by weather rather than an earthquake."

"Except there was no storm," Bastion added. "Nothing to cause it. Just the wave and more than a hundred miles of shoreline submerged."

And now she had the answer to the question that had kept her awake most of the night. Until sheer, crippling exhaustion had sucked her into sleep—around the same time as that wave had struck New York State. Seth had taken back his powers. He was gone. In spite of the veiled threat he'd made as he'd stormed out—"*We're nowhere near done, Alexandra Jarvis*"—he'd come around. Seen her point. And left without saying good-bye. Damn, but she hadn't expected that.

"You're not going to pass out are you?" Joly peered at her in sudden alarm. "You just went the color of the walls. Are you supposed to be here today? Shouldn't you be at home resting or something?"

Alex huddled into the coat she hadn't yet taken off. "I'm fine," she said gruffly. "Just tired. I should go check in with Roberts."

Her fellow detectives stepped back to make way for her. She passed between them, trying not to feel like she was running a gauntlet. She worked with these people. She knew them. They might have questions, but she was still one of them, wasn't she? They'd still have her back, wouldn't they?

Bastion's voice stopped her. "Jarvis. What Joly told you yesterday. He's right. We'll find her for you. Your niece, I mean."

Tears she hadn't been able to find the night before flooded her eyes. Gritting her teeth so hard they hurt, she nodded blindly, not daring to turn, and somehow found her way to Roberts's office door. Her supervisor looked up at her tap, scowled, and beckoned her inside.

"You look like death," he informed her when she pushed the door open. "Why are you here?"

"Could *you* stay home?"

He sighed and waved her to a seat. "Fine. I needed to talk to you anyway."

Her heart stumbled. *Jen?* She hadn't called the hospital to check on her, hadn't been able to work up the stomach for it. The thought of her sister tied to a bed—

"Jarvis?"

She realized Roberts had been speaking to her. "Sorry, I didn't hear."

"I asked who you pissed off in Ottawa. You've been seconded to the RCMP antiterrorism unit. They've set up a—"

Alex bolted upright. "That son of a bitch. I told him I wouldn't go!"

Roberts, his mouth still open to speak, regarded her. Then he stood, crossed the room, and closed the door, shutting out the others' voices, the ring of a telephone, a bark of laughter that was horribly out of place in her world.

"Sit," he ordered. "Talk."

She threw herself back into the chair, wincing at the pull of fabric against the stitches on her thighs and abdomen. "Where do you want me to start?"

Roberts returned to the desk but not his chair. He sat on the edge, one leg dangling, arms crossed, jaw set. "At the beginning," he said. "And I want all of it. It's time."

It took ten minutes to undo all the good accomplished by Michael's little memory-wipe trick two days before—and then some. She started with Caim and Aramael, continued with Seth and Michael and Lucifer, finished with the missing scrolls, her visit to Ottawa, and what Boileau had told her about the children at the study centers—now also missing. When she was done, Roberts remained silent for long seconds, hands on hips, staring out the window behind his desk.

"So let me make sure I have all this straight," he said at last. "Heaven and Hell are at war on some other plane, but the fighting might spill over to here. Seth, who you've been living with for the past three weeks, is the son of God and Lucifer—"

"The One," Alex corrected.

Roberts shot her a dark look. "Whatever. You think he's taken back his powers, which might have caused the disturbance in Lake Ontario last night, and gone back to Heaven."

She nodded.

"And now we've lost track of these Nephilim children, and your niece ..." He shook his head slowly. "You're sure it was Lucifer."

"Positive."

Roberts stared out the window in silence. Then, quietly and succinctly, said, "Fucking goddamn son of a bitch."

That pretty much encompassed it, all right. Alex waited through another silence. She'd had weeks to pull together the details she'd just given her supervisor. Weeks to absorb the new reality of her world. He didn't have that luxury. Roberts scrubbed a hand over his head and swung around to face her. His hands went back to his hips.

"I think I prefer Ottawa's alien theory," he muttered. "At least we might have been able to fight back. But if you're right about this, about angels and Lucifer and Armageddon—how the hell do we protect ourselves from that?"

"We don't. The war is between Heaven and Hell. We have no control over it and wouldn't want to get involved even if we could. What we need to focus on is the human reaction. World Health can cry virus all it wants, but once the rest of the babies are born—"

"Wait. There are *more*?"

She thought back over her explanation and realized she'd left out that little detail. Probably because it had become so personal now that Nina—she shied away from the idea. Bracing herself to deliver the news, she met her staff inspector's gaze as steadily as she could while wanting nothing more than to crawl under the desk and hide. From him, from the world, from the chaos, from the pain she knew still waited for her whether she found her niece or not.

The door opened, and Bastion's stammer preempted her. "The news—the babies—"

Without a word, she left Roberts to trail in her wake as she followed her colleague out to join the others. She knew what she would hear before she came in range of the newscaster's voice.

Knew, because it had been three weeks since the alley in Vancouver. Three weeks since Lucifer had announced his plans for an army.

Which meant the Nephilim pregnancies had reached term.

All eighty thousand of them.

Less Nina.

SIXTY-EIGHT

Striding up the boulder-strewn hill, Mika'el scanned the waiting Archangels and jabbed his finger at Uriel. "Report," he barked.

The fair-haired Archangel didn't so much as blink at the peremptoriness. "Major flickers along the entire length, but it's holding. For now."

"Was it down long enough to get a look at the other side?"

"Word is still coming in, but so far we think in the neighborhood of ten thousand."

"Ten—" Michaela's step hitched. He stopped and scowled. "That's a fraction of their number. Where in bloody Hell are the other ninety?"

"Nearly ten thousand are held in Limbo," Gabriel offered.

"That still puts them down eighty."

"Perhaps they're just not all waiting along the Hellfire border," Zachariel said. "We're not keeping our entire force there, either."

"No, but we have a great deal more there than they have. Sam—" Azrael shot a quick look at Raphael, whose expression had gone stony, then continued. "Samael knows how we think, and he's too good a strategist to leave their front line so weak."

Mika'el flexed his fingers, stiff inside their armored gloves. His glare passed over the group once, twice, and then a third time. He scowled. "Where the Hell is Aramael? Did he not get an invitation to the party?"

"He did," Raphael said. "I delivered it myself."

Mika'el considered asking if the other Archangel had delivered anything else at the same time, such as an incapacitating beating, but he refrained. Raphael had made his views on Aramael's appointment clear, but he was still one of them. Still an Archangel. He would follow his orders to the letter, whether he agreed with them or not.

Aramael, on the other hand—

He'd deal with that issue later. "I think Azrael is right. The Fallen have been waiting more than four millennia for the Hellfire to weaken, so they won't be just lounging around somewhere. If Samael doesn't have them on the front line, where are they? What are we missing?"

"The Nephilim," said a new voice.

Mika'el glowered over his shoulder. "You're late."

"Verchiel had news she thought you would want." Aramael climbed the last few yards to join them. "Some of the Guardians have reported that the Fallen are watching the pregnant women. They're stopping them from harming either themselves or the babies they carry. Verchiel has sent word to all the Guardians to check in on their wards and report back to her, but I'd say chances are good that's what's keeping the

Fallen otherwise occupied at the moment."

Of course. Lucifer would be taking no chances with his army. Mika'el stared out over the barren sweep of land below their vantage point. "If that's the case," he said at last, "this standoff could end at any moment. Let's be ready."

He watched the others depart, each to his or her own duties, and then, turning toward the Hellfire, he launched himself into the air.

SIXTY-NINE

Verchiel dropped to her knees beside the frail figure outstretched on the floor. She placed the back of her hand to the One's parted lips, exhaling her own breath only when she felt warmth stir against her skin.

"Who else knows?" she demanded.

The Virtue who had come for her shook her head. "No one, Highest. When I found her like this, I came straight to you."

Thank all of Creation for that. Sliding an arm under the One's shoulders, Verchiel looked up at the Virtue.

"You'd be more help getting her up than just standing there, Sachiel."

"Oh! Oh, of course."

The petite angel stooped to support the One's other side, and together they lifted her from the floor. Dark eyes, heavy with worry, met Verchiel's.

"She's . . . awfully light," Sachiel murmured.

Insubstantial, Verchiel mentally corrected her. *The*

word you want is insubstantial.

"Put her on the chaise," she directed.

Together they carried their Creator across the room. Pale silver eyes fluttered open as they laid her gently onto the chaise longue. The One looked between them, confusion furrowing her brow, and then her gaze settled on Verchiel.

"My dear, sweet Verchiel," she murmured sadly. "I think all might truly be lost."

Verchiel's stomach made a sickening lunge toward her toes. She leveled a glare at Sachiel, now at the foot of the chaise. "Mika'el," she snapped. "Find him. Now. And, Sachiel, not a word to anyone else. Am I clear?"

The Virtue nodded vigorously and scuttled from the room. Reaching down, Verchiel grasped the blanket folded near the One's feet. She shook it out and placed it over the tiny figure, tucking it tenderly into place. Then she perched on the edge, beside her Creator.

"You should rest before you try to talk," she said. She took the One's hand in her own, trying hard to still the flutterings of panic in her breast. Did they have time to let her rest, or . . . ?

"What can I do?" she asked.

"I'm afraid there's nothing anyone can do. Not anymore." Anguish clouded her silver eyes. "I thought I would be all right once Seth took back his powers, but I underestimated the effect on me. I'm worn out, Verchiel. Weak. Lucifer's army has been born, and now he will destroy everything I have ever created, everything I have ever loved, and I won't be able to lift a hand against him."

The One gave a bitter laugh and raised her free hand, frail and almost translucent. "At the rate I'm fading, I won't *have* a hand to lift. And all because I waited too long. Trusted too much. Loved too completely."

The One's eyes drifted closed as Verchiel sought words of comfort. But if such words existed, she couldn't find them. Not when she knew what was in store for humanity and angelkind alike. For all of them. She stared out the window at the gardens, gripping the One's hand and hoping that her presence brought some modicum of ease, until a small sound from the doorway drew her attention. Sachiel.

She raised an eyebrow, and the Virtue tiptoed in, glancing anxiously at the resting figure on the chaise.

"Did you find him?" Verchiel asked.

The Virtue shook her head. "He and the others are patrolling the Hellfire. I've sent a messenger, but it will take time."

She would have to handle this on her own, then. Verchiel waited for the tightness in her throat to subside before she dismissed Sachiel. The One's eyes opened and followed the Virtue's departing form. Then she withdrew her hand from Verchiel's and tucked it beneath the blanket.

"I think I'll rest for a bit," she said. "When Mika'el returns, will you send him to me?"

"Of course." Verchiel rose and then impulsively, swiftly, stooped to press her lips to her Creator's forehead. "Just so you know, none of this changes how much we love you," she whispered, her voice fierce. "Forever."

The One turned her head away.

Verchiel remained beside her for a few seconds more, staring down, hurting for herself and the others, but mostly for the One. To have been so much, so great, so powerful, and then—this. Condemned to fade away with agonizing slowness, knowing that all she had created would fade along with her? It was wrong. Verchiel lifted her chin.

It was wrong, and it wasn't going to happen.

Not if she could help it.

SEVENTY

Alex stared at the television screen long after someone—she didn't see who—switched it off. Silence hung over the room, heavy with unease, thick with disbelief. Beside her, Joly rubbed his mustache, making a harsh rasp of sound in the stillness. Alex inhaled. Exhaled.

"How many?"

Roberts's voice made her jump. She looked around and found him standing gray-faced and grim at the edge of the group.

"How many?" he repeated. He waved at the television. "Of them."

Them. The babies. Babies who would become soldiers in Lucifer's army against humanity.

"A lot," she said. She hesitated, debating the wisdom of holding this conversation in front of the others. But if the media were already reporting the births, there seemed little point in hiding what she knew from the people she worked with. The people she trusted most in the world. Especially when it was only a matter of time before the numbers became obvious.

Her gaze swept over her colleagues, returned to Roberts. "Eighty thousand."

"Eighty . . ." Joly trailed off. His shock was mirrored in the others' faces.

Roberts cleared his throat. "Damn," he said. "And the women—?"

"All of them."

"What the *hell*, Jarvis?" Abrams shoved himself upright from the desk he'd been leaning on. "How can you know numbers like that? What do you know that you're not—"

Their supervisor cut him off. "Not now, Abrams."

"But—" Abrams met Roberts's hard look and subsided with a mutter.

Roberts turned back to Alex. "This is why Ottawa wants you."

"Yes."

"Can you do anything?" he asked.

"I've already told them everything I know, so . . . no. I can't."

Her supervisor studied the floor at his feet. "My hands are tied, Alex. The order is signed by the security minister himself."

Damn Boileau.

"I'm not going. Not until I find Nina."

Alex watched Roberts's mouth compress. At last he nodded.

"I'll tell them," he said. "Is there anything else I need to—"

A shudder rippled through the floor. Before anyone could do more than look puzzled, Homicide's main door blasted inward. It sailed halfway across the room, narrowly missing Raymond Joly's head before landing at their feet. Detectives and office staff alike scrambled for whatever cover was nearest. Almost as one, those that were cops drew their weapons and pointed them at the man standing in the doorway. All but Alex, whose heart turned to lead.

"Seth," she whispered.

SEVENTY-ONE

Lucifer approached the lone figure waiting by the water, crimson robes billowing about her. Innate caution kept his gaze roving the deserted land and seascape, but he saw no other presence, angelic or otherwise. Felt nothing amiss. His hand closed over the folded note handed to him by one of the Fallen a few minutes before. He was still reeling from its receipt. Heaven's Highest Seraph, requesting an audience with him.

Not even demanding.

Requesting.

He reached the angel at the sea's edge and stood beside her. "You wanted to see me."

"Yes. Thank you for coming."

He raised an eyebrow. Shot another suspicious look at their surroundings. "Please and thank you. Not words I ever expected to hear from the Highest Seraph."

"She's dying, Lucifer."

Shock threatened to drop him to his knees before he shook it off. *Don't be ridiculous. She can't mean—*

The Highest Seraph turned to him, her face lined with weariness, worry, despair. His shock returned, ricocheting through his soul with the speed of an Archangel's sword and wreaking nearly as much damage. He staggered, caught himself, managed to remain upright. He was the Light-bearer. He would not fall before one of Heaven.

"I don't believe you," he said. *I can't believe you.* "She is the One, the Creator of All. She can't just die."

Destroy herself in the process of ending him, perhaps, but *die*?

"She can, and she is."

"But—*how*?"

"Seth. The powers he gave up were damaging the Earth. Controlling them, stabilizing them, took everything she had."

"He took his powers back. We all felt it. She'll recover."

The Seraph shook her head. "I hoped for that, too, but it's getting worse. She's . . . fading. She doesn't have much time left, and she no longer has the ability to do what she'd hoped."

"To what, lead Heaven against me?" he snarled. "You think I'm going to feel bad about that?"

"She wanted to bind with you."

It wasn't the response he'd expected. It wasn't even within the realm of what he might have imagined.

"*Bind* with me?"

"She never stopped missing you, Lucifer. You are her Light-bearer, her helpmeet, her other half. There was—is—no other way she can be with you again."

Odd, how difficult it had become to breathe. He

flared his nostrils. Narrowed his eyes. Regarded the Seraph with suspicion. "What exactly are you asking of me, Seraph?"

"I'm asking you to do what she cannot."

"Give up my fight, you mean?" He gave a bark of laughter. "You'd like that, wouldn't you? Did Mika'el put you up to this? Or was it she herself?"

"Neither of them knows I've come to you, and it's not about giving up the fight, it's about understanding that there is no more fight. Not for you, and not for her." Her pale blue eyes regarded him steadily, sadly, seeing far more of him than he would have liked. "Everything you've done, everything you are—all of it is because of the love you bear for her. Because you hope—have always hoped—that she would see her folly and return you to her side. But now—Lucifer, if she dies without you now, you'll have lost one another for eternity."

The words, stark and untempered, drove the wind from him as nothing else could have done. He walked away, to the very edge of the water washing onto the sand in slow, rhythmic waves. It was a trick. It had to be a trick, because it couldn't be real. The One couldn't simply stop existing.

But if he believed, even for an instant, that the Highest Seraph told the truth, that she might be right—

A great, shuddering breath rose in him. He had to know. Had to see for himself. Then he would decide what to do. He turned back to the crimson-robed angel who waited.

"The Archangels?"

"Patrolling the Hellfire, but I have sent for Mika'el."

He looked out over the water again. There would be

risks. A chance that the Seraph lied to him, that this was all an elaborate trap. He examined his heart to see if the knowledge changed anything. It did not. He still needed to know.

"Understand that I make no promises," he said.

The Highest Seraph nodded. "I know."

SEVENTY-TWO

Lucifer paused on the top step of the One's quarters and looked back over his shoulder at the gathering—and hostile—masses. Verchiel had assured him no one else would know of his presence here, but they had both underestimated the angelic grapevine. Within seconds of a startled Virtue crossing their path outside the rose garden, hundreds had blocked their route—grim-faced, silent, accusatory, giving way to the Highest Seraph's authority only with great reluctance.

"Do they know?" he asked Verchiel. "That she's . . . ?"

The Highest Seraph shook her head. "Not yet."

He raised an eyebrow. "And do you not think you should tell them they'll be without their Creator soon? If I were in charge—"

"You're not." Steady blue eyes met his. "Be very clear on that, Light-bearer. You are here for the One. Nothing else."

Her hands twisted into the fabric of her robe, at odds with the confidence in her voice. Lucifer waited for the surge of enjoyment at knowing he inspired such disquiet, but he felt nothing. Nothing except an overwhelming desire to be home. Not home like this—he looked beyond the gathering of angels to the lush gardens and woods—but home with the One whose very life spark he shared. Had always shared. He held his hands out, palms forward, in a gesture of conciliation.

"Forgive me, Highest. Old habits die hard. Shall we?"

Several seconds passed before she stepped clear of the door and pulled one hand from the crimson folds. "After you."

He preceded her into their Creator's simply furnished abode, taking a moment on the threshold to let his eyes adjust to the dimness. Verchiel's light touch against his back moved him forward, guided him toward the windows on the far side of the room, pressed him on when he would have stopped because his heart had already done so.

She sat in one of a pair of wingback chairs angled before the window, the light enveloping her body. Her eyes were closed, her hands folded in her lap, her face serene. Her demeanor spoke of one who waited, and his breath caught, rough and scraping in his suddenly constricted chest. He searched for but could not find his voice, and cleared his throat instead.

Silver eyes opened. Smiled. And instantly glowed with love.

Lucifer dropped to his knees before her and took her hands in his. Shock rippled through him at their fragility.

"Lucifer," she said. "Bearer of light and my truth. It is good to see you."

"And you," he said. Eyes closed, he pressed his lips to her palms, first one, then the other. Inhaling her, tasting her, absorbing her.

A sigh shuddered through her. Her hands turned in his until she gripped back, holding onto him as he did her. His heart swelled with sweet, aching joy. This. This is what he had missed so terribly, what he had wanted to come home to. Her love, her compassion, her—he felt the One go still beneath his touch and sensed her gathering herself. He remembered what would come next. What had to come next. He tried to pull back, but her fingers clamped onto his, holding fast.

"Lucifer."

Panic slammed through him. No. He couldn't let her see. She would never love him if she saw—if she knew—his pull became frantic. Hers was stronger.

"Let me look at you," she said.

He shook his head. "Please don't," he whispered.

One of her hands released his and lifted his chin. Her will surrounded him, pressed in on him, compelled him. He could have resisted. Fragility still underlay the All that had once been her presence, and it would have taken little effort to rise and walk away from her. But he did not. Instead, infinitely sad, he did her bidding and opened his eyes, the windows to his twisted, damaged, hateful soul. Opened them, looked into hers, and waited for the Judgment he knew was coming. Knew he deserved.

Tears gathered in the One's silver eyes. He blinked. She cried . . . for him?

"For us," she said, stroking his cheek. "I cry for

us."

He recoiled. *For us.* But that meant—

Truth laid open his soul, sudden understanding his heart. For the first time, he grasped the full impact of his actions. She was his Creator—his other half, his better half—and for six millennia he had allowed pride and jealousy to come between them, to divide not just the world, but the two beings who most belonged together. He had sacrificed all that he might have had, all *they* might have been, in favor of nothing at all. He had given up this—her touch, her presence, her love—for a thousand journals filled with a handful of fading memories, a lifetime of wasted wishes.

A groan surfaced in his core, ripped through his body, turned harsh with agony in his own ears. He—*he* had done this. Not only to himself, but to the one he loved more than any other. He tried to push away, but the One's arms went around him, pulling him close and holding him tight. Her presence seeped into him, scraping his soul clean, leaving him raw, bruised, achingly exposed.

"I'm so sorry," he whispered at last, when he could form words again. "I am so, so sorry for what I have done."

"Oh, my Light-bearer, it is I who should beg your forgiveness. So much I could have done to prevent all that came between us. To have created you as I did, and then refuse to understand you . . ." She rested her forehead against his. "I have wronged us both. Wronged all of my creations with my stubbornness. I am sorry."

It became his turn to hold her. He did so with tenderness and, as the years that had divided them began to slip away with every beat of her heart against his, a gratitude so intense that it took away his breath. Then, when she finally drew back, he pulled up the other chair—his chair, still sitting where he had left it six thousand years before—and settled into it.

"Tell me what you need me to do," he said. "I'm ready."

SEVENTY-THREE

Lucifer's presence in Heaven slammed into Mika'el like a fist, stopping him in midair. He dropped to the ground to get his bearings. A dozen feet away, the Hellfire flickered and danced without sound, its heat making the feathers of his wings smolder. He ignored it, trying to pinpoint the Light-bearer's whereabouts.

Had there been a breach? Why hadn't someone sounded the alarm? And Lucifer? It made no sense that the Light-bearer himself would—

Every atom in his body crystallized into ice.

The Creator.

Bloody Hell, he'd left the One unprotected. He'd put every Archangel on patrol, leaving none behind to watch over the One even though he'd known she was weakened. Now Lucifer was here, in his territory, threatening her. Mika'el's fury surged. He pulled his sword and threw himself from where he was to where he needed to be—landing in the One's quarters in a whirl of battle-ready feathers, cyclonic wind, and shattering glass as every window in the building blew outward.

His gaze settled on Lucifer, seated in a chair beside the One. A glow enveloped the two of them, binding them together.

"Light-bearer!" Mika'el's voice started as a low growl, rising to a shout at the end.

The glow wavered, settled, intensified. Sword high, he sprinted forward, driven by rage and hatred. His unfinished business with Lucifer was about to end. Here. Now. To—

"Mika'el."

He pulled up short, nearly running over the Highest Seraph as she stepped in front of him and placed a hand on his chest. Her calm radiated outward, countering his own turbulence. He sidestepped, trying to shake her off; she followed.

"Mika'el," she said again.

Her gentleness sliced through his fury, hobbling it. Hobbling him. He stopped trying to evade her and stared beyond, at the two seated before the blown-out window. She, the One, upright in her chair, eyes closed and face in deep repose. He, her Light-bearer, leaning forward, fingers entwined with hers. And around them both, that light. Emanating from each of them, encompassing them, tying them together . . .

Shutting out the rest of the universe.

His heart contracted. He was too late.

No.

He stepped forward again. Verchiel held firm against him.

"It's what she wanted, Mika'el. What we told her we would give her."

Mika'el shook his head, trying to reclaim his anger, needing it to hold at bay the grief clawing at his chest. His Creator, *their* Creator, the mother of them all, was leaving—and he hadn't had a chance to say goodbye. Hadn't told her how much he loved her, would always love her.

"She knows," Verchiel assured him softly.

He didn't want to listen. Fear—and the yawning emptiness looming inside him—demanded that he intrude, that he tear the One from the Light-bearer and insist that she stay and watch over her creations. That she finish what she had started. The weight of Heaven itself pressed down on his shoulders, his to bear when she was gone. His to lead in war, to watch over and protect, to hold together in her absence. He flinched from the enormity of the task—and from the part of him that silently raged against her for having left it to him.

But he said nothing, did nothing, because Verchiel was right. They had promised this to their Creator. Promised that they would let her go, that they would manage, that they would be all right without her. He released his breath in a long hiss.

The light from the two bodies surged, pulsed, struggled to merge. The look of concentration on Lucifer's face became fierce, then panicky. His own light glowed bright, but the One's began to fade. Beside Mika'el, Verchiel inhaled sharply.

Something was wrong.

"He's killing her!" He wrenched his sword free of its sheath again and started toward Lucifer.

"No." Verchiel caught his upraised arm, her hand surprisingly strong. "No, Mika'el, it's not Lucifer. It's you."

Me! But—

Comprehension kicked him in the chest, knocking the wind out of him. Of course it was him. He was the one holding on, unable to let go. The One knew he'd lied about managing without her. Just as she knew he doubted, knew he resented, knew he was nowhere near ready to let her go.

She knew, and in that knowledge, remained tied to Heaven. To him.

For a moment, a brief, wholly selfish moment, he hesitated. Lucifer had begun a conversion to incorporeal energy that he most likely couldn't stop. He would cease to be an issue for Heaven, no longer be able to interfere with the mortal race or rule over the Nephilim army he had created. Why not keep the One with them, then? Why not save her from this so that she could continue ruling, at least until they were ready to lose her? Until he was ready.

Words spoken by the One a few days before whispered again through his mind. *"Loss isn't something you're ever ready for, my Archangel. It's something you survive."* He shook his head at them, and his breath caught, harsh in his throat. But deny them as he might, they found a reluctant echo of truth in his heart.

His Creator was right. He would never be ready to lose her. None of them would, because the very concept of losing her was simply too big, too impossible. But the struggle to come to terms with it was his, not hers. And tying her to him, to them, because of his own shortcoming would be the ultimate betrayal of her love—and his own.

Lifting his head, Mika'el looked into the struggling glow around his Creator. A Creator that wanted—needed—to be more, to be whole again. Grief trickled into the vast hollowness that had become him. He studied the One, burning her every detail into his memory. He breathed in her presence one last time. And then he whispered the final words of release.

"I'll miss you," he said.

For a moment, nothing happened. Then the light around the One's form gave a sudden surge, burgeoning outward to touch that of Lucifer. It meshed, merged, grew so bright that Mika'el raised a hand to shield himself from it. But he didn't look away. He would not miss this last moment with her. He could not.

Eyes watering, he stared into the growing brilliance, watching the two beings within merge until one was indiscernible from the other. One that he loved with all his soul, the other he had detested just as much—if not more. Two halves of a whole, the yin and yang of the universe, united again at last.

The light flared outward . . . and was gone.

But Mika'el swore he felt the brush of the One's fingers against his cheek as it passed.

SEVENTY-FOUR

Alex watched Seth's advance across the office. Her brain screamed at her to run, but her feet were rooted to the floor. She schooled her features into a calm that couldn't be further from truth and cleared her throat.

"Seth," she said again. "What are you doing here?"

"I gave you what you wanted," he said. He spread his hands wide and smiled, oblivious to the weapons trained on him. "Your world is safe. From me, at least."

"I know," she said. "Thank you."

"And now it's your turn."

"My turn?"

"To give me what I want," Seth said, coming to a halt in front of her, mere inches away. "What we both want."

What we—? The question died unformed as she tipped back her head to meet the black void of what had once been his gaze. Her innermost self went still. She'd forgotten what his power looked like. No. Scratch that. She'd never seen his power look anything like this.

"Now that I have my power back," he continued softly, "I can make you like me."

Apprehension dug its claws into her shoulders. "I don't understand."

"Immortal, Alex. I can make you immortal, so we can be together always."

All around her, hands holding weapons wavered and then steadied. At her side, Roberts took a step forward, scowling. She put out a hand, stopping him, and regarded Seth. He couldn't be serious . . . could he? Was it even possible?

"You need to clear the office," she told her supervisor.

"There's no way—"

"Staff. This is between me and Seth. You can't do anything."

"There is no goddamn way—"

"You heard the lady," Seth said.

His voice held a dangerous edge that made Alex's fingers dig into Roberts's arm. The entire room seemed to wait. Roberts turned his head away from Seth and dropped his voice to a bare whisper. "Do you really think he'd . . . ?"

She wanted to say no. Wanted to believe the man she had loved was incapable of violence. But this wasn't him. This wasn't her Seth. Not anymore. This was the divine being from the Vancouver alley that she'd tried to save . . .

And failed.

"Just go," she told her staff inspector. "Please. I'll be fine."

Roberts's struggle with angry denial played out across his face. "Damn it, Alex—"

His arm ripped from her grasp as he lifted from the floor. He flew past and slammed against the wall of his office, ten feet away. A collective gasp ran through the office. Alex stepped forward to go to her supervisor's aid, but a single word stopped her in her tracks.

"Stay," said Seth.

She obeyed, afraid of what he might do otherwise. Heart hammering, she watched Roberts put a hand to the back of his head and bring his fingers away covered in blood. He scowled and climbed to his feet.

"I'm not leaving you with him, Jarvis."

Still blinking at the speed with which her supervisor had been tossed back—had Seth even *moved*?—Alex opened her mouth to argue. She snapped it shut again as, one by one, pistols held in trembling hands throughout the office turned to point at their owners' skulls. Fingers curled against triggers. Panic rolled through her, and she whirled back to Seth. "Don't!"

Seth stared past her at her supervisor. "It's not up to you, Alex. It's up to him."

"They'll leave, I promise. Just—don't." She looked over her shoulder. "Staff, *please.*"

Roberts's gaze held hers for a moment longer, his eyes wide with shock, sharp with denial. Then his shoulders sagged. He nodded.

"Put your weapons away," he ordered, his voice hoarse. "And clear the room. Alex, we'll be—"

"The building," she interrupted. "Clear the building."

Thank God it was Saturday, with so few people at work.

"I can't—"

Raymond Joly's weapon came up again, this time to point at the head of the administrative assistant who had taken shelter beside him. The woman's face lost all hint of color. Sweat broke out on Joly's forehead in his effort to redirect his hand, but to no avail.

"The building," Roberts agreed, his face as white as the assistant's. He limped forward from the wall to join the others, pausing at Alex's side.

"You're sure about this?" he asked. Then, turning his face away from Seth, he mouthed, "*ETF?*"

She shook her head. She couldn't risk it. Wouldn't risk it. If Seth could exert the kind of control he'd just demonstrated, not even the highly trained Emergency Task Force could do anything. And if he spoke the truth about making her the same as him, making her—God, she couldn't even *think* the word—then there was no telling what kind of power he'd have to bring to bear to do so, or what havoc such power might wreak.

"I'm sure," she told Roberts.

The slow sickening of his expression told her his thoughts had followed hers. He understood the risk would be too great. Anguish filled his face. His throat worked with the effort to speak, but in the end he simply gave her shoulder a squeeze and followed the others out of the office, taking his cell phone from his jacket pocket as he did so. His voice, gruff and authoritative, floated back to her as he gave instructions to clear the building.

And then there was only Seth.

Alex lifted her eyes to the awful emptiness of his.

Deep within her, her soul whispered a name.
Aramael.

SEVENTY-FIVE

Mika'el stood shoulder to shoulder with Verchiel in shared silence. The space that had been occupied by the One and Lucifer was now empty—bereft and oddly expectant at the same time. As if it couldn't make up its mind whether the Creator was really gone or had only wandered away for a moment and would return. Much like the hole in Mika'el's soul.

He squared his shoulders. "You'll have to advise the others," he said. "They'll have felt her leaving."

"Alone?" She cast a startled look at him.

"I need to ready the Archangels." He realized he still held his sword clenched in a near death grip and shoved it back into its sheath. "And an army. The Hellfire will come down soon if it hasn't already."

Her hands twisted into her robe. "Of course," she said. "Because it's just us now. You and me, leading all of Heaven."

He stiffened, hearing a note in her voice that he didn't like. Verchiel went to the One's chair and ran her hand over the back of it. She gazed out the window. Mika'el waited, bracing for what he suspected would come next. The Highest didn't disappoint.

"It won't work," she said. "We're not strong enough to fight a war and still hold all of this"—she waved—"together."

"Don't," he said. "Not yet."

Verchiel heaved a sigh. "We have to talk about it, Mika'el. She might be our—"

"I said not yet."

"Then when?" She turned to him, annoyance creasing her brow. "It could take us weeks to find her. We haven't heard so much as a whisper from her for six thousand years—or about her, for that matter."

They'd been watching for her? His mind answered the question even as it formed. She was the daughter of Heaven. One of its biggest losses—and greatest regrets. Of course they'd been watching for her . . . just as he himself had meticulously avoided doing so. He stalked past the Seraph, headed not for the door and the waiting throng, but for the glassless window and the eminently more manageable concerns of war. Verchiel's voice followed him.

"I know this is difficult for you, but at least let me begin looking."

Grief, guilt, and utter despair wrangled for the upper hand in his chest. He stepped through the floor-to-ceiling window and into the gardens.

"Mika'el!"

Unfurling his wings, he left her behind.

Her, but not the memories of Emmanuelle.

SEVENTY-SIX

S triding into the war council chambers, Mika'el unsheathed his sword. He laid it across the table with the others. Six Archangels fell silent. Six sets of eyes watched grimly. He didn't prevaricate.

"What you've heard is true," he said. "She's gone."

There was a collective inhale, and then chaos.

A dozen questions came at him in what seemed to be a single breath, battering against his ears, his skull, his already bloody heart. Resting his hands on the table, he dropped his head, waited for the accusatory voices to die down. They ended with a single harsh question rising above the others.

"Why in bloody Hell didn't you stop her?" Raphael demanded.

Mika'el lifted his head to glare at him. "Because she wanted this. It was the only way she could stop Lucifer."

The others blinked at him.

"She took him with her?" Azrael asked. "He *let* her?"

"Yes. To both questions."

Another jumble of voices ensued. Again he waited. Again one voice rose above the others.

"So that's it. Hell's ruler is gone. The Fallen are on their own," said Gabriel.

"No." Aramael pushed back his chair and stood, his hands fisted. "No, they're not. Seth will take his place."

"We don't know that for certain," Mika'el said, "but given Seth's lack of cooperation so far, yes, it's possible he'll step into the void."

"Not possible. Definite. I know him better than you do, Mika'el. He'll feel we forced him into this, forced him to give up Alex. He'll be bitter and angry, and this will be his way of getting back at us."

"Even if you're right, it changes little. We'll still be fighting the same war whether Seth is a part of it or not."

"Except the *Fallen*," growled Aramael, "will have a leader."

And we won't.

The former Power didn't speak the last part. He didn't need to. The words hung over the table all the same, stark and unforgiving in their truth. Drawing himself up to his full height, Mika'el glowered at him, hating that he was right but still refusing to consider the possibility raised by Verchiel. He would not— *could* not—go there.

"Then we'll just have to work harder at remaining united," he snapped. "Starting now. With us. Any objections?"

When no one spoke, he raised an eyebrow at

Aramael. Scowling, the other took his seat again. Mika'el nodded.

"Good. Then you each know what you're to—" He stopped as Gabriel, the only female among their company, cleared her throat. "Yes?"

"What about the Nephilim?"

"What about them?"

"The babies have all been born, and they've all disappeared. Do we just leave them out there like that, or—?"

Mika'el understood what she was asking. For a brief moment, standing there in the One's profound absence, he had wondered the same thing himself. He'd also reached a conclusion. He let his gaze travel the table, meeting each of the others' in turn.

"The One might no longer be here," he said quietly, "but her legacy lives on in us. All of us. We uphold her ways, is that understood?"

Slowly, one by one, the Archangels nodded.

"Then as I was saying, you know—"

A chair crashed to the floor as Aramael surged to his feet again. Mika'el sighed.

"Now wh—?" He stopped midword as the other Archangel grabbed his sword from the table, scattering the others—and their owners—in all directions. Mika'el leaned across the table and seized Aramael's wrist, holding him fast.

"Tell me," he ordered.

Ferocious eyes fastened on his, and Aramael wrenched his arm away. "Something's wrong," he said. "Alex needs help."

SEVENTY-SEVEN

It took every particle of self-control Aramael possessed to remain at the war council table and not bolt to Alex's side. His whole being vibrated with her need for him, resonated with his desire to respond to her summons. But with Mika'el scowling that way and Raphael's narrowed eyes grimly daring him to so much as twitch, he didn't dare. Getting into a fight with another Archangel—or several of them, for that matter, would only slow him down.

Gripping the tabletop with one hand and his sword in the other, he repeated his words, "Something is wrong. She needs help."

She needs me.

"Damn it, Aramael, you were to sever your connection to her," Mika'el said.

"The same connection you counted on to protect her from Samael when you thought he followed her?" Aramael snarled back. Painfully aware of the tension threading through the others, he reined himself in.

Made himself breathe. "Let me check on her. Please."

"This time and how many others?" Mika'el shook his head. "The Hellfire is down, Aramael. An attack is imminent. I cannot spare you."

You cannot hold me.

He bit back the ill-advised challenge and locked his knees against the need to leave. Whatever had drawn Alex to summon him, it grew more urgent with every second—and it wasn't going away.

"You don't understand," he grated. "I *need* to see her."

Raphael snorted. "I knew you'd be a liability."

"Raphael," Mika'el said.

His golden eyes venomous, the Archangel subsided.

Mika'el studied Aramael for what seemed eternity. "You're certain she's in danger?" he asked at last.

"What does it matter? She's a Naphil!" Raphael exploded. "His only loyalty is to—" He broke off, staring at the hand Mika'el placed on his arm, then at the warrior. "You have *got* to be kidding me."

"Well?" Mika'el asked Aramael.

Aramael noted distantly that the table had begun to smolder beneath his grip. Alex had called on him only twice when he hadn't already been there watching over her. Both times her life had been threatened. Neither time had ended well for her.

Putting any of that into words was beyond his current ability.

At his back, his wings quivered under the strain of holding them closed.

Mika'el rubbed at the back of his neck. "One time, and one time only, Archangel. Do whatever you must, but after this, you break your tie to her, do you understand? And be careful. I can't spare anyone to go with you, and if you're right . . ."

Aramael nodded his acceptance of the warning. And the risk.

"Go," said Mika'el.

Released at last, Aramael's wings shot open to their fullest, knocking aside chairs, taking out a wall sconce, and creating a wind that had the others grabbing to hold the table in place.

"Bloody Hell," Raphael growled. "You know better than to launch from insi—"

Aramael didn't hear the rest.

SEVENTY-EIGHT

As the last footsteps of her retreating colleagues faded down the hallway, Alex put the width of a desk between her and Seth. She searched his face for something familiar, something of the man she'd loved and thought she'd known. But while Seth's features remained the same, no *man* remained.

Seth stepped toward her. Instinctively, she shuffled away. He tipped his head to one side.

"What's wrong?"

Stay calm. "I was worried about you last night."

"And so you're running away from me today?"

Keep him talking until—

Until what, help arrived? *Not happening, Alex. There'll be no cavalry. Not this time.*

Her palms turned clammy, and her heartbeat thudded in her ears. She was on her own here. A deeply buried part of her stilled at the realization. The admission. There would be no peer backup, no divine intervention, no Aramael rushing in to save her. It had come down to her and Seth and a choice she desperately needed him to accept if she was going to get out of this alive. Intact. She took a deep, shaky breath.

"I was worried about you," she said again, "but it doesn't change what I said, Seth. We can't be together."

Dark brows met over the hurt in his eyes. "I don't understand. We chose one another. I love you. I gave up everything to be with you. *Always together.* You said that, Alex."

"I know. I know, and I'm sorry it couldn't be—"

Before she could blink, he stood before her, his hands on her shoulders.

"But it can," he said. "Don't you see? I meant what I said. I can make you immortal."

It took every ounce of willpower she possessed not to cringe from the word, the idea.

His touch.

She made herself stay soft under his hands. Unresisting. *No cavalry.* Hurt clouded his face. Betrayal twisted it.

"You don't want to be immortal." His voice was flat with dawning disbelief. "You don't want to be with me."

I did, she wanted to deny, *but we never had a chance. We were too different, too far apart. We should never have tried.* But she couldn't speak past the sorrow clogging her throat. Aramael had been right all along. This, human and angel—or whatever Seth was—coming together, was wrong, unnatural.

Seth turned from her. Bracing his hands on the edge of the desk, he lowered his head. Every rigid line of his body screamed pain. Alex's heart shredded. Whatever had happened, whatever decisions had brought them here, to this point, he didn't deserve this. No one did. She slid a hand across his bowed back and rested her forehead against his shoulder.

"Please," she said. "Try to understand. I belong here. On Earth, among mortals, doing my job. It's who I am. Just as this—this is who you are."

"But I don't want to be this," he snapped. "Not without you. I haven't wanted it since I first met you, Alex. When I brought you back from the edge of death, when I restored life to you"—he tipped his head to rest against hers—"touching your soul made me feel things I never knew existed. Never knew were possible. I can't give that up. I won't give it up." His voice dropped to a whisper. "Please. You can't save them. At least save yourself. Come with me. Be with me."

Alex swiped with the back of one hand at the tears on her cheeks. Not for a second was she tempted, but saying so, hurting him like this when she was the reason he had given up so much already—

Suddenly the One's voice filled her ears, as clear as if the Creator stood at her side. *"I know how much you love him, Alexandra. And I know why. But he's not your responsibility...When he chose you, he did so over the fate of all humanity. And he did it knowingly."*

Knowingly. Alex hadn't wanted to believe the One that night, but now, seeing what Seth had become, glimpsing what he was capable of...

She drew a jagged breath and stepped back, away from him. "I can't," she said.

For an interminable moment, Seth didn't reply. Then, slowly, he lifted his head, straightened, turned to face her again. His gaze met hers, no longer hurt or empty, but burning with a fierce, hot determination.

"Then I'll make you."

Her every fiber went cold. He wouldn't. Couldn't. "Seth—"

A gust of wind knocked her sideways. Papers and files scattered. Chairs tipped over.

From the destroyed doorway, a familiar voice growled, "She said no, Appointed."

SEVENTY-NINE

Mittron gazed down in mixed horror and fascination at the seethe of bodies below him. Every inch of every street within view held a Fallen One carrying a newborn infant. Even through the newly replaced window, the squalls were deafening. He shook his head. This chaos was to be Lucifer's legacy? The army that would destroy humankind? Samael might be a brilliant military strategist, but his organizational skills in this arena were severely lacking.

The door opened behind him, and he looked around. A Naphil girl-child of about six mortal years stepped into the room and surveyed him with large blue eyes. Mittron raised an eyebrow.

"You wanted something?"

"You don't look like the others," the girl said. "Where are your wings?"

"Where are your manners?" he countered.

She shrugged, her oversized gray T-shirt—the

uniform for all of Pripyat's Naphil occupants—sliding down her shoulder. She tugged it back into place. "I don't need manners. I'm a soldier."

"Indeed."

"Are you one of us?"

"A Naphil, you mean?" He shook his head. "No."

Her head tipped to one side. "Then why would Samael want to speak with you?"

"I'm helping him."

The Naphil considered his explanation for a moment, then gave him a bright smile. "That's nice of you," she said. She skipped to his side and took his hand, her fingers small and warm as they wrapped around his. "I'll take you to him. You can tell me a story on the way. I like the one about the Archangels getting burned in the Hellfire. Do you know that one?"

Of course he did, but as the girl led him from the room and down the dank, narrow hallway, she kept up an endless stream of chatter that made it impossible to get a word in edgewise, let alone tell a story. By the time they reached their destination, down four flights of stairs and through a maze of corridors, he was exhausted, annoyed, and more than happy to see her skip away after delivering him to Samael.

He threw himself into a chair and scowled at Lucifer's aide. "Let me guess," he said sourly. "You're planning on having the Nephilim talk humankind to death, right?"

Samael looked around from the window. "Don't get comfortable," he replied, ignoring the remark. "You have a job to do. Things are moving faster than we expected. Lucifer and the One are gone."

Mittron sat up straighter. "What? When? I heard about no battle."

"A short time ago, and there was no battle to hear about. Verchiel invited Lucifer to Heaven, he went, and now he and the One are gone. End of story. Except for this mess." Samael stared out again, feathers rustling irritably. He crossed his arms and scowled. "Already the Fallen are dividing, and I'm still not a hundred percent certain we have Seth on board. I need that backup from Limbo. How long to open it?"

Mittron tried to wrap his mind around the sudden turn of events. "There are no guards, so once you get me there, a few minutes at most. But remember the risk, Samael. Some of the Fallen have been in there for thousands of years. They'll be beyond reason. Beyond your control. Are you sure you want to do this?"

"If we're to hold on to Hell long enough to put Seth in place?" Samael's expression turned grim. "Yes."

EIGHTY

Alex's heart had leapt at the sight of the winged figure looming in the doorway. An Archangel, fully armored, sword at his side, controlled wrath rolling off him in waves. Aramael. But as Seth's face morphed into a mask of pure hatred, hope evaporated. She stepped forward, intending to put herself between them, but an invisible force knocked her from her feet before she could. She landed on the floor with a grunt of pain and surprise.

Aramael's scowl deepened. His expression granite-hard, he stalked across the room, shoving aside overturned chairs, ignoring the scattered papers beneath his feet.

"Leave her be, Appointed. You're done here."

"Oh, you'd like that, wouldn't you?" Seth snarled. "Do you really think I'll just walk away and leave her to you? Do I strike you as that stupid?"

"That's not what this is about. I can no more have her than you can. I told you that."

"You lied!"

A tiny blue spark snapped beside Alex's cheek. She cringed and, scrambling to her feet, flicked a panicked gaze over the room. She'd seen sparks like that only once before, wielded by Lucifer in a Vancouver alley. But there was no sign of the Light-bearer now. There was only Aramael, her—and Seth.

Another spark ignited beside her face. She inhaled sharply.

Seth?

"You lied," Seth repeated. "I have had her, Archangel. I've held her, and loved her, and possessed her, and I am *not* giving her up. Not to you, and not to the mortals. She belongs to me."

Raw pain flashed in Aramael's eyes at the words, but his voice held steady. "She belongs to no one but herself."

Seth stared at Aramael, his jaw clenching and unclenching. Then, after a long moment, he turned to Alex, his eyes tired. Sad. Lost. "You truly don't want to be with me?"

She hesitated, still loath to hurt him. Still hoping she could somehow make him understand. Uncurling her fingers, she spread her hands wide. Made her voice gentle. "It's not that—"

"Answer me!" he snarled.

She jumped. Then she straightened her shoulders. He was right. She'd tried explaining, tried to ease this, but no matter how she phrased it, Seth would never see it as anything more—or less—than outright rejection. He just had to accept it.

"No," she said. "No, Seth, I don't want to be with you. I'm sorry."

The blue crackles intensified, filling the air

around him. "So am I," he said. "I didn't want it to be like this."

Seth spread his hands wide in the gesture his own father had once turned against him. Alarm raced over Alex's skin, standing every hair on end. But before she could react, strong arms wrapped around her and held her tight against a broad, muscled chest. She barely had time to inhale the familiar warmth of Aramael before massive wings folded around both of them—and then chaos erupted.

From every direction, every angle, objects bombarded them. Desks, chairs, glass from windows imploding into the room, ceiling tiles, light fixtures. The very air itself turned solid, slamming into them with a force that made Aramael stagger and the cocoon of his wings open slightly. Alex looked up into his eyes and quailed at the grimness she saw there. It wasn't just her; he hadn't expected this force, either. Hadn't expected Seth to be this strong.

A shard of glass flew between the gap in his feathers, slicing open his cheek. The wound sealed itself almost instantly, but not before crimson spattered onto her own cheek and pain winced across his features. Behind him, a support post ripped out of its mooring and spun toward them. She closed her eyes as it thudded against the arch of Aramael's wing. The floor bucked beneath her feet. .

Dear God in Heaven, what had she loosed on the world?

"Enough," Aramael growled.

Her eyes shot open as he put her away from him, his hands solid and reassuring in their grip on her arms. "Stay behind me," he ordered. "My wings will protect you."

She clutched at him when he tried to let go. "What are you going to do?"

His gray eyes hardened with resolve. "What I should never have let you talk me out of in Vancouver," he said. "I'm putting an end to this. Now."

She wished she could object. Wished Seth had given her some reason—any reason, however small—to do so. But whatever Seth might have been, whatever he could have chosen to be, that chance had long since passed.

"He's not your responsibility," the One's voice whispered in her memory. Her throat tight with fear, regret, and a multitude of other emotions it would take a lifetime to identify, Alex let go her hold on Aramael's sleeve.

Metal hissed against hardened leather as he drew the sword from its scabbard. It glinted dully in the light coming from the broken windows, plain, unadorned, built for one purpose and one purpose only. His wings lifting clear of Alex, he turned.

"Be careful," she whispered.

EIGHTY-ONE

With his wings unfurled to their fullest to protect the woman sheltering behind them, Aramael raised his sword to deflect a jagged piece of metal aimed at his head. "By all that is holy, Seth Benjamin, *enough*!" he shouted.

Nostrils flaring and chest heaving, the Appointed hesitated. Then, returning Aramael's glare, he let his arms drop to his sides. The power that had pressed in on Aramael subsided to a low, sinister pulse.

"You cannot stand against me forever, Archangel," Seth panted, sweat trickling down his forehead. "I'm not one of you. I'm more, remember?"

"Mika'el stood against your father," Aramael reminded him grimly. "And I will stand against you."

"Mika'el had five others of your kind with him. You have a *Naphil*." Seth spat the word.

"Fine. If you think you can take me, let's not waste time." Shifting his grip on his sword, Aramael spread his feet apart and settled them into the remains of the thin carpet. "Take your best shot."

Seth narrowed his eyes. Shook his head. "You really do care for her, don't you? You can't help but try to save her. It's a compulsion for you."

"And it always will be."

"Then save her from this."

An ominous rumble sounded behind Aramael, followed by the screech of metal tearing under stress. Alex gasped. Whirling, Aramael lifted his wings up and over her just in time to shield her from the collapse of a section of the floor above them. Concrete chunks showered down, battering outspread feathers hardened against attack. Twisted steel beams followed, and then a desk and—

He felt a sudden, sharp pain centered in his back, between his wings. Instinctively, he arched away from it, but it followed, pressing into him, piercing deeper. More pain erupted in his chest. He looked down at the jagged metal he had deflected only seconds before, its now crimson tip protruding from the breastplate of his armor. From the inside. Fury at himself joined his rage at Seth. Damn it, he should have expected that. Wrapping his free hand around the projectile, he braced himself to pull it through—and then stopped. Stared. Went cold. There, mixed in with his blood, traces of phosphorescence.

Seth's makeshift weapon had pierced his immortality. His gaze sought Alex's, and he saw his shock mirrored there.

Bloody Hell.

Steps sounded behind him. Warm breath stirred against his ear.

"There you have it, Archangel. My best shot. Good enough for you?"

Aramael felt Seth seize the metal projectile and twist it. White heat seared through him. His sword dropped to the floor, and he lurched forward, trying to escape.

Too late.

The metal left his body with a wet, sucking snick. His own roar of agony filled his ears even as a part of him distanced itself, shutting out the pain. His knees buckled, and he dropped to the floor. His voice became hoarse, trailed away. Another sound penetrated his awareness.

"Aramael? Aramael! Goddamn it, how do I get you out of this?"

Alex.

She knelt before him, her hands roving frantically over his armor, trying to remove it, to get to his wound. He tangled his fingers in hers, holding fast, shaking his head. Lifted his gaze to hers. To the terror, the denial, the anguish. Failure swelled in him.

"I'm sorry," he whispered.

"Don't. Don't you dare. You're not going to die on me, Aramael. I won't let you." She pulled her hands from his and cupped his face. "You can call someone. Call Michael. He'll—"

The pain in his chest sank deeper, radiating inward, brushing against his core. He swayed and would have toppled but for Alex's hold.

"I can't," he said. "I can't call from here. It's too—"

The word *far* died on his lips. He had been in Heaven when Alex called him. Somehow her voice had done what no angel's could and reached across two realms to pull him to her side. Not even their soulmate connection could fully explain that.

"Alex." He cradled her face, smearing her cheeks with his blood. "Where is Seth?"

"He's over there, watching. He said—" Her voice broke, and she made a visible effort to recover. "He said he would give us time for our goodbyes before he—he—"

"Sh." He laid his forehead against hers. The pain sank into his center. He fought it off. "There's one last thing we can try. I can't call Mika'el from here, but you can. Just like you called me."

"But you and I—we're soulmates—"

"It doesn't matter. He'll hear you. I'm sure of it."

He has to.

The pain took on an exquisite edge that stole his breath. He was running out of time. Pulling his wings over her, he tried to shelter her one last time, if only for a few seconds.

"Call," he whispered, willing her to stay strong. "Call Mika'el."

Her eyes—the color of a summer sky—brimmed with tears, and she covered his hands with hers, squeezing fiercely. Desperately.

"I love you," she said. "I tried not to, but I do. I always have."

He pressed his lips to her forehead, drawing on her warmth to ward off the cold in his core for another instant. Another labored heartbeat. "I know," he said. "Now call."

Her gaze locked with his, and he felt her go still. Felt her reach inside herself, past the fear, past the pain. Heard her whisper the name of Heaven's greatest warrior in the very depths of her soul.

Aramael's world went dark.

EIGHTY-TWO

Mika'el strode through the great hall, angels scattering from his path, the other Archangels fanned out behind him in tight-lipped silence. Raphael followed closest, his glowering disapproval a near palpable weight across Mika'el's shoulders. A justified one.

The One had been gone for less than an hour, and already cracks were appearing in Heaven's foundation. For the first time ever, the others questioned Mika'el's judgment. He slammed a fist against a bookcase as he passed by, and a collective gasp went through the hall.

He'd been certain Aramael could overcome his connection to the Naphil, but he'd obviously underestimated the former Power's feelings for the woman. Now his newest recruit was imagining a call for help across two realms, and Mika'el had believed him. Let him go. What in the name of the Creator herself had he been thinking? He had bloody Armageddon looming and—

Michael.

He stopped in his tracks, and the boulder-solid form of Raphael slammed into his back. Armor clanged against armor, underscored by cursing.

"Damn it, Mika'el, warn me when you're going to—"

"Quiet." Mika'el held up a hand. "Did you hear that?"

Raphael looked up from buffing a scratch on his breastplate. "Hear what?"

Mika'el scanned the faces of the other Archangels. "A voice. Saying my name. None of you heard it?"

Blank looks met his. Heads shook. He scowled. Wonderful. Now *he* was imagining—

Michael!

His head snapped back. That wasn't just his name, it was his Earth name. One that none in Heaven ever called him. He went still, stopped breathing. *Impossible.* Not even an angel could send forth a summons between Earth and Heaven. There was simply no way a Naphil, thousands of generations removed from her divinity, could achieve such a thing.

Could she?

He whirled. "Azrael, you're in charge here. Nothing gets past that border, understand? The rest of you, with me."

Raphael caught his arm, fingers almost as dark as the armor on which they rested. "Mika'el, what the Hell is going on?"

"Aramael is in trouble."

Instinctively, almost as one, every Archangel's hand went to the sword hanging at its owner's side. Including Raphael's. Whatever doubts they might have about the Aramael's appointment to their ranks, he was still one of them. Then Raphael's golden eyes narrowed.

"Wait. I thought he went to Earth. To the Naphil."

"He did," Mika'el said. "And I think she just summoned me."

"It's over, Alex."

The voice struck with physical force, each syllable a hammer blow against Alex's soul. Cowering, she held fast to Aramael's hands beneath the protection of his wings.

Hands still warm to her touch.

Still alive, but barely—and for how much longer?

Feathers shifted above her, and for an instant—a brief, cruel instant—her heart soared. It plummeted again when she saw Seth's fingers grip the limp wing and shove it aside. Aramael toppled sideways, resisting her attempts to hold him upright, landing with a soft grunt amid the rubble on the floor. His hands pulled away from hers and dropped to nestle against dull black feathers. The final loss of physical contact was more than she could bear.

She exhaled on a moan of denial, a harsh, monstrous sound that came from the very core of her being. The place where her soulmate resided. Aramael of the stormy gray eyes and bolt-of-lightning touch; Aramael, who had risked falling from Heaven itself for her; Aramael, who had stood by her and protected her life with his own even after she had chosen another over him.

Another, whose hand stretched down to her

now, waiting to pull her to her feet.

Fighting to control her breathing and unlock her throat, Alex stared at the outstretched appendage. Slowly, she looked up, following the arm to which the hand was attached; tracking along a shoulder and then a neck; settling on a face. Calm and expressionless, with no reflection of what its owner had just done. No acknowledgment. No remorse. Nothing.

"It's over," the voice repeated, the face's mouth moving with the words.

Rage obliterated all else. Knocking the hand away, she surged to her feet and shoved against Seth's chest. He didn't so much as sway.

"Fuck you!" she bellowed. She shoved again. Then a third time. And a fourth. Each with more fury, more despair, more impotence. The One had been right all along. Seth's choices were at the heart of all of this: Armageddon, the Nephilim babies, everything— and Alex had lost everything because of those choices. Her sister, her niece, Aramael—even the love she had once felt for Seth himself. All were gone from her world, and she could do nothing to bring them back. Nothing to stop what would come next, what hovered just beyond her ability to reason. Panic licked at the edges of her anger. She stopped shoving and started shaking, vibrating from head to toe.

The emptiness that had once been Seth—funny, wry, loving Seth—reached for her. He held her against his chest, his face buried in her hair, and heaved a deep sigh.

"There," he whispered. "Now you're free. There's nothing to stop you from being with me anymore."

"Don't," she choked back. "Please, Seth. Don't."

"Shh." His hands crawled over her, one tangling

in her hair, one stroking her back.

She pushed against him. His grip tightened. It began. A tiny, sharp tingle, sparking along the skin of her extremities, crackling with heat. She writhed against his hold.

"Damn it, Seth, *no!*"

He ignored her. The heat slithered beneath the surface and traveled along her nerves, her veins. Trickling at first, then increasing to a rush toward her center. Toward her chest. Her struggles increased tenfold. He paid no attention. The heat pooled, intensified—and turned to pure, liquid agony, as if her very heart were melting.

She tried to scream but had no voice.

Then, through the haze that descended, a hand. Strong. Clamping onto her shoulder. Pulling her back, flinging her away. Other hands catching her, pushing her to the floor. The rustle of many wings. And a voice. Michael's voice. Snarling, furious, agonized.

"In the name of all that is holy, Appointed, *what have you done?*"

EIGHTY-THREE

Mika'el grabbed a panting Seth by the shirtfront, threw him against the remains of a support pillar, and held him there. He shot a look over his shoulder at Uriel, who was bent over the prostrate Aramael. The other Archangel shrugged and shook his head.

Not dead yet, but nothing we can do, the gesture said.

Mika'el turned back to the creature he held. Fury and an overwhelming sense of failed responsibility rolled through him. Aramael had said something was wrong, and now he was dying because Mika'el hadn't believed him. Hadn't bothered to send someone with him. How in all of Creation had he let this happen? He seized Seth by the throat and slammed his head against the pillar.

"Damn you, Appointed! What in bloody *Hell* were you thinking? Aramael is the only one who stood by you. He helped you save his own soulmate, knowing she had already chosen you. Do you have any idea what that did to him? What it cost him? *This* is how you repay him?"

Seth's gaze met his—empty, awful, wrong. "He interfered," he said coldly. "He tried to protect her from me, but she's mine."

"Mika'el," said Raphael.

Mika'el ignored him, glowering at Seth. "He was right to protect her," he snarled. "She has free will. She doesn't belong to anyone. You know that."

"Mika'el."

"I saved her life, Archangel," Seth spat back. "Twice. My soul touched hers. Twice. A part of me resides inside her forever."

"That doesn't make her—"

"Mika'el."

He rounded on Raphael. "*What*?"

"He made her immortal."

The words hung in the air. Stark. Vast. Impossible. Raphael shifted his grip on his sword. No one else moved. Turning his head, Mika'el took in the wreckage that had once been an office. The fallen Aramael. The crumpled woman on the floor.

A dozen thoughts collided in his head, all clamoring for his attention. That Seth would dare to inflict immortality on a human was one thing, but that he *could* presented another problem altogether. When—and how—had he become so strong? He looked at the hand he had wrapped around the Appointed's throat.

And how long before Seth recovered from what he'd just done and became that strong again?

Triumph illuminated Seth's face, as if he knew exactly what the Archangel was thinking. "I told you," he said. "She's *mine*."

He seized Mika'el's wrist, tightening his fingers until bones ground together. Staring into the emptiness of his eyes, Mika'el shut out the pain, stilled his mind, and let clarity descend. Swiftly, surely, he sifted through to the core of what mattered. The only truth.

Seth should have died three weeks before.

He hadn't.

It was time to set things right.

Seth's windpipe rattled against Mika'el's fingers as the Appointed struggled to breathe. The bones in Mika'el's wrist began to splinter. He reached with his free hand for his sword, closed his fingers around the hilt, pulled the blade from its scabbard, stepped back, and swung.

Steel met steel in a shower of sparks.

"I think not, warrior," said a new voice. "He belongs to us now."

There was an indrawn hiss beside Mika'el, and then a guttural roar, starting low and building to a bellow that shook dust from the shattered ceiling.

"Sam-a-el!"

Mika'el threw out an arm in time to stop Raphael from impaling himself on the half dozen blades suddenly ranged against them. The other Archangel fought his hold, subsiding only after Mika'el's harsh "Stand down!"

Fallen Ones. But not just any Fallen Ones. Mika'el skimmed the lineup of faces, the hollowness of their eyes. He stared. Withered inside. Only one place could turn eyes that dead, that empty. They'd escaped from Limbo.

But there were only a dozen of them. Six with

swords leveled at their throats, six others behind those with weapons also drawn. Thousands had been trapped there. Where were the rest? His eyes settled on the one in the center. Samael.

So. The brother to Raphael and the only Archangel to follow Lucifer was now laying claim to the Appointed, was he?

Still holding Raphael back, Mika'el scowled. "Explain yourself, traitor."

Samael raised an eyebrow. "I thought it fairly self-explanatory. The Appointed isn't yours anymore. He's ours. Therefore, I object to having you impale him."

"You want Seth to lead Hell."

Samael shrugged. "I think the idea has merit, yes."

"No."

Samael's eyes hardened. "I don't think you understand, Mika'el. I'm not asking your permission."

"In that case, you seem to have forgotten who you're dealing with. There are four of us"—Mika'el indicated the Archangels flanking him—"and only a dozen of you. How long do you think a fight will even last?"

Samael smiled grimly. "Long enough," he said, and lunged forward.

EIGHTY-FOUR

Alex jolted back to consciousness with a gasp. She lay without moving for an instant, trying to get her bearings. Then, just in time, she rolled clear of the many booted feet trampling near her head. The clang of metal on metal reverberated, mixing with shouts and grunts of pain, coming from what seemed to be every side. Instinctively, she sought cover as her brain scrabbled for a frame of reference, trying to piece together where she was, what was happening. Cool softness pressed against her cheek. She put out a hand—then recoiled when her fingers found the long, limp curve of a wing.

Remembrance flooded back.

Aramael. *Dying.* Seth. *Murderer.* Michael. *Here.*

Horror churned together with agony and emerged in a harsh gag.

Aramael was dying.

A rough hand hauled her to her feet. She struck out blindly, viciously, her training and experience forgotten in a vortex of pure terror. Her black-armor-clad captor shook her.

"Knock it off, Naphil. I'm trying to help," the female Archangel growled. With no hint of effort, she hoisted Aramael's body upright with her other hand and towed both it and Alex unceremoniously through the fray. Surges of sparking blue power battered them, but the Archangel seemed oblivious, intent on her destination, shoving their heads down as a black wing, edged with razor-sharp feathers, whistled past.

By the time they reached the washroom corridor at the back of the office—the only area that had so far escaped devastation—Alex bled from a at least ten wing-inflicted wounds and felt as if she'd gone twice that many rounds in a fight ring. The Archangel thrust her into the ladies' room and dumped Aramael on the cold tile floor.

Alex dropped onto her knees beside him, one hand searching for a pulse at the side of his throat, the other trying again to stem the trickle of blood from his chest. The blade of a sword came between them.

"Take it," the Archangel said. "You might need it."

Alex recoiled from the blood-spattered blade. "What do I look like, a goddamn ninja?" She tugged her sidearm from its holster, ignoring how it trembled in her grip. "I have my own weapon."

"That"—the Archangel plucked the gun from her and tossed it aside—"will have about as much effect against one of us as a peashooter against an incoming comet."

She shoved the sword into Alex's hand and forcibly curled her fingers around it. "This is Aramael's blade. It needs to be wielded by an Archangel to kill, but it contains enough power on its own to hold off a Fallen One until we can get to you. Stay here. If anything other than one of us comes through that door"—she pointed—"swing first. Then scream. Clear?"

Alex stared at the broadsword in her hand, its steel glinting dully. *Aramael's blade, because Aramael can't use it himself.* She tried to release it, but the Archangel's grip was unyielding. A shriek of agony rose above the clashes and clangs of battle, then cut off abruptly. The Archangel seized Alex's chin and forced it up. Sapphire blue eyes glared at her.

"Take it," she snarled. "Aramael protected you with his life. You owe him nothing less."

Alex shrank from the words. Another hand, warm and familiar, closed over her fingers. Aramael, alive and awake.

"Do as Gabriel says," he whispered. "Take the sword."

Meeting his pain-clouded gaze, Alex swallowed, nodded. She let her fingers curl over the hilt. Seeming satisfied, her rescuer whirled in a metallic whisper of feathers and, her own sword in hand, leapt for the door. The clashes and clangs of battle grew louder and then muted again as the door swung closed on its hydraulic hinge. Alex stared down at the figure on the floor, nested against his own black wings, deathly pale and unmoving. His eyes—his magnificent, fierce, stormy gray eyes—closed once more.

Grief clawed at her chest, fighting for release. She clamped her teeth against it. With her free hand, she brushed back the hair from his forehead.

Don't you dare lose it, Jarvis. Aramael didn't save your life so you could play wilting violet. You're going to get out of here—Michael and the others will make sure of it—and Aramael will live, and then you're going to find Nina . . .

Find her and hold her and watch her die.

God.

Clang. Crash. Scream.

Christ.

The cut on her arm gave a twinge, and she glanced down. The other cuts she'd sustained had been superficial, but that one had looked—

Gone?

The air wheezed from her lungs. She took her hand from Aramael's forehead and swiped at the drying blood. Licked her fingers. Scrubbed harder. Stared. Not so much as a scar remained. Aramael hadn't saved her after all. Seth had done it anyway. He'd made her immortal. She couldn't die. She was going to live forever.

Horror swirled in her chest, slammed into her belly, rose again in her gorge.

Still clutching the sword, she lunged toward a sink.

EIGHTY-FIVE

Alex braced one hand against the smooth porcelain sink and used the other to carry cold water to her face, her throat, the nape of her neck. Nausea still churned, but the retching had finally stopped—although that could simply have been because there was nothing left to purge. She eyed her wan, dripping reflection. While the physical shaking had also ended, her insides continued to vibrate at a pitch that would have shattered her if she'd been made of crystal.

She looked at the forearm supporting her. She hadn't been able to bring herself to wash the blood from it—or from any of the other injury sites. It was as if, on some visceral level, she needed to retain evidence of her wounds. The only evidence she had of what she'd become. What Seth had made her. Her mind veered away from the idea, and she splashed another handful of water over her neck. Beyond the washroom door, the sounds of sword fighting continued.

Swords. With all the power these beings possessed, who would have imagined they'd resort to swords for battle? She looked at the blade she had propped against the wall by the sink. Simple, unadorned, crafted for nothing more than service. She turned off the tap and tore a length of rough brown paper towel from the dispenser to dry herself. Tossing the paper into the garbage, she turned to check on Aramael.

Outside and across the hall, a door thudded shut.

She stared at the washroom door just a few feet away. Was the fight over? No—she could still hear the clang of metal on metal. Then who—

The door cracked open, and Seth stepped inside. Hysteria bubbled up in her chest as he stared at the prone Aramael. She shoved it ruthlessly back down, swallowing against it. Seth looked up and smiled at her.

"There you are," he said. "I thought they might have taken you away."

His matter-of-factness hit her like a shock of ice water, erasing the vestiges of panic, replacing it with a vast, disorienting disbelief. After all he'd done, he behaved as if none of it had happened at all. As if none of it mattered. Was he really that unfeeling? Had she made that monumental a mistake in saving him from Michael and the others in Vancouver?

She shifted to block the sword from his view. "What do you want?"

He raised an eyebrow. "A little gratitude for the gift, to begin with."

"*Gift*?" She choked out a laugh. "I've lost everything I ever loved, everything I ever cared for, and now I get to live forever? How in hell is that a *gift*?"

"You haven't lost everything, only the distractions." He put out a hand to brush the hair from her face. "You still have me, remember? It's what we always wanted."

Another blast of ice water. He thought—he'd convinced himself—oh, dear God. She breathed carefully around the knot unraveling in her chest. Forced her hands to remain at her sides and not strike out at him while she worked through her realization and its terrifying consequences.

A stalker. Seth Benjamin, son of the One and Lucifer, bearer of immeasurable power, had become nothing more than a classic, delusional stalker—on a cosmic scale. Even now he was convinced she wanted to be with him for eternity. He had arranged for exactly that. Horror bubbled up in her again, this time on a whole new level, a whole new scale.

Seth's arms slid around her.

I'll never escape.

He buried his face in her neck . . .

I can't escape.

. . . murmured her name . . .

Not even through death.

. . . whispered, "I love you, Alex Jarvis. Forever."

"Leave...her...alone," grated a hoarse voice.

Aramael. For an instant, sheer, wanton relief surged in Alex's breast. He was conscious. He could hold off Seth until the others arrived. But then Seth went still—terrifyingly so—and euphoria turned to panic. Dread.

Aramael could never survive another fight. Not wounded as he was. Seth would kill him this time, finish what he had begun. Pain squeezed through Alex's chest. No. She wouldn't let him. She put her hands up to Seth's face, forced herself to hold it. To hold his attention. To lie.

"I love you, too," she croaked.

Sudden joy flared in Seth's black eyes, and he cupped her face gently, reverently. Locking her gaze on his, she tried to project the adoration he craved from her and not let him see the desperation crawling along her every fiber, turning her inside out.

Oh please oh please oh please don't do anything more to him.

"I said *leave* her!" Aramael snarled.

Seth's jaw went rigid beneath her touch. She tightened her hold, clinging to him, clinging to hope, searching for the right thing to say. If she could make him believe her, if she could keep him focused—

His fingers wrapped around her wrists. He pulled her hands from his face and pushed her away. Blue crackles snapped in the air around him. He turned. Over his shoulder, Alex saw Aramael standing tall and straight, his wings spread as wide as the tight space would allow. She caught her breath. He looked so capable, so confident. Had he recovered? Was he—

A fresh trickle of phosphorescence welled from the hole in Aramael's armor. His glorious, powerful wings trembled ever so slightly. Hope morphed into despair and sent cruel tentacles to wrap around her soul. She grabbed for Seth's arm, but he shook her off, forcing her back a step. Stumbling, she put a hand out to steady herself against the counter. Her fingers closed over the hilt of Aramael's sword.

"*Take it,*" the Archangel Gabriel's voice whispered through her.

"Again, Archangel?" Seth snarled at Aramael. "How many times do I have to kill you?"

"How many times does Alex have to say no?" Aramael countered. "I won't let you take her."

Alex lifted the heavy, hardened steel blade. Gabriel had said it would slow down a Fallen One, but that's not what Seth was. He wasn't an angel at all but something other. Something more. What if it didn't work against him?

The blue crackles came together, weaving themselves into a wall before Seth. "Then you'll die," he told Aramael. "Again."

Over Seth's shoulder, Alex met her soulmate's calm certainty. Aramael's mouth curved upward in the slightest of smiles. He knew what she considered. Nodded his approval. Blinked his good-bye. He turned his attention back to Seth.

"So be it," he said.

Alex stretched a hand toward him. *No. Oh, God, no . . .*

Aramael threw his wings and arms wide. Hardened feathers splintered the wall tiles and tore through a metal stall door with a screech, then swept toward Seth. Power struck crackling energy with a force that gusted outward, shattering mirrors, sinks, toilets. And then Alex swung the sword with all the strength she possessed, down in an arc toward Seth.

"You owe him," whispered the memory of Gabriel's voice.

The blade sliced through the flesh between Seth's ribs and hip. An unearthly bellow ripped through the washroom. The clash of divine energies exploded into a blaze of white.

Aramael dropped like a stone.

EIGHTY-SIX

Mika'el's blade sliced through collarbone as if it were butter, cleaving all the way down to the center of the Fallen One's chest and shattering the hardened sphere of immortality hidden within. He tugged the sword free with grim satisfaction. The third kill in a fight only fifteen minutes old. Samael truly had forgotten the power with which he dealt.

A hand settled on his shoulder, and he looked into Gabriel's piercing, deep blue eyes. Impeccably trained, the others closed around them in a protective ring, blocking them from harm while they spoke.

"The woman is safe?" he asked.

She nodded. "But we have another problem. A Guardian is seeking our help. A Fallen One is wreaking havoc in a crowded gathering place not far from here—a mall, he called it."

"All right. We can take care of those remaining here. You go—and Gabriel, fly there. Use your physical approach to draw him out and away from the mortals."

"I'll be seen."

Thou shalt not interfere with the human race.

His grim gaze swept over the wreckage surrounding them. The cardinal rule might have had its place once, but no longer. Not after this. "I'm pretty sure our secret is out."

Gabriel nodded, turned, and launched herself through what little remained of the exterior wall. Mika'el turned back to the fight, but before he could choose a target, a small hand tugged on his sleeve. He glanced down at the ethereal, almost translucent figure of a Guardian, its fierce look of concentration a measure of the effort it took to achieve even this much physical form.

"It's all right," he told it. "Gabriel has gone to the mall. She'll look after the Fallen One there."

"But I haven't come from a mall," the Guardian objected as he turned away. "There is a museum a short distance from here. Two Fallen Ones have attacked the patrons there."

A second attack? Hell. Mika'el caught Zachariel's eye and the Archangel raised an eyebrow. Mika'el nodded. Stepping back from the battle, Zachariel launched himself in Gabriel's wake. The wisp of a Guardian followed.

Mika'el raised his sword. Two Archangels remained, along with nine Fallen. The odds were still firmly in their—

"Mika'el!" Raphael's voice pulled his attention away from the battle yet again.

Mika'el looked toward him, then followed the tip of the other's head. Another Guardian had shimmered into form along the wall, and two more were taking shape on either side of her.. In an instant, Mika'el understood.

"Stop!" he roared.

Silence dropped over the assembly, broken only by the harsh breathing of winded fighters. And Samael's chuckle.

"You've figured it out."

"How many?" Mika'el demanded. "How many have you sent out?"

"As many as I needed to. One more activates every three minutes until I say otherwise."

"Call them off."

"Not until I have what I came for."

"I can get more help," Mika'el said. "Heaven still outnumbers you."

"You can," Samael agreed. "It wouldn't bother me in the least to fight the entire war right here on Earth. But are you sure that's what you want?"

Mika'el bit back what he would have liked to reply and growled again, "Call them off. We'll talk."

"We have nothing to talk about, warrior. I'll call off my soldiers when I have Seth safely away from here. Not a minute before."

Impotent fury snarled through Mika'el. He'd been outmaneuvered, and every soul in this room knew it. Viciously he sheathed his sword and motioned for a reluctant Raphael to do the same.

"Fine," he growled. "Go. Take your new leader and—" Breaking off, he spun on his heel, his gaze raking the destruction around them. He swung back to a calm Samael. Too calm to have lost what he'd come for. "Where is he?"

"Claiming what's his, I should imagine."

Claiming—the woman.

Before Mika'el could move, Samael's sword came up, blocking his way.

The traitorous former Archangel *tsked.* "I wouldn't," he said. "The next Fallen releases in two minutes."

Fists clenched, Mika'el glared at the angel who had once fought at his side. Naphil or not, the woman deserved better than this, and yet he could not go to her. Could do nothing to save her. Not without unleashing Armageddon itself, here and now.

Samael smiled, smugly, unpleasantly, arrogantly. He lowered his sword and sheathed it. "I knew I could count on your sense of honor, Mika'el. It has always been your greatest weakness. One day it will be your undoing."

"And arrogance yours," Mika'el retorted. "Now collect your prize and—"

A bellow cut him off, filled with rage and a deep, gut-wrenching anguish.

Without a word, Samael bolted for the back of the office where Gabriel had stowed the Naphil. Mika'el followed.

EIGHTY-SEVEN

Bloodied sword still in hand, Alex stared down at the two figures lying amid the wreckage. Water from the broken toilets swirled across the floor, running crimson where it mixed with blood, trickling into the emergency floor drain with a hollow musicality. Seth writhed in agony; Aramael lay motionless. Shattered glass and porcelain littered the room.

From beyond the washroom, she heard the sound of footsteps running, then the door burst open. A Fallen One skidded to a halt in the opening, his gaze going first to the bodies on the floor, then to Alex. Jaw hanging open, he struggled visibly to piece events together.

He staggered aside as Michael shoved past him into the washroom. Seth's convulsions slowed, and he groaned, a low, agonized sound that twisted inside Alex's belly. She backed away until she came up against the wall. Gripped the sword tighter, needing to hold onto something concrete, something real.

Something to connect her to the soulmate she knew without doubt she had just lost. The agony of grief squeezed inside her chest until she gasped.

Michael's gaze burned into her. "What happened?"

"I—he—" Alex closed her mouth, gritted her teeth, and shut herself off from the part of her mind that wailed its anguish. She'd been here before, in this place of loss. She'd handled it then—a mere child of nine—and she would deal with it now. She raised her chin and met the emerald blaze of Michael's eyes. "He wanted me to be with him. Forever. Aramael tried to stop him, but he wasn't strong enough. I had no choice."

Michael scowled. "*You* did this?"

Suddenly the sword felt wrong in her grip. Awful. Murderous. She tried to hold it out for Michael to take, but her arm refused to lift it. She opened her hand and let it fall. It landed with a thud deadened by the water covering the floor. Seth groaned again, and she looked down at him, at the gaping wound in his side where the sword had bitten so much deeper than she'd expected it to, at the blood pooling beneath him. Despite herself, she felt a twinge of something akin to regret.

Choices have consequences, the One had told her. She'd spoken of Seth's choices, but how much of this could Alex have prevented if she herself had made other choices? How much of it would have ended differently? With Seth in Heaven where he belonged, and Aramael still alive . . .

Michael stared at her for another second and then turned to the Fallen One. "Take him," he said harshly. "And call off your dogs."

"I'll take him, all right," the Fallen One snarled, "but I'll be damned if I call off my dogs, as you put it. Not after this."

Before Alex could blink, Michael's sword clashed with that of the Fallen One.

"Yes," he growled back. "You will. We both have better things to do than engage in a pissing contest right now, Samael. You can't lead Hell into battle without a leader any more than I want that battle to take place here, so put your goddamn tail between your legs, be glad you have him at all, and go back to where you belong."

The two of them stood locked in silent, unmoving combat until the Fallen One finally blinked and Michael stepped back. With a last, vicious snarl, the Fallen One sheathed his sword again. Then he stooped, hoisted the semiconscious Seth to his shoulder, and vanished. Alex slid down the wall to the floor. Her hands limp in her lap and water seeping into her clothing, she stared at Aramael's body until a pair of black boots blocked her sight line.

"I have to go. I need to make sure Samael recalls his Fallen. Your rescue people are on their way up."

She said nothing.

"We'll talk," he said. "But later. When you're stronger."

He lifted Aramael's body into his arms. Black wings, dulled by death, dragged through the bloody water pooled on the floor. The arm not supported by Michael's body hung limp. Vacant gray eyes stared back at her, devoid of all that had been divine, all that had been alive, all that had been Aramael.

Heat burned behind her eyes. Raw pain sliced

down her throat, making her voice harsh. "Michael."

Heaven's greatest warrior stopped in the doorway with his burden and waited.

"I'm sorry." She looked away, swallowing against her loss. "For everything."

"We'll talk." he said. "Soon."

EIGHTY-EIGHT

Mika'el strode down the short corridor, the slain Aramael heavy in his arms, grief heavier in his heart. They had lost so much today. Too much. Stepping into the former office, he found the remainder of the Fallen had left. Raphael stood watch at what had once been the windows, waiting for him. He turned at Mika'el's approach. Mika'el shook his head at his unspoken question.

A shadow darkened the other Archangel's expression. He sheathed his sword and stepped forward, indicating Aramael. "Let me," he said.

Mika'el raised an eyebrow. They'd only ever lost one Archangel to death before and so there wasn't much in the way of precedent, but still, as the choir's leader, it was up to him to carry their dead.

Bleak golden eyes met his. "I told him he wasn't one of us." Raphael's voice was rough. "I owe him this much."

Without comment, Mika'el handed over the

body. There would be no burial on their return to Heaven, no ceremony. When Raphael moved between the realms, the energy that lingered, forming Aramael's corporeal body here on Earth, would dissipate. Aramael would disappear, Raphael would cross over alone, and there would once again be an empty seat at the Archangels' table.

"What about Seth?" Raphael asked.

"Gone."

"So Aramael was right. Hell is getting a new ruler." Raphael shifted his burden. "And we're down not just a ruler but another Archangel, too. Samael's screwed us over again."

"Not everything went the way he'd planned. The woman wounded the Appointed."

Raphael's golden eyes narrowed.

"The Naphil? With what?"

"Aramael's sword."

"That's not possible."

"Neither is summoning me across two realms."

"What the Hell is going on with her?"

"I'm not sure. Her Nephilim blood, the soulmate connection to Aramael, being brought back from the verge of death—or a little past it—twice by Seth." Mika'el rolled his shoulders wearily. "A combination of everything, perhaps. Go. Take Aramael. Tell Azrael what has happened. I'll clean up here and foll—"

A dozen heavily armed mortals poured through the shattered office door and brought weapons to bear on them. Shouted instructions followed, all muddled together and ringing with fear and tension.

"On your knees! Now!"

"You holding the guy—put him down!"

"Hold your hands away from you where I can see them!"

And on it went.

Mika'el closed his eyes. He and Raphael had to leave: Raphael to transport Aramael's body; Mika'el to locate the remaining Archangels and deal with the Fallen. They didn't have time for this—or to oversee another memory-wipe by the Guardians.

The mortal shouts continued.

Mika'el saw the question in Raphael's eyes and knew the other agreed. They had only one way out of this, but while it might be too late to pretend Heaven had any secrets remaining, it was still damned difficult to flaunt themselves.

Difficult but, at this point, necessary. He nodded. Standing tall and straight despite his burden, Raphael instantly unfurled his massive black wings to their fullest and shot upward—

Into nothingness.

A slow, collective lowering of weapons and stunned silence followed, broken by a murmured and heartfelt, "Holy Mother of God."

Mika'el studied them, one by one. He had spent six millennia on Earth, long enough to know humans better than any other angel did. Long enough that, though he could not save them, his heart ached at knowing what they faced. Their lives would never be the same after today. Not ever.

"Your colleague is in the washroom," he told them. "She's unharmed."

And then, opening his own wings, he followed the other warrior.

EIGHTY-NINE

Alex sat on the narrow platform at the rear of a paramedic bus, apart from the hive of activity even in the midst of it. Yellow wooden barricades held back a throng of onlookers. A group of officials stood off to one side in earnest discussion. Dozens of emergency personnel moved from one place to another, tending the wounded, checking the building, their feet crunching through piles of tempered-glass pebbles from dozens of disintegrated windows.

Her colleagues were clustered together, as far from her as the emergency vehicles and barricades would allow.

Cold from the hard steel seeped into her.

She burrowed deeper into the blanket's folds. Her eyes burned from holding them open too long, hardly daring to blink, because every time she did, she saw it again. Aramael sprawled amid the black feathers of his wings. Dead. For her. Because of her. The image burned nto her brain for eternity, because that's how long she would live without him. With this loss and all the others to follow.

Forever and ever, amen.

Hell.

The platform beneath her gave a little, and a second blanket settled around her shoulders. She looked over to find Joly at her side, Abrams and Bastion standing beside him. Bastion held out a paper cup, steam curling up from the hole in its plastic lid.

"Probably not what you could use right now," he said gruffly, "but it's warm."

Her *thank you* wouldn't emerge, but she accepted the cup and managed a nod. Bastion reached across Joly to pat her shoulder. The three of them joined her in staring at the scene.

"The others?" she asked after a while.

Joly cleared his throat. "They'll come around. You're one of us, Jarvis. We watch out for our own."

Except maybe she wasn't one of theirs anymore. Not after what Seth had done.

"Those things that came out of the window up there," said Abrams. "The ones with the . . ."

"Wings," she supplied, when it was apparent he wouldn't—couldn't—finish.

"Yeah. Those. They looked like . . ."

"Angels."

His skin tone took on the same gray as the November afternoon. He exchanged looks with Joly and Bastion—or tried to, but they were wholly focused on the pavement at their feet. "That's insane," he muttered.

She neither confirmed nor denied the conclusion.

After a moment, he scuffed at the street. "Jesus Christ Almighty."

There seemed no point in contradicting him on that. More silence ensued, and then a new set of legs entered her field of vision. She looked up at Roberts. Someone had loaned him a firefighter's coat, but despite the day's chill, he hadn't closed it to hide the dark brown streak of dried blood marring the shirt and tie beneath. Seth's blood, acquired when Roberts had enveloped her in a wordless hug on the washroom floor.

He stared pointedly at her companions.

"Give us a minute?"

With more awkward pats on her shoulder, Joly, Abrams, and Bastion wandered back to join the others. Alex felt her supervisor studying her.

"You all right?" he asked.

Damn. Was she going to tear up every time someone asked her that? She nodded and tugged the blankets closer.

"There's an awful lot of blood on you for someone who has no injuries, Alex."

Hers, Aramael's, Seth's. But they'd found only her at the scene.

"You want to talk about what happened?"

"Nope."

Roberts sighed. "I'm going to have someone take you home. Is there any chance Trent . . . ?"

Her tears overflowed, sending hot trickles down her cheeks. Clamping her lips together, she shook her head. Quickly, fiercely. Roberts's hand settled onto her shoulder and squeezed.

"I'll get Joly to drive you, and I'll have Dr. Riley meet you there. No argument."

The latter as her head snapped up in objection.

Her supervisor shook his head, compassion and

concern clouding his eyes. "There is no goddamn way I'm leaving you alone, Jarvis. Not tonight. Which reminds me—" He held out his hand. "I need your service weapon."

She stared at his open palm. It was on the tip of her tongue to tell him he didn't have to worry, that even if she did eat her gun, it wouldn't kill her.

That nothing could.

Not anymore.

Instead, she reached to her hip, unholstered the weapon she'd retrieved from the washroom floor, and held it out to him. "I wouldn't, you know."

Roberts pocketed the gun without comment and turned to go.

"Staff."

He looked back.

"Not Joly," she said. "Make it a uniform."

Someone I don't know. Someone I don't have to talk to.

He regarded her for a moment, then nodded. "I'll let you know where our new quarters are," he said. "Take a few days off, then—"

"Monday," she said. "I'll see you Monday."

ALEX LET HERSELF INTO the apartment and dropped the keys on the table. She didn't lock the door—partly because she knew Riley was coming, and partly because she didn't care. Because it didn't matter.

She turned to stare at the home she had shared with Seth. The hallway stretched before her, empty and accusatory, still resonant with the anger from the last time they'd stood in it together. She flinched, reliving again the slam of the door as he'd left. Her breath stabbed beneath her ribs. So much accusation and betrayal—so many dead because of it.

How in hell could she have been so wrong?

She leaned against the wall. A thousand little details crowded in on her. A thousand misgivings that she'd ignored, dismissed, convinced herself weren't real or important. She'd been so determined to love him, so set on saving him as he had twice saved her, and now . . .

Now she'd lost it all, everything that ever mattered to her, and because of Seth's *gift* to her, she would live forever with those losses. Jen, Nina, Aramael.

Her legs slowly buckled beneath her. Beneath a past, a present, and a future that had become too heavy to bear. She slid down the wall until the floor prevented her from sinking any farther. Wrapped arms around knees. Held on tight as the first tear fell. A second followed, then a third—and then the dam inside her gave way to an anguish that enveloped her, sucked her under, closed over her soul.

From a long way off came the sound of knocking and Elizabeth Riley's voice calling her name. A part of her tried to respond, but the rest of her wouldn't cooperate. Couldn't through the spasms racking her body. Then a door opened, footsteps approached, and gentle hands lifted her chin. Soothing murmurs washed over her, then something sharp jabbed into her arm.

Too late, Alex tried to pull back, to reassure Riley that she was okay. Still sane. Wasn't she?

She slid beneath the surface.

NINETY

Alex stared at the pale light creeping around the edges of the window blind. Outside, a truck rumbled by, a distant siren wailed, a plane droned overhead, a car alarm shrieked a summons to which no one paid attention. The sounds of a city stirring to life on a Sunday morning.

Inside, the rhythmic inhale and exhale of her own breathing, the faint tick of the clock in the living room. The sounds of an empty apartment bereft of all life but hers. No Seth. No Jen. No Nina. Everyone important to her, everyone she had ever cared about . . . taken. And the one soul who might have heeded her call for help?

Also gone.

She turned her mind inward, found her center, whispered his name. *Aramael.* But her soulmate didn't hear her. Didn't come to her. Never would again.

Curling into a ball, she bunched the covers beneath her chin and waited for tears. They didn't come either. She closed her eyes. Without hysterics to distract herself, it was time to focus on the realities. Realities such as the three weeks Nina had before she would die giving birth to Lucifer's Naphil bastard. The same length of time Alex would have to find her so she didn't die alone. *Fuck.*

Alex bit down on a scream of pure fury. Tempting as it was to give voice to the frustration building inside her, it would not help to have the neighbors calling 911 on her behalf. She tossed back the covers and swung her legs out of bed. On the bedside table, her cell phone rang. She reached for it, thumbed the answer button, and put it to her ear.

"Jarvis," she croaked. Lord, was that *her*?

"You sound like you've had a rough couple of days or something," Henderson said.

At the sound of his voice, the tears she hadn't been able to find a moment before flooded her eyes. She blinked them back furiously, shrugging a shrug he couldn't see, and cleared her throat. "Nah. Same old, same old. Nothing exciting ever happens around here, I swear."

Her Vancouver colleague gave a soft snort. "You are so full of shit, my friend. How are you?"

Remembering his aversion to her usual *fine*, she hazarded, "Alive?"

"I'd rather you said that with a little more conviction."

"And I'd rather I felt it with a little more conviction."

The reply earned her a chuckle. She smiled a little in return and blinked away the rest of the tears. It was good to hear a friendly voice. "Seriously, Hugh, I'm okay."

"Want to fill me in?"

"How much do you know?" She lay back against the pillow and tucked her feet under the duvet.

"I've seen the news footage from Parliament Hill, Riley filled me in on your sister and your niece, and I know that Seth came after you. You can go from there."

"Seth took back his powers. Turned out it wasn't such a good thing for us after all. Or for me. He wanted company in his new abode. Ara—" She choked on the name and tried again, her voice husky, "Aramael tried to stop him."

Henderson was quiet. "Tried?" he asked at last.

She squeezed her eyes closed. Put her forearm across them. Curled her hand into a fist so tight that her fingernails bit into the palm. "He's gone."

"Ah, hell. Alex, I'm so sorry."

She had to work to find her voice. "Yeah. Me, too."

"So how—?"

"Michael. He and the other Archangels—" She broke off. Opening her eyes, she peered at the sleeve of her pajamas—wait, how did she get into her pajamas? She mentally shoved aside the distraction and scowled. How had Michael known that Aramael needed help? That she . . .

"*Call,*" Aramael's voice whispered in her memory. "*Call Mika'el.*"

She scrambled into a sitting position. Stared at herself in the full-length mirror hanging on the opposite wall. Holy hell. She'd called Heaven's greatest warrior. And he'd heard her. Was that even possible?

"Jarvis? You there?" Henderson asked.

The bedroom door opened to her left.

Instinctively, she cowered, the events of the day before still alive and well in her memory. Elizabeth Riley held up both hands in a gesture meant to calm and reassure. Because it was Riley, it didn't have the desired effect.

"I'm here," she told Henderson. Her heart hammering, she swung her legs out of bed for a second time. "And apparently so is Riley. Can I call you back in a while?"

"Ten minutes. You can call me back in ten minutes, or I'm getting on a plane and coming out there myself."

She didn't bother pointing out that the flight would take him the better part of the day. "Ten minutes," she agreed.

Dropping the phone onto the covers beside her, she met Riley's bright blue, too observant gaze. At least the psychiatrist's presence explained the pajamas. Alex shoved aside the usual prickle of antagonism and mustered a smile.

"You didn't have to stay the night."

Riley shrugged. "I promised your supervisor I would. Did you sleep all right? I only gave you a mild sedative. I wasn't sure it would be enough."

"It was," Alex assured her.

"Good. I've made coffee if you're interested."

"Very."

The psychiatrist disappeared from the doorway, presumably headed for the kitchen. Alex frowned. That was it? No other questions? No probing her psyche to ascertain her level of sanity after yesterday? She scooped up the cell phone and padded after Riley. If the promise of coffee hadn't been enough of a draw to get her out of bed, curiosity would have been.

NINETY-ONE

Riley turned from the counter as Alex entered, handed her a mug, and watched in silence as she added cream and sugar. Alex lifted an eyebrow.

"None for you?"

"I prefer tea. I couldn't find any, so I'll get some at the hospital."

The sip of coffee Alex had taken turned tasteless. She forced it down just to get rid of it. The hospital. Jen. She stared into her cup at the brown-paper-bag colored liquid.

"Is there any change?"

"They've removed the restraints, but other than that, no. I'm sorry. She's moving up to the psych ward this morning. I'm going to stop in and check on her, then I have a meeting with your chief and Dr. Bell before I catch my flight back to Vancouver."

Alex set her mug on the counter, wondering what Riley would think if she poured herself a Scotch instead. She studied the petite woman. Which of those topics did she want to take on first: hospital, meeting, or flight out? Riley forestalled her.

"You don't need me here, Alex. After what's happened in the last few days, the very fact that you're upright and not curled into a ball in the corner proves it. I plan to tell your chief exactly that—and I'll probably tell your department shrink to go screw himself."

Alex's jaw dropped. "You—I—that's it? No questions, no trying to get me to talk?"

"Do you want to talk?"

"Not particularly."

"I wouldn't either, if I were you," Riley said. "So. I guess that's it, then. I'll make sure the hospital has your contact information. They'll notify you of any change in your sister's condition, so unless you hear from them . . ."

Alex set her mug on the counter with an unsteady hand, finishing Riley's sentence in her head. Unless she heard from the hospital, she didn't need to go to the place that had housed her mother on so many occasions—the place that had now claimed her sister. She folded her arms across her belly.

"Thank you."

"Will you return to work?"

She nodded. "That and look for Nina."

Riley hesitated. "Part of me would like to ask what's coming," she said. "What we should expect. The rest of me thinks I'm better off not knowing."

"I couldn't tell you if you did want to know, because I have no idea."

"None?"

"Apart from a feeling that the rest of you is right? None."

Riley nodded. "In that case, I should go. I've left my card on the hall table for you in case you change your mind about talking. My cell phone number is on the back so you can call anytime. And if you don't call me, at least stay in touch with Hugh and let him know how you're doing. Please."

Alex gave a soft laugh. "I don't imagine he'll give me much choice."

"Good point."

Then, before Alex realized her intent, the psychiatrist wrapped her in a quick, hard hug. "Look after yourself, Alex," she whispered. "Stay strong."

Stay sane.

She'd reached the door at the end of the hallway before Alex found her voice.

"Elizabeth."

Riley looked over her shoulder.

"Tell Bell I said ditto."

A smile. "I'll do that."

The door closed, the click of its latch near deafening in the silence left behind. Alex stood for long minutes without moving. The emptiness of the apartment closed in on her. Pressed down. Squeezed the air from her lungs, the life from her heart.

She looked around the kitchen, at the bananas on the counter that were Seth's favorite fruit, at the dish of chocolate-covered almonds that he'd bought for her , at the dishwasher needing to be emptied of the dishes from the last meal he had made for them. The meal she hadn't come home for because he'd been right. She *had* been torn between him and Aramael, and work had been an excuse—a way to keep her distance. And now . . .

Now this was it. This was all she had left. An

apartment filled with memories and a life that would let her remember for eternity.

She dumped the coffee into the sink and reached for the Scotch.

NINETY-TWO

"The Fallen are gathering."

Mika'el looked around at Gabriel, who stood in the doorway of his private quarters. He went back to adjusting the scabbard at his side. So. The time for war was come at last. He had never doubted it would, but oh, how he had wished he might have been wrong.

"Did you hear me?" she asked.

"I heard." He picked up his sword and slid it into its sheath. "The others are at the border with our forces?"

"Waiting for the first strike."

"And the Guardians?"

"Recalled as ordered, except for the patrols. Still no word on where the Nephilim have been hidden."

"Then we're ready."

Gabriel said nothing. Mika'el watched her tight-lipped reflection in the mirror. He knew what she was thinking. It was the same thing they all thought, that in truth, they had no idea if they were ready. If they could be. Heaven's forces had always been driven by the will of the One. Without her—

Without her, they had no idea what to expect. What they could do.

What they couldn't do.

He picked up a second sword from the table beside him and slid it into a second, smaller scabbard. His fingers closed over it tightly. He turned, donning the familiar persona of military leader as he faced the other Archangel.

"You know what to do, then," he said. "I'll join you shortly."

Gabriel's sapphire gaze settled on the sword in his grasp, then rose to meet his again, clear, calm, determined. She nodded her understanding.

"I'll tell the others," she said.

ALEX CLIMBED the stairs from the parkade toward Homicide's temporary new quarters on the ninth floor. A uniformed officer getting into his cruiser had assured her the elevator was working again after the terrorist attack—was that really what they were telling people?—but she'd taken the stairs anyway. It was quieter here. She could pace herself, steady her nerves, give herself time to plan how she would handle the questions, the concern . . .

The search for Nina.

Gripping the handrail, she paused and closed her eyes, listening to the sound of her own breathing, the beat of her heart. Roberts had called the night before to check on her and give her the option of taking another day or two off. She'd turned him down. It was best to throw herself back into the fray where she wouldn't have too much time to think. Or too much time alone with a bottle of Scotch.

She began her climb again, turned a corner on a landing. Only four flights left. Four flights to get her focus together and pretend she could do this. Pretend she could—

A sudden shadow loomed over her.

Instinct drove her sideways into the protection of the corner.

"It's me," said a familiar voice.

She remained where she was, her hands braced on her knees, waiting for her heart rate to return to normal. Wondering if her nerves would ever do the same. She glared at the black-winged, black-armored Michael.

"You scared me half to death!" she snapped.

"I'm sorry, but I promised we would talk."

"I don't want to talk."

"We have to. There are things—"

"Can you stop the Nephilim?" she interrupted.

"No."

"Help me find Nina?"

"No.

"Undo what Seth did to me?" she asked.

He sighed. "No."

"Then we have nothing to talk about."

She moved to go around him, but Michael's wings opened, blocking her route. She stared at the glossy feathers, near enough to see the barbs along each of them, and then stepped back. Crossing her arms, she waited in tight-lipped silence.

"Lucifer is gone," he said.

"So what? In case you hadn't noticed, the damage is already done. Eighty thousand women are dead, the babies they carried have disappeared, and he impregnated my niece." Her voice wobbled on the last bit. She lifted her chin to continue. "Whether he's here or not doesn't matter anymore because he already accomplished everything he set out to do."

"The One is gone, too."

"Again," she said harshly, "so what?"

Pure fury flared in the emerald gaze holding hers. For a moment, she quailed. Then she stood taller. Grew angrier.

"Damn it, look around you, Michael. Look at the mess we're in—at the mess she left us in. Seth has stepped into his father's shoes, you're at war with Hell, Aramael is dead, and I'm going to live for goddamn forever. Where, in all of that, is my reason to care about the being who's responsible?"

"The fault wasn't only hers. We all made mistakes."

"Yes, and now the world gets to live with those mistakes. I get to live with them."

For a long moment, Michael said nothing. Then he held something out to her that she hadn't noticed him holding. "It was Aramael's," he said. "I had the armory make it over for you so it would be easier for you to handle."

Alex stared at the sword in its hardened leather scabbard. Remembered the feel of it slicing through Seth's flesh, biting into his bone. Crimson washed across her vision. She blinked it away.

"I don't want it."

"He would have wanted—"

"I said I don't want it." She raised weary eyes to his. "I don't want anything of his, or yours, or any other part of Heaven, Michael. I'm done. I don't want to see you again. I don't want to know what is happening in your world or with the fight between you and Hell. I don't want anything to do with any of you."

He continued to hold out the weapon. "If the Fallen come after you, it could save your life."

"You assume I want it saved," she said quietly. Pushing past the sword, past him, past his wings, she resumed her climb up the stairs.

Michael's voice followed as she reached the top of the flight and turned another corner. "Free will is a messy thing, Alex. For what it's worth, I'm sorry."

Not until she stood on the ninth floor landing did it register that, for only the second time ever, he had called her *Alex* and not *Naphil*. She hesitated then, and despite her better judgment, looked down over the railing to where she had left him four floors below.

The stairwell was empty.

Heaven's greatest warrior was gone.

Alex pulled open the door and stepped into Homicide.

It was time to find Nina.

LINDA POITEVIN is a writer possessed of both a light side and a dark one. On the dark side, she's the author of the Grigori Legacy, an urban fantasy series featuring a hard-as-nails cop caught up in the war between Heaven and Hell. In her lighter moments, she writes the sweet and funny Ever After contemporary romance series. And when she's not plotting the world's downfall or next great love story, she's a wife, mom, friend, coffee snob, gardener, walker of a Giant Dog, minion to the Itty Bitty Kitty, and avid food preserver (you know, just in case that whole Zombie Apocalypse thing really happens). She loves to hear from readers and can be reached through her website at www.lindapoitevin.com.